Kane

Kane

An American Extreme Bull Riders Tour Romance

Sinclair Jayne

Kane

Tule Publishing First Printing, August 2017
The Tule Publishing Group, LLC

ISBN: 978-1-947636-14-9

Dedication

I'd like to dedicate Kane to the Tule Book Girls – Meghan, Michelle, Sarah and Lee – for all their inspiration, encouragement and help. It is no easy feat to get a book to "print"–hard copy or digitally, and everyone works so hard and juggles so many moving (and sometimes running away) pieces. And finally, I owe so much to the original Tule Book Girl–Jane Porter, who is so passionate about story and never let me give up or slow down or phone anything in. She also introduced me to the art and thrill of professional bull riding–and she made me sit on my hands instead of cover my eyes after the fourth rider had hit the dirt. For that, I bought her a cute t-shirt with a bucking bull and wrote her a book. Jane has taught me so much and she's in every book I write.

Dear Reader,

Writing *Kane* was one of the most exciting and creative projects I have tackled. It was exhilarating and terrifying. I was so fired up to have the opportunity to participate in Tule Publishing's American Extreme Bull Riders Tour (AEBRT) series, and to work with so many talented authors including Sarah Mayberry, Barbara Dunlop, Kelly Hunter, Megan Crane, Amy Andrews, Jeannie Watt, and Kathy Garbera. Brainstorming with the Tule team and hearing all the other authors' ideas was very inspiring, and a little intimidating. Researching bull riders and what it really takes to stick a ride for eight seconds and what happens when they don't was fascinating, but also terrifying. I had the hardest time watching the YouTube videos, and when I actually attended a Professional Bull Riders Tour show in Portland, OR, and the riders walked out and then the fire was lit…I was hooked–watching much of the show through my fingers over my eyes–but definitely entranced.

Kane was also close to my heart because he is my youngest Wilder brother–of my Wilder Brothers series set in Marietta, Montana. Strangely, he was the first brother I created, but I didn't have a story for him yet, a purpose, a heroine, a conflict, and so I hung on to him, dreamed about him, waited. All I knew was what he looked like and that he was a fiercely intelligent and driven cowboy. Being part of the bull rider series gave Kane a home, and I hope you enjoy reading his story.

-Sinclair

Prologue

KANE WILDER STRADDLED the top of the chute and looked down at the broad black back of Rocket Launcher. He breathed in deep—the familiar scents of bull and dirt settled in his lungs. He let out his breath twice as slow. Again. And again. His heart rate slowed further and the clash of the music, the fired-up cheers and whistles of the sold-out crowd, and the deep, practiced voice of the announcer all faded away.

He leaned down and put his boot on the bull's back to let him know he was about to get some company he didn't want. Then he dropped down, legs wide, knees bent and feet angled back so they couldn't get caught up in the rails when the bull shifted. Immediately he began to wrap his rope, sliding it back and forth between his glove to test the friction, warm the resin and get the feel of the rope for his hold hand.

He tested the hold, his position, rocking back on the bull and trying to feel the exact center of gravity. There was a science to it. And an art. Kane always felt the animal. The mood, the energy, and he never gave the nod until he felt the connection. Some of the American Extreme Bull Riders Tour front and back office teased him about being a bull whisperer—because, when he got what he thought of as his alignment, his belief that he'd ride the full eight was absolute. No doubt.

And usually he was right.

His focus was on the shoulders, the dip, and angle of the head. Yeah riders could get a read on a bull from watching the spot between the ears, but the massive shoulders held the power. Kane thought of himself as floating slightly above the thrashing shoulders. If he could keep his hold hand anchored and his weight light so he could rock back and forth, countering the moves while his hold hand held the plane, he was golden.

The trick was to move with the bull, but in the opposite direction, synchronously, anticipating and countering each roll, kick and whatever else the bull wanted to throw at him on any Friday or Saturday night.

Kane hadn't been one of the AEBR's top bull riders for the past four years because he often ended a ride tossed in the dirt on his ass.

He was golden for sticking, winning, earning cash and landing sponsors.

"Rock and roll," he said softly.

He angled his pelvis up toward the bull's shoulders, nearly sitting on his hold hand wrapped up tight in the bull rope.

He kept his body loose, but his thighs tight. He held his left hand high, rocked a little on the bull, shoving his hold hand a little higher on the rope. He could feel the tension, the restless energy of Rocket Launcher beneath him.

Felt good. Real good.

Kane kept his chin tucked, his gaze glued to the point between Rocket Launcher's massive shoulders that lined up with his hold hand. He gave the nod. There was a slide of metal and Rocket Launcher—true to his name—shot out of the chute, immediately dropped his head and shoulders, and kicked his back legs high, nearly perpendicular to the ground, his massive, one-ton body already shifting into his trademark roll to the right.

Fuck yeah.

The noise of the crowd would be deafening except Kane always screened it out to the point of white noise. At six seconds Rocket Launcher pulled his namesake move and jumped forward, kicked up and jumped forward again, spun a one-eighty and kicked up and came down hard.

Kane stayed welded—left hand extended up and fingers spread. He saw the light but couldn't hear the bell—the music and the crowd drowned it out, but the change in the ambient light hitting the arena from the jumbo screen graphics showing a full ride gave further proof. Kane judged the bull's next move and dropped his bull rope and launched himself free over the top and to the right of Rocket Launcher. The bull had run left after the flank rope was released seventy-eight point three percent of the time in the last two years on the tour. Immediately, Rocket Launcher calmed and ran a half circle around the arena as if taking a victory lap.

Kane jumped to the top of the fence, took off his helmet, popped out his mouth guard, and did a quick wave to the crowd as his score flashed. Ninety-two. Kick-ass.

Thank you, Rocket Launcher.

Four points higher than Casey, who was having a year and had too much to prove after ducking the finals last year. Five points higher than the nineteen-year-old Brazilian, Gonzalo, who thought he could kick Kane's ass, but he couldn't. Gage was only two points behind.

Rocket Launcher ran through the chute and Kings of Leon's *Sex on Fire* blared. The crowd went crazy and the announcer, Jessie, did a little move to set up and face him.

Fuck he was sick of this part.

Why the hell had he chosen this song?

He wasn't an asshole, well, not really. And he wasn't twenty anymore. He'd thought Alicia Flores who managed PR like he rode bulls would axe it. He'd suggested the song as a joke, a play on his image, but nope, she'd let the song slide. Probably because she knew he'd regret it after his fourth or fifth stick. It was only April, and he wanted to swear each time he heard the opening guitar lick. The pogo stick style drumbeat made him want to stick a screwdriver in his ears.

Alicia always gave the riders their own noose. And she

made sure his was tighter than most. His fault. But hell, she'd been halfway drunk. One time. And he'd been in the wrong bar and his offer to take her home had not been greeted in the way his twenty-two-year-old self had anticipated.

All kinds of awkward apparently. But even though he had a reputation and cultivated it, he still had rules. No one on the tour. No employee of the tour or employees of tour sponsors. No one else's girl. And not when he had a girl. Which had happened a grand total of once.

Damn the song. And Jessie staring. Fans stomping.

Kane laughed. Jumped down, rested his thumbs lightly on his belt buckle and the crowd erupted. He did the quick Texas two-step for six beats and then a tight spin, head fake, shoulder dip and quick hip check while Jessie did the same only with a bit more free styling because he was allowed. Kane finished with a quick four beat hip-hop-style walk and hand pose before flashing his commercial merchandising smile, opening his arms wide and then vaulting up and over the fence and dropping down on the other side.

He'd done the dance one night when he'd been a punk and drunk on love. Showing off to his girl, Sky, because she loved to dance. The crowd had gone wild that night, and Alicia Flores—head of the PR machine and hell on wheels if you said no or expressed an opinion contrary to her own—told him to do it again each time he stuck a ride, only with Jessie. It would be his move, she said. One of his signatures when he performed. Get his name out there more.

Kane still remembered her intense assessment.

"You'll need a look." She'd walked a critical circle around him, two of her ever-present assistants who seemed to change every six months or so watched, tablets palmed, fingers ready to type notes. Always notes.

Kane had felt like one of the bulls being assessed. Only less important.

It could have been hot. Alicia was damn attractive and ten, maybe fifteen years older than him, but usually no cowboy impressed her, which was why he'd been so shocked by the buzzed proposition during his second year when he'd been climbing the rankings.

He still remembered how her appraisal after the dance had unnerved him. He'd barely been twenty-two when Alicia hammered home the lesson that he was product. And if he didn't win, he'd be cold product, bumped down to the pro circuit. He was on the tour to make them money and create prestige for the AEBR. Cowboys came and went. Interchangeable.

Alicia had circled around him, watching. Thinking. Critical.

The meeting had reminded him of his childhood. His mother was always push, push, push pushing him to be better. Smarter. More ambitious. More accomplished. But more had never been enough. The bar just kept getting raised.

"Grow your hair," Alicia had said fingering one of his curls that he usually just finger combed away from his face. "Women will love the curls almost shoulder length. It'll be different. And win. Keep winning." Alicia had made it all sound so easy. Like anyone who didn't place top three, maybe four, just wasn't trying hard enough. "Or you're out."

So he'd won because that's what he did. And it had been fun until Sky left. Didn't come back.

He'd been fucking twenty-two and he'd felt empty, tired, worn.

So he'd ridden harder. Grittier. Fiercer. Got sponsors. Earned more money. Rode in the top three to five the last four years since Sky left because he had nothing else in his life. Nothing better to do. Alicia and the AEBR could kiss his ass. He was going to win on his terms. Quit on his terms. And he was going to earn enough money to give his mom some peace after the hell he'd put her through. And he'd still have enough money for himself so he could have a moment of quiet where he could finally sort through all the shit in his head and figure out what he wanted to do next.

And finally exorcise Sky's ghost. Move the fuck on. Get a life like his brothers—all three of them now—had.

Kane tucked his helmet under his arm, palmed his mouth guard and shrugged out of his protective vest as he walked down the long narrow hallway toward the dressing room. He was ending Friday night in top place. Tomorrow he had to do it again. But tonight he'd head back to the tour hotel, hit the gym, soak in an ice bath and watch the tapes for the bull draws tomorrow.

Kane saw a few of the riders grouped together talking outside the dressing room as he approached. Cody looked up and Kane was pretty sure if an expression could be a middle finger, he'd just been flipped off. He smiled back with his best *fuck you too.*

"Where we drinkin' tonight?" Kane called out just to piss them off. Not that he'd be there.

"Cactus," Paulo, always cool with every rider on the tour, said.

That was the real bar they would hit after a few of them showed their faces at the sponsoring bar, shoot shit or pool, drink a beer and then head out with the excuse that management kept them on a tight leash so they had to get up early in the morning. And then they'd gather at the real bar to try to cut some of the adrenaline with booze and women. Or they'd hit the gym. Or bed if they had a woman.

"What the hell, Kane? This image is trademarked." Alicia advanced on him down the long hall of the staging area toward the dressing room where five bull riders lounged and now smirked at him. Her stilettos clicked on the concrete like automatic weapon fire. She clutched a glossy brochure "And no shirt. We talked about that damn tat. Violation of your contract."

All the bull riders shut up. Alicia didn't usually blow up publically, but she'd always been harder on him since the act of chivalry that his mom had drilled into him since birth had been shoved back down his throat and perceived as a rejection of her as an attractive woman. Saying no hadn't been personal. It had been him adhering to his rules.

"Explain." Alicia bore the brochure like it was a shield and she was Perseus about to slay Medusa.

He read the words.

Scottsdale Austen Sheridan Orthopedic Guild Auction. Starry Night Art Auction.

Seeing the despised name, he pushed the brochure out of his face.

"The amount of fucks I give is less than or equal to the numerical value of zero."

"What?" Alicia stared at him, her dark eyes blank. Casey shook his head and coughed instead of laughing. Kane noticed that Cody, who never appeared to give a shit about saving anyone's feelings or pride, huffed out a lazy laugh.

"Just the professor talking dick again. He takes online classes and majors in *I'm smart. You're stupid.* So don't even fucking try to communicate with the prick." Cody sauntered by and seized the brochure. He took one look at it and barked out a laugh. "You might not give a fuck Wilder, but AEBR legal and PR sure as hell will. That picture was on the AEBR tour program last year."

Kane was still trying to figure out how Cody of all the riders knew he was working on his MBA online. He grabbed the brochure back and glared at the glossy print advertising an art auction set for the following week. There was an exclusive preview brunch tomorrow at nine a.m. for the heavy hitter patrons and then the art exhibit opening Saturday evening. The name of the hospital guild and the hospital burned his ass, because they were unpleasantly familiar, but he finally lassoed his ire and focused on the art.

"Where'd you get this?" he kept his voice quiet and cold.

"Not the point," Alicia said.

Kane looked at the image of the bronzed sculpture of a bull rider defying the odds of gravity.

Fuck.

"I'm sure you cowboys all have something better to do." Alicia walked over to the growing group of curious bull riders in various stages of dress and undress.

"Not really." Cody crossed his arms. "Free at the moment."

"Got an answer yet, Kane?" Alicia demanded.

Kane, coiled tense as a rattler about to strike, smiled, lazy and confident, and walked toward Alicia, his body fluid.

"Don't even give me that walk," Alicia hissed at him, holding up a small, neatly French manicured hand like a school crossing guard. "Save it for the buckle bunnies in the bar. We have a situation. And I don't want a situation especially this week. You are booked tomorrow with interviews, meet and greets. Next weekend you have a commercial shoot and two meetings with two potential sponsors in addition to everything else."

Where was this coming from? He never missed an event.

"How did this artist get your image? And your…?" Alicia trailed off biting her red lips, clearly agitated and not trying hard enough to regain her regal cool.

His large, elaborate tat of a furious bucking bull that scrawled across his back had been a crazy impulse according to Alicia. She'd been incensed. The AEBR was family-friendly and the riders were not tatted up like bikers. The rules on other tours had relaxed some, but the AEBR, not so much. Kane had caught a lot of heat for the tat. Management figured he'd been out of his mind drunk—as if a tat that detailed and stylized could have been inked in a couple of heavily under the influence hours. But the art had been an analytical decision. A declaration. A promise. A reminder. It had taken several sessions to finish. And he'd been utterly sober each time. And irrevocably in love.

Idiot.

Kane didn't break his rolling stride or eye contact.

"No worries, Alicia." He took the brochure from her stiff fingers, rolled it and slid it in the back pocket of his jeans. Her dark eyes narrowed in doubt and challenge. "I got this."

Chapter One

SKY GORDON RESISTED the urge to fidget in her electric blue sky-high heels. Who wore high heels and a ball gown for brunch? She looked ridiculous, like a child playing dress-up. Although a lot of women were also coiffed elaborately. Why had she succumbed to peer pressure? And professional pressure. These heels were going to kill her or force her to take a dive into a waiter circulating with mimosas and champagne.

She was short. She needed to deal. Most days she did, but this morning was big. Big money. Big donors. Big-name artists. Bigger egos. And she just felt so small. Even though she was a featured artist, she felt like she was pretending, like her father was going to show up any second and remind her how she didn't belong, wasn't wanted.

No.

She wanted to kick herself with the hated heels. She was not going to be that bewildered lonely girl anymore, seeking attention, seeking warmth, seeking love from her parents who'd had none to give. All of it had been spent on Bennington. And she'd loved her brother. Hadn't begrudged his all that love, but she'd wished there'd been a little bit left over for her.

But enough of the past. That was one of the reasons she was here—to kick the past in its tight ass. Move on.

Sky had donated the signature piece to the upcoming auction benefiting the most prestigious hospital in town. She was virtually an unknown artist, but one of the hospital's premier orthopedic surgeons, Dr. Austen Sheridan, had seen her work at a local juried art fair. He'd come by her studio. Asked her a million questions. Asked her about her life. Her schooling. And then to see her work. All of it—works in progress, but especially the metal sculptures comprising her MFA portfolio. She worked in a lot of sculptural mediums, but metals were her favorite. She loved the fire, the heat, the chemistry, the raw earth-element nature of working with materials from the earth. She felt like she was a part of history when she thought of the thousands of years people had been honing metal to their will.

And now here she was at a brunch art preview—who knew such a thing existed?—with some of the richest people in Scottsdale. This opportunity and event was something she could only have dreamed about last year when she'd come home to Scottsdale—a juried artist with her sculpture, a distressed copper and bronze figure of a bull rider defying gravity and probably other laws of physics, holding center court in a high-end art gallery and being ogled by a lot of women.

Just like the cowboy.

Jerk.

She'd really done exquisite work. That's what obsession did to a woman and to art. The bull rider looked vividly alive, even a faint smile curved his lips.

Not his corporate shill smile. His real one. The one with the left dimple and the chin cleft.

Damn.

Sky kept her bare back toward the sculpture she'd labored over for months as she mingled with the crowd. Or pretended to mingle. Jonas Richards, the rich boy gallery owner mingled for her, doing all the talking, the smiling, the lingering touches on her bare back and shoulders when he introduced her, steered her around the room like a toy car. Her skin crawled.

He'd picked out this gown and rented it for her despite her strenuous and repeated objections. And now she knew why.

"Smile, babe," he said through his perfect, bleached teeth. "You're hot. The patrons will love you."

Disgusting.

She didn't want to be hot. She wanted to be gone. Working in her studio. She had preliminary sketches finished for another western theme set of sculptures for the mountain rodeo circuit. Cowboys on bucking broncos. No bull riders, thank God. This smiling and pretending part of the art business would better suit the cowboy who'd inadvertently posed for her sculpture. More of them if she were honest.

No need to go that far.

He was so hot he burned. He could have melted the bronze with his smile, not a forge. He was so charming women creamed themselves just to stand near him. She was a mere mortal, devoid of most social skills. She fought her tremble just standing in a room with so many people. Her breathing was shallow. Sweat beaded in her hairline, and her pulse was a rapid reminder of her fear of crowds, closed-in spaces, and forced socializing.

"You can do better than that." Jonas looked down at her, his brown eyes narrowed with disappointment.

She nodded and concentrated on her mouth and pushing it into the correct shape, but she was so bad at this. Jonas's face blurred as she tried to gasp in a breath deep enough to stop the light-headedness. The black dots danced in front of her eyes. Her skin prickled with him standing so near her, but she forced a deep breath, bit the inside of her lower lip to center herself and made her mouth comply with, if not a natural smile, at least a better imitation.

Her face hurt she was so smiled out. And this was just the brunch. Tonight's event was even bigger. Jonas had chosen a red strapless dress for her for this evening. She grimaced. She knew she should be grateful. This was an unheard of opportunity for a new artist. She wouldn't get any money, but she would get recognition and cache and access—if she could summon the nerve to seize them. Sky had received so many rave reviews from the press and from many art patrons over her work, as well as admiration for her generosity, but she wasn't donating the sculpture for a good cause so much as she was giving it away. A cleansing. A quiet middle finger to the man and their past. And the hope that she could finally move on.

"I need to check my phone," she whispered under her breath.

She couldn't be unreachable. She had responsibilities that extended far beyond schmoozing to build her career.

"No calls, no texts," Jonas brushed off her concerns like he did everything else. "I'd feel it." He patted his pocket, but Sky was too uncomfortable to look down. And she didn't like the thought of her phone anywhere near down there. Jonas was getting sexually pushy. And no way was that happening with him. She'd flung herself into the deep end once with a dominant and ambitious man. She wasn't even getting her newly manicured toe wet again.

"I just want to check in with Brandy."

"Sky, you look enough like a teenager. No need to waste the power of those drop-dead gorgeous baby blues by gluing them to a phone screen. You haven't even taken a sip of your champagne," he said, critically. "This is a party. A cel-e-bration."

She didn't trust him or the situation. She felt like a Barbie all dolled up according to his specifications. Yeah, she was chasing money and a career as an artist, but she was starting to feel pimped and the last thing she needed was to self-medicate like her mother, who'd done it to cope with her father even before she dove deeper into the bottle after her brother… Sky had to stop thinking about everything except this moment.

Why did she always do that? Fall into the past? Get stuck. She was an adult. Independent. No longer hoping for affection or acceptance, much less admiration from her parents.

"I'd just feel more comfortable checking in," Sky said in a low voice, clinging to the last of her patience and trying to push down the panic edging her voice. She hated crowds. Being in the limelight. Being looked at and judged. She tried to tune Jonas out. Ignore the conversation, the string quartet, the pop of champagne corks and just breathe.

"Who the hell is that hick with the cowboy hat, and what's he doing heading into my gallery?"

Sky looked toward the door. Her heart flailed wildly. The "hick" was no hick and mercury eyes slashed hers before he'd cleared the door. Met. Clashed. Melded. Her breath tangled in her throat and four years crashed around her unsteady feet.

Kane Wilder strode through the gallery door. Past the men in tuxes. The women in floor-length sparkling gowns. Black western-style shirt fitted to his highly sculpted athletic form, black Wranglers that hugged his thighs and butt like he was in an ad, black, highly polished, hand-tooled cowboy boots, black Stetson molded to perfectly frame his high-cut cheekbones and the aggressive jut of his jaw, and a tuxedo jacket casually dangled by one finger over his shoulder. The collar of his shirt was open, two buttons undone revealing a strong, tanned neck and enough of his chest to remind her what he looked like and felt like naked when he'd been above her.

She couldn't swallow. Couldn't tear her hungry gaze away. It was like watching a crash in slow motion, aware of every detail—his appearance, the way he moved, his eyes that had always sucked her in way too deep, and of course, her reaction to him. Breath knotted uselessly making her dizzy. Her blood scorched her veins, her tummy tumbled sickly and her core heated and slicked as if he'd flicked a switch. And he saw it all. His pale blue almost silver eyes were those of a hunter, and she knew she looked like prey.

"Who does he think he is?" Jonas demanded stepping forward and slightly in front of her as if to intercept. "He's wearing jeans at a brunch and a gaudy belt buckle the size of Vegas. In my gallery!"

It was completely unconscious, but Sky adjusted her body so that she was still facing Kane, aligned with him and creating a clear path, as if an invisible steel cable connected them—heart to heart, mind to mind, soul to soul—and she'd be lying if she didn't admit the rest. The sex. Kane Wilder had owned her body as much as her heart. She'd been his, and even after four years just the sight of him made her melt into a puddle of want and despair.

God, she had lived to touch him. Be with him. Smooth his dark curls away from his forehead. And she'd always, always loved to watch him walk toward her. He made her feel alive. He made her feel like the only woman in a room.

Six foot one plus some of confident masculinity cut through the crowd like he was a knife, and everyone else was butter. His legs ate up the ground, his body long, lean, fluid and so toned. In her first anatomy and sketching class in college she'd learned why Kane moved so beautifully. Symmetry and perfect alignment. His pelvis and spine, head and shoulders were all on the same plane, and as he moved, they stayed there as if he were in his own dimension. Science hadn't diminished his magic.

And time away hadn't dimmed his pull.

"That joker doesn't have an invitation." Jonas was still talking and he took an aggressive stance as if that would deter Kane Wilder.

Sky tried to stifle a hysterical burble of laughter. No. No. NO. This could not be happening. She wanted to run toward Kane as much as she wanted to run away. She was still crazy. She was done with Kane Wilder. She had to be done. She'd hugged her secret and burned that bridge with a flamethrower. And then tossed a grenade.

Bye-bye.

Hardest thing she'd ever done. Worst thing she'd ever

done.

Sky stared, frozen as he continued that rolling stride, his long, honed legs that were used to gripping thrashing bulls ate up the floor until the last possible moment. She could feel the heat from his body, and it was like she combusted.

Her body was no longer hers. She actually swayed toward him like a damn magnet.

In one fluid move he swung his jacket around her bare shoulders, enveloping her shivering frame. His knuckles brushed against her bare skin and then without breaking his body's flow, he pulled out the jeweled clip that she'd used to twist her long dark hair into some pretense of sophistication and tossed it over her shoulder where it pinged on the ground near some patron's expensively shod feet.

Sky couldn't look away from the churning emotion in his eyes. They were turbulent, the gray and darker gray of a brewing storm. No heat and light and amusement like she'd seen since childhood.

Kane Wilder was angry. She hadn't seen him angry. He'd always protected her. Made her feel safe and cherished. Without thinking, one hand reached up and a finger twirled in one of his dark curls. He'd always worn his hair shaggy. Usually his beautiful glossy curls had brushed his high angled cheekbones or he'd get a little edgier and let his hair grow almost to his jawline, before lopping off length, but now his hair brushed past his shoulders in thick whorls that begged to be speared and stroked and brushed over bare skin, preferably hers.

He looked raw and masculine and timeless and so beautiful her eyes stung. Her heart ached. Her blood burned.

He cupped one large, tanned hand on the back of her head and then ruthlessly reeled her in for a kiss.

Her lips parted automatically, shocked and thrilled and remembering, and he caught her betraying gasp as if it were the price of admission to heaven. His lips were firm and before Sky could even marvel that Kane had appeared back in her life after so many years, his tongue traced her inner lip, sending darts of heat arrowing low in her tummy and peaking her nipples beneath the thin blue material of her gown. The way he stepped in closer, closing even the concept of distance between them, pebbled her nipples almost to the point of pain, and it took all her willpower to not rub against the smooth heat of his shirt.

Sky hummed as she drowned in pleasure from the kiss. God, could the man kiss, and her whole body got in on the action. Her breasts had always been embarrassingly sensitive, and Kane clearly hadn't forgotten, as one hand splayed rough, hot and hard on her back to press her more deeply into his body. His lips continued to move over hers, tongue stroking. Every cell in her body rejoiced, and she couldn't begin to muster the presence of mind to shut any of this down.

"Hey, baby." Kane paused the kiss, but instead of reining in any scrap of sanity, Sky stood on tiptoe and tilted her head back, hungry to reignite the smokin' hot moment. "You missed me."

A statement. Typical Kane. No doubt. None.

"No." Her voice was low, shaky.

He laughed. Smiled. Oh God, not the famous marketing smile—the full-on left dimple, cleft chin, probably insured smile that crinkled his eyes and stretched across his beautiful, masculine face, and that made her want to slap him—but his real smile. The one that kicked up his sensuous mouth at the corners for a second and then painted warmth in his cool, watchful eyes. No dazzle. No sparkle. But that simple smile with the left dimple that had never failed to make her want to rip off his shirt.

He smiled her smile.

"Liar."

"What the hell are you doing, Sky?" Jonas grabbed her arm and tugged her away from Kane. Or tried to.

Of course she stumbled in the stupid heels. Kane easily righted her. His arm circled her waist, firm, but not digging into her sensitive flesh. His attention honed on Jonas.

"Hands." Kane's voice was quiet, but threaded with steel.

"This is my gallery," Jonas said fiercely, but he did drop her arm, and Sky couldn't help but try to rub away his touch. Her skin had pinked because Jonas had grabbed her hard. Kane didn't miss her reflexive gesture as she soothed her smarting skin. Jonas sneered. "And Sky is my..."

"Nothing," Kane said. "She's not yours. Not now. Not

later. She's mine."

Sky startled at that bold assertion. She hadn't been his in four long, empty years. And he hadn't lost a moment's sleep without her. He'd replaced her in an afternoon.

"Who do you think you are?" Jonas sputtered, so outraged his normally precise and well-modulated diction skewed all over the place. "What do you want?"

"Sky's got something of mine. I've come to get it back."

Panic kicked in. Her newly manicured nails dug hard into her palms. The room swam in front of her. How did he know? What would he do?

"And that..." Kane tilted his head toward the sculpture that rose up like a taunt to physics and to civilized society "...is also mine."

"The hell it is," Jonas said fiercely.

Sky felt incased in ice. Kane had come for the sculpture? Not her. He hadn't discovered her secret. He just wanted his darn image! Figured. Four years later she was still so stupid. Of course he hadn't come for her, but she'd jumped into his arms and his kiss like he'd just left for the weekend.

Ashamed, Sky willed herself to not inhale Kane's scent wafting from his still-warm jacket draped around her body—pine, cedar, and sandalwood. She loved sandalwood.

God, Kane was like a drug. She an addict.

And that thankfully kicked up her anger.

"It's mine," Jonas said sounding like a truculent fifth grader.

Sky tugged against Kane's casual hold around her waist. Useless. She narrowed her eyes at him warning him to back off, which he didn't.

"It's mine," she stated coolly as irritated with Kane as she was with Jonas and his posturing.

No way was Kane Wilder striding back into her life and saying squat about her art. "I'm donating it to the Pinnacle Peak Hospital's Austen Sheridan Guild art auction.

She felt the press of Kane's body jerk tighter like a cable cranked, but the arm at her waist didn't hurt.

"And it's my art and I'm doing what I want with it."

Trying to erase you from my heart. Finally.

She wasn't nineteen and obsessed with him anymore, although her body had yet to get on board with that concept.

The guild, her donation along with many better-known artists' donations, the preview brunch—those were the reasons she was here. The auction was next weekend. She was wearing this Barbie dress and heels for this stupid preview, and even in these stiletto skyscrapers she barely made it to Kane's shoulder.

Kane had no say.

She was moving on. She had moved on.

See?

She notched her chin at him, like a childhood dare when he or her brother Bennington, Kane's best friend, had told her she was too young or too little or too much of a girl to come with them on some fantastic boy adventure.

Only now Kane ignored her and instead walked around the piece, his eyes intense, his face lit with concentration. She tried to ignore the lines of his body. Failed. So instead she tried to see what he was seeing. She'd lived with the sculpture for three years. She could trace each line with her eyes shut. Remember the placement of each groove, the etched texture.

The bull rider, left hand high, fingers wide like he was high-fiving God, was parallel and in alignment with the bull's bucking, writhing body, precariously balanced on one hoof so that it appeared that both man and bull were standing vertical. The rider's corded thighs gripped the heaving, thrashing animal's sides, the fringe on the chaps seemed to ripple, and the rider's sculpted ass kissed air. The two other points of contact were the rider's hold hand, wrapped tightly in the bull rope that had taken her hours to texturize, and the spurs lightly touching the bull's sculpted sides.

The sculpture screamed power and grace; the defined muscles of the bull mirrored those of the rider. The energy from the heaving body, counterbalanced the Zen-like fluidity of the rider.

The sculpture had garnered a lot of praise and attention after the press release, newspaper article and the glossy brochure that had been circulating around town. Just like the man. Sky swallowed hard, unable to breathe. She'd never thought Kane would see this sculpture. She knew how much it revealed about her feelings toward him, and he didn't know half of it.

"Uncanny how you captured the exact angle. Like the photo. Brilliant, Sky. I love it," he said, finally looking at her, and Sky hated how his praise was like a supernova in her chest, even as it struck terror there as well.

She hadn't been able to show the sculpture to her parents. It had been part of her final portfolio, yet she'd left it out of her graduate show because if her parents had seen the sculpture they would have known. And they would have been devastated. Beyond furious. One more way in which she would have hurt them. But in the end, they hadn't even shown up to her MFA showing. The rift she'd created by leaving home and lying and moving across the country to pursue art had just kept growing. She'd stopped trying to bridge the gap that had become a chasm worthy of the Grand Canyon.

More secrets. They'd kept so many from her she'd later learned and then she'd added a few of her own.

"You are so talented, baby. Incredible, but I am not surprised. Not. At. All."

Tears pricked her eyes at his sincere and open praise. Stupid tears. Stupid swelling heart.

Jonas was clearly pissed, and his tension was starting to attract attention. Conversations faded. People looked. Gravitated toward the center of the gallery as if being sucked into the vortex of the building drama. Or maybe they realized the model, one of the top bull riders in the world, had arrived.

"It's so raw. The power's fierce. Radiates," he assessed her as he made another tight turn, his focus intense, until he flicked his eyes to hers again, and she couldn't breathe. "You've blended metals."

"You're no art critic, cowboy," Jonas derided.

"No. And I'm not an attorney but I got one and I do recognize trademark infringement when I see it."

"Come again?" Jonas demanded.

"Kane?"

"I remember that day, Sky."

Obviously.

"Your first win on the AEBR Tour." She stated. They hadn't even been a couple yet except in her dreams.

"That's not the first I was remembering," he said softly. His eyes lit up with something she didn't want to think about, but the innuendo made her pale skin flush all the way down to her collarbone, which of course Kane noticed. His smile kicked up and ruined her breathing.

"But for that part at least—" he indicated the sculpture with his head without breaking eye contact "—I was wearing a shirt. And a protective vest although I appreciate the sentiment."

He ticked his finger at her and mouthed 'dirty girl.'

It was stupid to blush. She was an artist. She'd drawn hundreds of naked men and women of all ages and sizes. And she shouldn't be embarrassed about her artistic choices, but she felt pervy now—the sculpture was too revealing: man and bull nearly vertical, symbolizing oneness, half man half beast like a Minotaur. The only hint of clothing, of civilization, was the chaps, the fringe giving the illusion of movement. And boots with spurs prickling the tough hide in warning and daring. A dark edge. A hint of power and violence. Danger lived in every line. Spurring was worth extra points. And Kane was all about extra points.

Sky had still been an undergrad when she'd started the project. Scared. Grieving. Lonely. Broken. Sure she'd never again be whole. Never be loved. She'd felt dead, and the project had started first as a memorial, and yet in the end, she'd felt fierce. Determined to pick up the pieces of her life. Move on. She'd been angry at so many things, unable to articulate any of it, but her roiling emotions had led her to push the symbolism and the sexuality by having the bull rider's heavily muscled torso bare, to mirror the bull's musculature.

As a final flourish, she'd precision etched the tattoo of a bull in full competition mode across the rider's broad, sculpted shoulders. And then the hat. Always the hat, although Kane hadn't worn a Stetson that day or ever to compete. And he hadn't worn one around her until she'd bought one for him for his birthday before their first kiss. She'd used a chunk of her summer job money from teaching dressage lessons to have it custom fitted.

"Like hell that's you," Jonas jeered interrupting her self-flagellation. "Sky's an artist not a sports fan. And no way in hell can a man do that. Please. Copyright infringement my ass."

"Sky was on tour with me that summer. She took the photo. And she sold the rights to the AEBR."

Sky winced. She'd been nearly nineteen and stupid. Then her art had leaned toward charcoal and oil pastel sketches and photography. She'd sold the picture because the AEBR had wanted it for a future cover of their annual tour book. She'd been thrilled for Kane to be profiled and then on the cover. She hadn't even asked for money, just a photo credit. She'd received both.

"That pose is trademarked by the American Extreme Bull Riders Tour. You want to use it, you gotta ask real nice." He ignored Jonas and winked at Sky.

Then he looked away, his eyes caught by someone in the crowd. Sky noticed the tick in his jaw. She followed his gaze, wondering what had upset him as Kane always kept himself in complete control. She'd only seen the tick in his jaw at the hospital the night her brother had been severely injured and Kane had stayed with her while she waited for her parents to arrive.

What had upset him? All she saw was the doctor who had come to her studio. His attention was riveted on Kane. His expression was so strange that she stared back at him. What was it? Unconsciously her fingers danced, imagined quickly sketching him. Awe? Desperation?

"But for you..." Kane looked back at Jonas, his gaze cold, face shuttered, all emotion shut down "...and the hospital fundraiser for the Austen Sheridan Orthopedic..." his low deep voice, always smooth so people told him that announcing for the tour or doing TV or radio commentary would be a natural fit once he retired from the tour, roughened "...no way in hell. The sculpture's mine."

Jonas hissed his annoyance. "Get out. Get the hell out or I'll call the cops."

Even though Kane had kept his voice low and perfectly modulated, people were noticing. The attention was probably Kane's fault for being so masculinely beautiful. Charismatic. He looked like a movie star. It would take a giant screen to contain that much sexuality, confidence and magnetism.

"Kane," Sky said softly, wanting to defuse the situation, but not knowing how, but then she saw Brandy outside the gallery, peering in, holding Montana's hand along with her car booster seat and a travel bag. Montana saw Sky first, squealed and wrenched out of Brandy's grip and ran into the gallery, her little light-up sandals tapped out an excited rhythm on the terrazzo floor.

"Mama!"

Sky couldn't breathe. Couldn't move. It was her biggest nightmare.

But seeing her three-year-old daughter rush toward her kicked in her mommy instinct and Sky hurried forward, silently cursing the heels and the long hem of the rented dress.

"Hi. Sorry." Brandy rushed up, out of breath. "My niece is real sick and had a febrile seizure. My sister called 911 and is in the ER freaking out. Her husband's on a fire department call, and I don't want her to have to wait in the ER on her own. I tried calling and texting you."

Damn Jonas.

Sky automatically picked her daughter up and squeezed Brandy's hand in reassurance. Jonas hadn't wanted her to carry her phone around today as she greeted gallery guests and donors so he'd held on to her phone and hadn't let her know the sitter was trying to reach her.

"Go. Let me know how your niece is doing later," she said.

Her throat dried and her heart pounded. She didn't want to turn around, but knew the one moment she had dreaded above all others had inexplicably arrived. Anxiety was alive slithering through her nerves, knotting her stomach, and for a moment she thought she'd throw up. She could hear her heart thundering in her ears and her voice sounded as if she were underwater.

Get a grip.

She was an adult. She had managed her own life for four years without any help, but still her past hurts, her fears, her inability to deal with confrontations crashed around her, and this confrontation was about to reach critical mass at the worst moment and in the worst place imaginable.

He'll be shocked. You can deal. It won't change anything.

She turned around, shaking, and reflexively clutched Montana to her chest like a shield. Kane stared at her, and for the first time in her life she had no idea what was going on in his head. He looked at Montana, then back at her and then his eyes fixated on her daughter's large pale blue almost silver heavily lashed eyes that were replicas of his own. So beautiful and so distinctive that no one would have any doubt. Montana's dark curls also matched her father's. And her jutting chin with the little indent already starting to form.

Montana stared back at him. Eyes huge and curious. Then she grinned. Twin dimples whereas Kane only had one.

"Mommy," she said, pressing her small hand on Sky's cold cheek and forcing her to look at Kane, who was pale beneath his golden tan. She could see his chest rise and fall with shallow breaths that made him seem human for a moment. He looked like he'd just taken a toss from a bull and then a hoof to the gut. Maybe another to his chest.

Montana blissed out in her toddler ignorance took her wet finger out of her mouth and pointed at Kane like he was an unexpected gift instead of her mother's biggest nightmare. Fear circled like buzzards ready to pick apart her carefully constructed, hard-won life.

"Look, Mommy, look. Daddy. My daddy."

Chapter Two

MONTANA SANG OUT the last word crystal clear and then because she had none of her mother's shyness, tongue-tied tendencies or fear of strangers, she dive-bombed into "Daddy's arms."

Sky should have been prepared for that move. Montana never wanted to be held for long, and maybe if she hadn't been shaky with shock and wearing heels when she normally only wore athletic shoes to teach, flip-flops when running errands or steel-toed work boots in her studio, she wouldn't have toppled with her daughter. Kane, being Kane, didn't miss a beat. He caught his child in one arm, pulled her to eye level. Tucked her in close.

Sky's arms were empty. They hung at her sides, useless.

He wrapped his other arm around her daughter. Father and daughter's eyes met. Held. Kane's eyes blazed, and Sky felt the threads connecting them, pulling her child away from her.

"Give her back, Kane." She tried to control her voice, but the words bounced around like bingo balls rolling out of the spinning basket. "Right now."

He didn't even spare her a glance. He and his child just stared and stared and stared. Pale, silvery blue-gray mirroring pale, silvery blue-gray. Sky swallowed sickly and stepped forward. She grabbed Kane's arm. It was a steel cable, with hard, outlined muscles. Kane didn't budge or seem to notice.

Jonas said something, but she couldn't hear over the roaring in her head.

"Kane. Give her back right now." She tried to prize his fingers open, but she might as well have tried to bend the upraised hand of the sculpture.

"Mine," he said. His eyes blazed with absolute possession.

"Give her back." Fear was a smothering cloak. "You have to give her back right now. Kane."

Montana had slapped her wet hand on Kane's cheek. She smiled.

"Daddy on a horse." She pointed to the sculpture.

Kane looked awed. "You want to watch Daddy ride for real, baby girl?"

Her little dark curls bounced as she nodded enthusiastically.

He grinned back like this was the most normal situation in the world, and Sky thought she was really going to lose it because there was nothing normal about this, and Kane had a will more honed than anything she could hammer out on an anvil. He was wild, unpredictable, and didn't know the meaning of back off or back down. He didn't lean in to anything. He flung himself in, and she so didn't like the way he was holding her little girl.

Their little girl.

Oh. God.

"Please, Kane. Please you're scaring me. Give her back now."

"No." The word was quiet, nearly a whisper, but it sounded like a gong in her ears. And his eyes finally cut into hers. They blazed heated mercury and Sky took an unsteady step back.

"Kane." She could barely force out the whisper.

"Hey, asshole. Give the kid back and get out of my gallery before I call the cops."

"Call them," Kane said casually, still smiling at his child. "We're leaving."

"Wait, what?" Sky yelped.

"My daddy." Montana pointed to her heart and smiled so eerily like Kane that Sky's heart skipped a beat, and still seemed to flounder in her chest like a trapped bird in a too small cage.

"My daughter." Kane's eyes blazed into Sky's. "My woman. My sculpture."

And then he picked up *The Ride*. One-handed. Like it was a box of cereal on a shelf he was going to put in his basket. Sky blinked. Two men had carried the crated sculpture into this gallery last night in a wood box. And Kane now held it tucked under one arm.

"All of it mine."

Kane strode toward the exit of the gallery with the same fluid pace he'd entered only this time he had her daughter and her signature art piece in his hands.

"Kane, wait." Sky ran after him, awkward with the long clingy dress tangling around her legs and the heels making her sprint precarious.

The doctor blocked his path.

"Kane," he said quietly.

Kane didn't even slow or make eye contact, just neatly dodged around him not even breaking his flow.

"Wait! What are you doing! Where are you going! You can't just..." Sky broke off not wanting to alarm Montana although the only person the least bit fazed was herself.

Kane clicked the alarm on a huge black truck parked illegally. Sky stumbled to a stop. He was really planning to take her daughter. Put her in that monster truck and drive off. Without her.

"You can't take her, Kane. Really you can't." She lurched forward and grabbed his arm as he slid her little girl into the back seat. "Stop playing games," she hissed dimly aware that Jonas was standing at the gallery door, phone in hand. "This isn't funny."

"No." Kane finally turned to look at her, and Sky wished he hadn't because the ice in his eyes, and the barely leashed tension in his body, scared the hell out of her. And then her mind and body did what they always did when primal fear kicked in. She froze. She felt herself do it, and she screamed inside. She had to focus. She had to get Montana back.

"You're right about that, Sky. Keeping my child a secret is not funny."

"You can't take her."

"You did."

She opened her mouth but nothing came out. No words. And she couldn't breathe.

He really intended to take her child.

"Un-for-giv-a-ble." His voice usually so deep and warm and sexy was the slash of a whip. Each syllable was enunciated and cut through her tender flesh. She felt like he'd flayed her soul open. "And I'm not driving off without her, and hell no I won't play nice and make this easy for you. Mine."

She felt so stupid trying to gather her wits in the blazing morning light on the sidewalk of Scottsdale's arts district with a gallery full of potential clients staring at her while she shook and tried to think of words to make Kane drive out of her life and their child's life again.

"Kane." She forced his name out through cold, stiff lips that no longer seemed to belong to her. His name had always been her talisman when she'd been scared or lonely or hurt. He'd been so strong. So confident. Her opposite. Now she could barely say it, could barely look at him without feeling slashed and burned.

"Get in the truck, Sky."

Relief made her sag. She nearly sat down on the side-walk. He wasn't taking Montana away from her.

She sucked in a shaky breath, tried to lock her knees. "Kane." Her words trembled and tumbled out of her mouth in a frightened whisper. "You need to let her go. You can't just take her with no warning."

"Like you did?"

"I can explain." Sky stared hard at his black boots, handtooled Tony Lama cowboy boots, and winced at her words because really she couldn't, not in words that he would accept, and she couldn't make herself that vulnerable to Kane ever. Tell him about her life. Her fears.

"You stole my child. You stole my life. You stole her father."

Sky wrapped her arms tightly around her slim, shivering body, each accusation another flick of the whip. She looked at her bare arms almost expecting to see blood. Kane Wilder had never once mentioned wanting children, and he didn't remotely live a lifestyle conducive to having a wife or a kid. She'd done him a favor. At least she'd tried to while also protecting herself.

"I'm not wasting one more second not being a father to our child. Our daughter. Not yours. Now get in the truck."

Kane pushed past her and strode to the other side of the truck. He placed the sculpture on the seat and buckled it in. Like it was a person. Kane neatly hung his tux jacket on a hook behind the passenger cab. He opened the passenger door and then loped around the truck to the driver's side. He opened the door and climbed in.

"Get in." He jerked his head toward the passenger door. His voice roughened. "No way would you rather stay with that gallery idiot. You can do way better."

"What?" She stared at him blankly. Kane's mind was crazy quick and often left others straggling behind, but she couldn't comprehend this shift.

"He was more pissed that I grabbed the art than you."

He'd grabbed his child and the art. Not her.

And then Kane looked at his watch like he had somewhere to be. Like he had some appointment and she and Montana had just been a little detour. Kane Wilder was a jerk. And a lot of other four-letter words. She'd done the right thing running away from him. In four years he'd only gotten cockier, and more beautiful and honed and... She had to stop noticing him physically.

She was responding to him when Kane was pissed and vengeful and determined. Imagine if he ever decided to turn on the charm. She'd be as helpless as a frog in a high school biology lab.

Again.

"What's it going to be?" He rolled up the sleeves on his silky black shirt and looked like he didn't care if she agreed or not. "Climb in or I'll toss your ass in the truck," he said in a low, conversational voice.

Sky stared at his muscled, tanned forearms. She remembered working out in the gym with him. How fit he was. Strong. Driven. God he still cast that physical spell on her. Four years she hadn't noticed another man. Two minutes with Kane and she couldn't think beyond his physical attributes even in a stage-four, all-sirens-screaming panic attack.

"She can't be buckled in like that. You need her booster seat."

"Get it."

"I…" Sky avoided his eyes. "It's heavy, and these heels."

"Lose the shoes. Get it."

"Please, Kane."

"Not going to be fucking stupid again." He spit each word at her.

Again?

"You were never stupid," she whispered.

"I trusted you," he said. "The only woman I've ever trusted and that includes my mother. You told me you loved me over and over and I fucking believed every one of your lies."

Lies?

She couldn't even move beyond that way-off-the-mark accusation. Kane had been her whole world. She'd been so terrified of him becoming bored with her, of cheating on her, that she'd left him first.

"Get the booster seat and whatever was in that backpack the sitter dropped off."

"You won't leave?"

"Like you did?" he taunted.

Any other woman would have been playing this better, Sky thought with a familiar burst of self-recrimination.

"Our daughter needs both her father and her mother, and lover boy's about to make a call to the cops so we gotta roll."

Sucking in a deep breath Sky willed her thrashing heart to settle so she could maybe think and react. She glanced past Kane's shoulders to where she could see Montana sitting cross-legged in the truck and clapping and singing to some song in her head. Sky bit her lip, crossed her fingers and said a little prayer.

"She likes to sing," she whispered wanting to give him something to hold on to. Something to make him stay long enough for her to grab the car seat and whatever Brandy had thought to pack in the owl-shaped backpack. Sky didn't even know where Kane intended to take them.

"I'll get the booster seat," she whispered, trying to move her body toward the door and away from her entire world that was now in a stranger's truck. Because Kane was a stranger, she fiercely reminded herself. They'd been apart almost four years. They were different people. And he'd been with a lot of women since her.

Why did she have to think of that?

She didn't care. That was only one in a long list of reasons she'd left him.

"What the hell is happening?" Jonas demanded as she reentered the gallery. "He's bringing that sculpture back, right? What was the trademark issue he babbled about? What an asshole. Who dresses like that? And that kiss. Where the hell did that come from? That cowboy pawed you like he owned you."

If her reaction to his kiss were anything to go by, he clearly still did.

Despair swamped her. She was scared yet worried that some stupid part of her still wanted him.

Something was seriously wrong with her head.

Sky kept walking, having to concentrate on putting her feet one in front of the other, not just because of the heels but also because her limbs felt like they belonged to other people and couldn't quite coordinate with each other. And she was tired. So tired. The after effect of too many shots of adrenaline hitting her system at once.

And yet she had to stay alert. Get the booster seat. The backpack. She should sprint, not walk like she weighed four hundred pounds and was on a tightrope.

"Wait, what are you doing? You're not really going with him are you?" Jonas demanded, outraged as he saw her pick up the discarded large, plush Britax booster seat complete with two cup holders and an adjustable five-point harness restraint. Sky had skimped on many things in her adult life, but safety for her child was not one of them.

"He's got my daughter. Of course I'm going with him."

"This is the preview brunch of the biggest art show of the season. A privilege I extended to you, an unknown, I'd like to remind you." Jonas could barely speak around his clenched teeth. "And what about tonight? It's one of the biggest art openings of the year. The party will spill out into the street. Art patrons from all over the country will be here. I need that sculpture."

The sculpture not her.

"It's the centerpiece of the art auction. Dr. Sheridan and the guild worked with me to choose that one to highlight over many art pieces from better-known artists.

Sky tried to push past him, conscious of time slipping. Jonas had reminded her many times of how lucky she was. Theme of her life. She was lucky. Even when she didn't feel lucky at all. Jonas reached out and stroked one finger along her bare arm.

She looked out toward the street where Kane waited, framed by the truck's open window. His eyes were watchful, and tightly focused on her. She pulled away from Jonas and scooped up the booster seat and the little owl backpack that Montana had seen at a street fair and had fallen in love with. The booster seat seemed like a lead weight, even though she was strong from wielding heavy materials for her sculpting and from teaching Pilates, yoga, pump and spin classes to supplement her income for the past five years.

She kept her eyes on Kane as she walked back across the terrazzo floor that had seemed so beautiful to her when she'd first seen it last week, but now seemed fraught with peril. She expected to stumble in the shoes and long skirt at any moment, and her legs were trembling so violently she thought they'd snap in two.

She tried to ignore the stares and whispers.

"Sky, you dropped this." An older woman held out the jeweled stick that she'd used to pin up her hair. She'd forgotten Kane had tossed it.

"Sky, excuse me. Do you remember me? Dr. Sheridan. You kindly let me into your studio."

Sky looked up into his dark blue eyes. His smile seemed tense, and his tall frame even more so.

"I…" She paused. "I'll get the sculpture back." He must be worried by the bizarre scene. God, she hated being the center of attention. "Or I will donate another. I have six others from that series."

Not like that one.

She didn't even know when she'd get back to her studio to pick another. Didn't know where Kane was taking them, but she had to make him see sense. She had a life. She was finally getting traction on her career. He couldn't toss her and their child in his truck and head out across the desert. The truck's deep engine rumbled to life. Her heart leapt painfully.

"Jonas, I have to go," she said softly when she should be firm.

"Sky, you are going to ruin your career before it gets

started." Jonas was back in her ear like the bad angel.

"I'll return and will have another sculpture for you. Please just give me a little time," she pleaded.

"Let me call the cops."

Police. That was all she needed. Kane in jail.

"No," she snapped. "Montana is his daughter. He's not doing anything illegal."

"You can't walk out on a showing. I'm calling the cops." Jonas was furious, and his grip on her shoulder and arm hurt. "He's stealing my art."

She tugged herself to get free just as she heard the truck door slam. Oh no. Kane could not come back in here. Then Jonas would really have a reason to call the police. The felony charges started racking up in her head and she jerked out of Jonas's grasp and rushed toward the door. Her heel caught on the doorjamb. She face-planted, barely managing to break her fall with her hands. The booster seat hit her in the ribs and the backpack was flung across the sidewalk.

Strong hands lifted her up. Thinking it was Jonas she struggled briefly.

"Baby, you okay?" Kane's strong hands swept down her body. "Are you hurt?" His hands parted the long, sexy slit in the skirt, probably searching for blood, but screw that. She slapped at his hands, her embarrassment monumental. Worse, his knuckles brushed along her thigh and shivers of awareness heated her skin.

She'd not only just had her budding art career destroyed

by the most unwelcome blast from the past ever, but due to the local press for the gallery showing and the upcoming auction coupled with Kane's celebrity—not likely he'd be unrecognized for long especially with the AEBR Tour hitting Phoenix next weekend—it was highly likely her unglamorous and clumsy face-plant would grace far more than a few snarky FB, Instagram and Twitter posts.

She didn't need to top off the disaster by flashing her sexy blue thong at the rich and connected of the valley. Coupled with being in the arms of one of the top bull riders in the world who was celebrated equally for his skills on bulls and in bed while their secret baby sat in the back of his idling truck, she'd never be able to show her face in public again.

A starring role in her own soap opera. And her parents would know!

Sky felt sick.

"Talk to me." Kane tried to tip her face up so he could see her, but Sky thought if she had to look him in the eye one more time she'd hit him. Better than crumbling. "Are you hurt?"

"Let's just go."

"Dammit, Sky, you're bleeding." His hand swept apart the slit, but at least his body was blocking her from the wall of gallery windows.

He paused and sucked in his breath.

"Were you wearing those panties for him?"

"Really, really off topic," she whispered again, the pain

and the shock starting to catch up with her and pull her under.

"You never wore anything like that for me."

"It's not a contest."

Although for Kane, probably everything was a contest.

And he won.

"Please can we just go?"

Only they couldn't. Kane had to install the booster seat. She tried to show him how, but Kane being Kane and perfect at everything, slid the belt through the back of the Britax like he did it every day. Montana hopped up and wriggled into the five-point harness. Kane buckled her in and checked the fit before Sky noticed she was bleeding down her right leg. Great. She'd probably stain the dress. She winced thinking of the deposit. The night just got worse.

She'd been excited about her art being included in the auction, but nervous about the showing. And now her emotions seesawed everywhere but where she wanted them to be. Calm. Over Kane Wilder.

Nope. Not even close.

She tried to move around Kane to check on Montana, but her ankle wobbled and pain shot up her leg.

Kane didn't say anything as she sucked in a breath and grabbed the doorframe for stability, but he definitely acted. He reached down and pulled off one shoe and then the other and tossed them against the gallery wall. "Now you can walk."

She stared at the shoes tumbled together in a graceless tableau of electric blue silk and crystal beads. Didn't that just symbolize her night, heck, her life?

"Those aren't even my shoes," she said pointlessly. "I rented them. And the dress."

"I'd pull that off too and leave it for your most recent lover to deal with, but since you're not wearing a bra I'll refrain," he grit out.

He was pissed about Jonas? Her latest lover? As if! Kane was the serial sex machine not her. He could have a parade in downtown Phoenix with all his ex-hookups.

Kane picked her up and put her in his truck, even shocked and angry, his hands were gentle. He slid the seat belt across her body, his arm—in the silky western-style shirt—brushed her body and his heat and the hard muscles jangled her nerves with memories she really wanted to forget.

He hesitated, but didn't meet her shattered gaze. Shaking, her hand reached to touch his silky hair even though she silently screamed no.

Kane's eyes glittered, and he sucked in a quick breath. Time seemed to stop. The past four years apart fell away. Her awareness of the world narrowed to Kane. His arm across her body caged her in, and the tension pulsed between them like a drum that beat in her chest in time with the one that beat between her thighs.

Sky wanted to hold him as much as she wanted to cry.

She'd spent four years trying to rip Kane Wilder out of

her heart, and with one look, all those efforts were doomed. She was lost.

"Kane," she whispered her voice unbearably husky. She barely bit back an apology. She'd spent her childhood apologizing. When she'd left home at seventeen, she'd vowed to be different. To find a place to belong. To shine. It couldn't be in Kane's world. She wouldn't survive that. "You have to let us go."

"Hell no."

He slammed the truck's door and before Sky could even process she didn't have her cell phone back from Jonas, her purse, her keys or her change of clothes, Kane was back in the driver's seat. He shifted into drive and they sped off.

Chapter Three

SKY CLENCHED BOTH hands together and winced at the pain. She'd fallen hard. Stupid heels. Stupid dress. Stupid her. How could this be happening? Kane back. Kane turning onto Scottsdale Road. Kane in a truck with her. More beautiful and potent and take charge than even she remembered. And she'd thought about him constantly, especially when she'd been trying not to.

She was living the moment she'd hoped to avoid for so many reasons. And though she had wrestled hard with her decision to not tell Kane, especially the first few months after discovering she was pregnant, she'd never planned for what she would do if he did find out. It wasn't as if he'd ever loved her. His silence had screamed 'not that into you.' So she'd given him what she thought he wanted.

Freedom.

And why not? Kane could have most any woman he wanted and judging from so many pictures she'd seen of him over the last few years, he had. That alone had reinforced she'd done the right thing—protecting her daughter's heart from a father who would resent her existence, but Kane's simmering barely repressed tension was digging sharp claws of guilt into her, and all of her rationalizations over the past few years were starting to seem awfully flimsy.

She sucked in a shaky breath and looked back at Montana. The movement caused her to wince. Her ribs ached from the fall and her knees stung as did her palms.

"How bad?" Kane asked, his voice low and tense.

"What?"

Montana stared out the window, her feet bouncing to some internal rhythm and her lips moving to the notes in some inner song.

"You went down hard."

Sky watched a freeway sign blur by.

"Wait! Where are we going? My studio is…"

"I've got to get back to Santa Fe," he interrupted. "Finals are tonight and I have a preshow interview and a quick meet and greet with the local tour sponsors."

"Wait. What?" She spun now in the large truck seat to face him but couldn't suppress her yip of pain.

"Jesus, Sky, how bad?"

"You don't really think you are driving to Santa Fe today?" She stared at him like she'd never seen him before. "With us?" Kane had always been calm and reassuring. Not a man given to impulse or irrational behavior.

Kane again looked at his watch, his face grim. "No choice."

She willed herself to remain calm. She taught yoga. She got paid to intone about breath. She should not be on the verge of hyperventilating.

"You need to take us home," she said gripping the edge of the seat and ignoring the sting of pain. "I am not prepared to go to Santa Fe."

She had no shoes, an inappropriate dress to walk into a bull-riding event, no wallet, no phone. And that was just the beginning of the list of why this was a disaster.

He didn't answer. His face looked carved. Beautiful. Remote. Sky felt panic wash through her. She didn't know him like this at all. She had no idea what was roiling through that big brain. He was overreacting, wasn't he? Her Kane had always been in control. Thinking.

"You need to be in Santa Fe," she said coldly, crossing her arms to ward off the icy blast of the air conditioner. "We don't."

"I go. You both go," he said. He turned down the AC fan on her side and raised the temperature a little.

She tried not to notice the unconscious action—to remember how he'd always taken care of her without ever making a big deal of it. As if it were natural when no one else ever had. Even shocked and angry he'd noticed she was cold and done something about it.

But the rest of his behavior this morning stomped out the blossoming warmth, and alarm blared through her. He was acting out of character. Unpredictable. He didn't want her. And what was he going to do with a three-year-old? He wasn't thinking. He was reacting. Badly. With his primitive brain. But why?

Sky couldn't even get her own brain to kick in. She still felt like she was reeling—stuck back in the gallery, hating the crowd and Jonas's sexual interest. Then she'd looked up Kane Wilder, hero, man of her dreams, sexy cowboy personified and trampler on her heart strode across the gallery like he'd been expected.

His reaction had been over the top. Like a movie. And that had been before he'd kissed her.

And you kissed him back like you were thirsty.

Breathe, she reminded herself. In through her nose for seven. Out for seven. Five cycles. She didn't even make it through one.

"You're not being practical, Kane."

Nothing.

"You don't want me."

"I want my child."

She flinched. She was irrelevant. Just like she'd feared. Life with Kane would be her childhood all over again. She'd be an inconvenience. But what about her precious daughter? No way would she let Montana experience what she'd had—wanting love but never understanding why she didn't quite deserve it, never feeling like she'd been wanted or belonged. Trying desperately to please when no one could be pleased.

"We'll fly to Vegas Sunday." His beautiful face briefly

twisted with distaste. "Get married. Fly to Phoenix for the competition. Pack up your things. Move them to my family's ranch in Montana."

She stared at him.

"Or better yet…" He handed her his phone. "Check the marriage requirements of Arizona."

Sky shoved the phone back at him.

"You don't mean that." She squeezed the words out. This wasn't the Middle Ages when women were property and did what the big heap of a man said. "I have a life. I'm not trailing after you city to city," she said outraged. "I'm not going to sit in a hotel room or a trailer and wait for you to come back at night after your ride and your whooping it up with the boys and the women in the bar so you can grace us with your fabulous, god-like presence."

Like a dog waiting happily for its master.

But the worst part of it, Sky thought dismally, was what hurt the most was how his face had twisted at the word *marriage*. She was *not* going to live her life unwanted one more moment. Not one!

Without thinking she grabbed the truck's door handle.

"Stop the truck. Stop it. I mean it, Kane. Stop. I'm not going to Santa Fe."

He didn't reply. His calm made her reckless and she yanked on the handle, which didn't budge.

"Take me home. I mean it. I am not marrying you."

"You will." His voice sounded cool, far away, as if his

attention were somewhere else. Then he looked at his watch again, which really made her want to toss it out the window. Again something chased across his face before he shut it back down to his remote mask. "Sunday if we can swing it. Monday at the latest we will marry, which is already four years too late."

Marry.

The word conjured up every stupid childish fantasy she'd harbored since she'd first spied him with her brother when she'd been eleven. She'd stupidly dreamed about him since that day until reality had slapped her besotted idiot face when Kane dropped her off on an airport curb clutching the boarding pass he'd printed off to send her back to school a few days before fall term started after they'd spent three months together—him riding bulls and then riding her just as hard for the entire summer. He'd smiled, kissed her cheek and then had returned to his truck with that deadly sexual swagger. No promise to call. No turning around.

And a week later, her churning worry that had dogged her the past month had been realized with a positive pregnancy test.

He hadn't wanted to marry her, and he hadn't wanted a child. Oh, she'd known he would have tried to control his dismayed expression. Would have married her because it was his duty. Like military service. A sacrifice for his child. But he wouldn't have wanted to.

"I am never marrying you."

If possible his features cranked even tighter. God, any more and his skin would tear with the pressure from all those arrogantly perfect, sculpted bones.

"Too bad," he said coolly. "I am not raising my child without being married to her mother. And I sure as…" he lowered his voice even more so that she had to strain to hear it over the whir of the air conditioner "…hell am not letting any other man raise my child, so ditch Gallery Boy."

His lips were tight. His mouth tight. He spit the words like pebbles. Each one hit with deadly accuracy, and Sky found herself recoiling, wrapping her arms tight around her bare skin and trying to find a safe zone that didn't exist.

"Just stop talking." She hunched in her seat, wanting to slap him, which was an impulse she'd never had in her life. "Just shut up. Now, please."

Maybe it was the 'please,' but Kane huffed out a laugh that definitely mocked her.

Sky balled her fists and slapped them on her legs in frustration and then yipped as pain shot up from her knee and both hands.

"Dammit," he hissed and instead of getting on the freeway, he signaled and pulled off into a shopping plaza. "Tired of asking, Sky. Open the glove box. There's a first aid kit in there."

"I'm fine."

"Open it. You can clean the scrapes on your hands. And I want to see what the fffff…what is going on with your knee."

No way was she lifting up her skirt while sitting next to him.

"I'm fine."

Kane made a sound of supreme irritation that sounded ominous. She had the idea that if Montana weren't in the car he'd be expressing himself far more colorfully, and in some small compartment of her overwhelmed brain she marveled at how he was already making adjustments. He'd never once raised his voice in the truck, and she too had been whispering even as they argued.

He shoved the truck in park but left the engine and AC blasting him, while it whispered over her. He opened the glove box and pulled out a substantial sized medical kit.

Given his profession, he probably needed it, but didn't the bull riders have team doctors? Please let them have team doctors. She might have finished with Kane Wilder years ago but imagining him injured and trying to bandage his own wounds made her feel sick to her stomach.

"Really." She caught his hand as he slid her skirt up her leg. "I'm fine."

"Mama, what's wrong?"

"Nothing," she said quickly.

"Mama hurt." Her daughter's voice hitched, and so did Sky's heart. Kane's beautiful, mystic pale blue eyes that turned silver during high emotion narrowed when they flicked over her face.

"I'm fine, sweetie."

"She's fine, baby girl."

They answered at the same time.

"I want to see."

"It's nothing," Sky insisted, trying to tug her skirt free from where it was bunched up in his hand. She pulled hard again, but no give.

Like the man.

"Seriously?" His mouth quirked. "You do remember what I hold on to for a living?"

She bit her inner lip hard to try to suppress her irritation and embarrassment. Kane reached back, unbuckled the struggling child and Montana clamored on the console, rolled into her lap, and righted herself kicking Sky's bruised ribs. She hugged Sky hard, and Sky tried to swallow her umph of pain.

"I need to see, baby." Kane tried to work Sky's body-hugging dress higher even as she clung on.

"Daddy kiss you all better, Mama," Montana said, straddling her and holding her face between her palms.

Kane stilled. Sky could feel the flush from her chest to her face. Damn her fair skin for betraying her every thought and emotion. She should have grown out of blushes after the first time she and Kane had had sex. She'd been so wanton and had only become more shameless during their summer together. The things she'd let him do to her. The things she'd done to him.

Another flush warmed her. Why did it have to be 9:30 in the morning? Midnight would have at least given her blushes a bit of privacy.

"Me kiss you too." Montana kissed Sky's palm and pressed it to her cheek and then kissed it again and pressed it to the other cheek. "Hold."

Sky sucked in a breath at her daughter's sweetness and now she hurt on a whole different level. Beside her Kane was rigid as a steel beam. Where was all that easygoing charm when he needed it—heck, when she needed it?

"Thank you, sweetie. But really I'm fine. You don't need to worry," she reiterated, pissed at Kane for making a big deal of her graceless public tumble.

That seemed to galvanize Kane. He opened the box and took out several small squares and ripped them open with his teeth. Ignoring her, he gently dapped at her scraped palms. They were actually worse than Sky had realized, and she tried to hold back her wince. Dirt was imbedded.

She tried to close her palms, suddenly remembering another time when Kane had stepped into medic mode. For all the years of ballet she was an astonishing klutz. She and her brother and Kane had been swimming. She'd been climbing out of the pool and had been distracted by the water sluicing off Kane's chest when he'd paused on the edge of their diving board. She'd slipped on the pool deck, and Kane had carried her into the house, her soaking bikini leaving a trail of water across the living room.

He had treated her injury then too, but the gouge in her chin had been so bad that her brother had driven her to an emergency clinic for stitches. Kane had carried her to her brother's jeep, wrapping her in a towel and putting his T-shirt carefully over her head so that it fell like a dress over her thirteen-year-old body. He'd sat in the back seat with her, talking, distracting her from the pain, but none of that had been necessary because sitting next to her superhero and wearing his shirt obliterated the throb in her chin and jaw and the bruises forming on her hip.

Sky was jarred from the memory when Kane pulled out a bottle of water from the middle console, which Sky realized was a cooler. It was loaded with several bottles of water and cold packs. He reached behind her and pulled out a slate blue T-shirt from an athletic bag he had tucked behind his seat. He cradled her hands on the shirt. Then he poured a little water in her hands and let it drip through. Next he dabbed at the scratches again.

He deftly picked up a small white and green tub of ointment.

"Really, Kane," she whispered. "That's a waste of a T-shirt. It's not that big of a deal. And I know you've got to be really…angry and reeling from this so you can stop pretending that this is normal," she finished in a whisper.

"If I even begin to stop and try to wrap my head around what you've done to us, we'll really be in trouble," he said his voice tight but otherwise without inflection. "I have to ride tonight."

His words sent a chill through her, especially his use of us and we, as if the three of them had already merged into one. She trembled.

"Hurts or still cold?"

Of course he noticed. She met the blank pale blue of his eyes, and that chilled her even more because Kane's eyes had always been his emotional bellwether—amusement, desire, turbulent disappointment in his performance, determination, possession—it had always been there.

Never blank. A mask.

"What's this?" Montana lifted up the tub and stuck a finger in it.

"Tea tree ointment. It fights infection. Don't eat it. Hungry?" Kane asked conversationally.

The care he was taking with her scrapes, and now her knee, was undoing her. She felt like all the knots of tension that had been holding her together for as long as she could remember were being untied and she would fall apart, a ball of tattered ribbons on the ground. A woman. A mother. A lover. An artist.

"Starbucks." Montana pointed across the parking lot. "Mama likes chai."

"I know," he said softly.

"No food coz she's gluten free." Montana said the words carefully.

"Yes," Kane said, his voice gentle now as if the earlier

emotion had been poured back into the cauldron where it had boiled over. "I remember."

He knew things about her. A lot of things. And the things he didn't know she didn't want him to ever find out. And now she was in his truck. And his hand was up her skirt. And their daughter was in her lap.

"Kane. Really." She tried to pull away, but there was nowhere to go. Again he cleaned the deep scrape with gentle fingers and put on the tea tree ointment. She sucked in a breath, holding her body rigid. Pissed that for some reason her eyes began to sting and burn along with her palms and her knee.

"Ow ow ow," Montana chanted, laying her head against Sky's chest. She folded her tiny hands together as if in prayer and tucked them under her cheek. Montana stared into Kane's eyes and he stared back. Everything in Sky stilled, even the air in her lungs. Time slowed. It was a moment. Small in time but epic in emotion and significance, and for the first time ever, Sky felt cut out of her child's life. It was as if they were in a picture frame, and she didn't belong and could get up and walk out and no one would know she was missing.

The story of her childhood.

The story of the life she'd been afraid she'd pass on to her child if she'd told Kane, and allowed him to do "the right thing," as she'd known without a doubt he stoically would. He would have even been nice about it, but inside, she'd imagined that he'd die a little. Her father certainly had. And he'd let her know it in so many ways.

A tear splashed on her hand. And another. She didn't dare move in case the dam broke. Silently she counted. It was too much. Everything just kept hitting her one thing after another.

Her daughter looked so serious. How did a three-year-old look so full of wonder and wisdom at the same time, as if she were looking through a portal at the mysteries of the universe? Sky was riveted by the expression. It hurt, but her artist's eye once again protected her from reality, from the pain, from the moment, because it was already focused on the lines of Montana's face, the light and shadow, the tilt of her chin, the tiny cleft there already forming like her daddy had.

Her pink lips tilted into the beginnings of a smile, and her expression changed from wonder to possession.

"Mine," she said eerily reminiscent of Kane earlier remarks. "My daddy. Mine."

Sky felt like Montana had just gouged out her heart and tossed it on the seat between them. Her daughter had never once indicated that she was unhappy that the daddy she'd seen in the pictures Sky collected of him from his career stats and articles and their summer together and her tween and teen years were only in a book, not real life.

"My baby girl," Kane said softly. "Mine."

Montana slid off Sky's lap and onto Kane's. She laid her

head against his chest, and one of those strong arms that could hold onto a resin-wrapped rope and keep him on top of a pissed and thrashing bull held her so sweetly. Her eyes drifted shut and then opened. She reached out and caught one of Kane's dark curls that brushed his shoulders. She speared one with her finger and pulled a little. She laughed as it bounced back and then she tugged one of her own curls.

"Daddy's hair. My hair, Mama."

Another punch to her gut.

"Yes," Sky said at a loss because every moment of this day, which should have been such a triumph, just kept getting worse.

Montana stared at Sky with the same eyes as Kane's, and it hit her then how alike they were. Not just in appearance—eyes, smile and dark curls—but in temperament. The independence. The confidence. The determination. She had none of that innately. She struggled for it all. And once again, Sky felt like she was on the outside looking in. Forbidden to enter the place that should be where she felt the most loved and safe—her family and home.

Kane's hand remained on her bare thigh. She could feel the imprint on her bones. Her breath feathered in her throat. Instead of looking at him she stared at the dash. At the digital glow of the clock.

"Eight minutes," she whispered.

"What about it?" He moved his hand, and perversely she missed it so she tugged the skirt of the long blue dress back down.

"You walked through the gallery door eight minutes ago."

Eight minutes to turn her world upside down.

What else could she expect from a man who could win a championship in a handful of eight-second rides?

Chapter Four

SKY PALMED HER grande almond milk chai and stared at the green straw poking out. They'd gone through the drive-through, Kane letting Montana hang out the window, his hands large and protective as he held her while Montana waved at the video of the smiling barista taking their order. He'd been charming to the barista, who was blonde and cute and perky and patient with Montana as she changed her mind so many times until she'd eventually settled on a berry and yogurt parfait and a bag of dried fruit and nut snacks and a water.

Kane had remembered Sky was dairy free, conferring only with her about almond, coconut or soy milk. Her stomach twisted. They'd sounded so much like a normal family, like a couple, that tears had burned her eyes. Of course he'd noticed that. She'd seen his infinitesimal pause. His brain had kicked over, and she'd become fascinated with the skirt of her dress, the flow of blue lace that tumbled like a waterfall over her legs, while Kane had turned back to the video of the barista and finished the order.

"That's a lot of food." Sky tried not to sound critical, but she shouldn't have bothered. Most everything seemed to roll off Kane's back where all the worry, doubt, anxiety and insecurity kept sticking to her.

"It's a six-hour drive."

She swallowed hard.

Back on the road as the truck ate up the miles, Sky fidgeted. Tried and failed to think of something to say. She wanted to sit in the back and help Montana eat. Mostly to escape the potent masculinity and pheromones that Kane exuded. There was no escape.

"Daddy, music!" Montana sang out after a while. Sky's heart pinched to hear the word daddy on her daughter's lips, and also at the familiar request.

"What would you like, sweet girl?" He flipped down a mirror that was below the rearview mirror so he could see the rear seats. Jonas had one of those but he hadn't used it the one time he'd driven Sky and Montana to downtown Scottsdale to an outdoor art festival when her car had once again been in the shop.

"You want country? Disney? I got satellite radio and anything you want on my phone.

The conversation unnerved her. One more slap in the face about how differently they lived their lives. But again, his reaction to Montana's request made it seem like they were a normal family. Kane turned on the satellite radio. Found the Disney station. Of course the song from *Frozen* was playing. Of course Kane knew the lyrics. He knew everything. And he had a beautiful voice. He had a beautiful everything, she thought resentfully and hunched in the seat, but her ribs pinched and she shot up.

"Sky, I'm losing my mind here. Do you think you need an X-ray on your ribs? Let me feel…"

"No!" she snapped. If he touched her she'd break. "I'm fine. I always bruise easily."

He'd remember that. He remembered everything. Anything with numbers he was practically a savant. He remembered every rider's stats each year. He also knew the bulls' stats. And facts? All stored in that computer brain and easily retrieved. She sighed. She had liked his quirky nerdiness almost as much as his devastating confidence and sex appeal.

His lips tightened. "I'm going to want to see later if not now." He was stating a fact, but his voice was laced with threat. "Are you still taking iron supplements? What was your last red blood cell count?"

She really wanted to smack him.

Anemia. Of course that hadn't slipped his mind. Her health wasn't any of his business. He was so fit and healthy and bursting with energy that her food sensitivities, overly sensitive stomach and anemia had always made her feel less than.

"I'm fine," she reiterated trying hard not to snap at him as Montana built up to the chorus in a little girl voice that was unerringly melodically on key. "Let it goooooo."

"Let it go, Let it go," Kane harmonized with Montana. Sky, who usually took so much pleasure in her daughter's love of music and voice, stared out the window thinking that Kane had ruined one more simple pleasure. Being with him like this was making her question all her decisions. And she wasn't liking the answers. And she didn't want to listen to the stupid voice that mocked her—she'd never let Kane go, not really.

She really couldn't take this anymore—being on the outside of her own life again.

"How do you even know the lyrics?" she demanded in a low voice as he sang out in a beautiful baritone giving the "cold never bothered me anyway" line a whole different spin.

"Disney, seriously." She glowered. "Wouldn't imagine too many buckle bunnies want Elsa's theme song crooned in their ear."

His features, tight and remote now that he wasn't looking at Montana, shut down even further.

"You'd be surprised," he bit out.

"Really don't want to know about your personal conquests before or after."

She couldn't begin to count how many women he would have been with during the past four years. Dozens. Hundreds. Maybe even some when they'd been together. She didn't know. She had been too afraid to ask questions. He'd been gone a lot. Sky felt more than a little sick.

"Not one word," she reiterated.

"Not really something I brag about," he said coldly. "But every woman after you is on you, not me."

Every woman!

Sky spun to face him. She'd been right. Dozen. Hundreds. He was lucky his penis hadn't broken off from the arduous work. Sky turned the music up. Predictably Montana got more excited and sang more loudly. Finally something going her way.

"How is your ravenous sexual appetite on me?" she demanded.

"You dumped me."

How was going back to school dumping him?

"Yeah you were so brokenhearted you had your hands all over two blondes in a club that night."

"That was work."

"Right," she said flatly. "That's a hard job," she snipped.

She was officially becoming her mother. Damn.

"You can't claim higher ground. You dumped me for some Italian exchange student." His voice was hard, low and fast and she had to bend closer to hear him although she really should be leaning away because the heat from his body and his citrus and faint sandalwood scent were making her feel warm and light-headed and relaxed, almost as if he were exuding some narcotic that was making everything warm and dreamy.

"You replaced me," he reminded her. "Pretty damn fast

although discovering yourself pregnant with another man's child at the beginning of your grand love affair must have put a damper on your vive amore. Finding another passenger on board definitely cuts into the libido."

Between the music and Kane's low voice, Sky wasn't catching every word but she heard 'libido' and yeah he had enough for five men.

"You'd know," she tossed at him, feeling like for the first time in her life she was holding her own during a confrontation, although between the Disney love theme songs and Montana's belting out the lyrics, it was hard to concentrate and seemed surreal.

"Bedding an Italian exchange student was cliché. Italians are notorious."

Again Sky couldn't hear everything clearly, but she caught the last word.

"Bull riders are notorious," she said like she was a snotty eleven-year-old again. And Kane was the most notorious of all.

"A rebound fling with an Italian just sounds like a dumb plotline from a movie. Even his name was lame. Lorenzo."

"Who?"

The minute she opened her mouth and saw the change in his expression she remembered the stupid story she'd concocted when Kane had shocked the hell out of her and shown up at her campus apartment and leaned on the buzzer until she'd finally been forced to answer through the intercom, terrified that someone else would eventually let him in and lead him straight to her.

She'd looked like hell. Exhausted. Not keeping much food down. Her body changing. She'd needed an iron infusion. He would have noticed. Nothing slipped by Kane. And no way would she have had the ability to resist him if he'd made it to her doorstep. Although maybe if he'd seen her, he would have run in the opposite direction.

"There was no Italian boyfriend," Kane said flatly.

Sky flinched and turned away toward the window.

Of course there'd been no Italian. The thought of another man replacing Kane was absurd. Kane had always been the one and only. But she knew she'd just been another notch on his bedpost. The virgin. A novelty. He'd probably thought he was still watching out for her as a favor to his dead friend, her dead brother. Make the girl's first experience in bed memorable. But then she'd had to go and fall in love. Desperately.

Humiliating.

"So why'd you dump me?"

"Not talking about this."

"I was worried about you," Kane said, his voice laced with frustration. "I flew across the country just to see you for one day because I was due in Little Rock the next day for competition."

Her stupid heart quivered at the memory of the gesture, but she stomped on it. Don't talk. Don't engage. He'd figure it out, and he was already barely leashing his temper. They were in a truck barreling down the freeway toward Santa Fe.

Kane turned down the music to half volume. Montana pouted but compensated for the silence by singing even louder and banging her plastic yogurt spoon rhythmically on the cup holder of her booster seat.

"Why wouldn't you see me if there was no Lorenzo?"

He sounded hurt.

Don't let him get to you. Again.

Why was she still so susceptible? Kane radiated confidence and sex appeal and success. He'd had women proposition him right in front of her, actually elbowing her aside to get to him. And she'd been this little mouse so grateful for the crumbs of his attention. She wasn't going to get caught up in that again. He didn't need her. She hadn't hurt him. No way in hell.

Theirs had not been an equal relationship. She'd adored him. He'd been her first and only, her world, moon, stars, and sun. She'd been his summer fling—a limited shelf life on their affair. A convenience. The girl he'd mostly kept under wraps in his trailer while he'd been working, attending sponsor events, interviews and then riding the hell out of bulls. He'd come back high on adrenaline ready to ride her all night, and she'd let him. She'd loved his intensity, how hot he burned for her, how hot she'd burned for him.

"You knew."

Oh God, the calculating would start. Her eyelids fluttered shut. Of course she'd known. She'd been a month late in August. Almost two months late and nearly always nauseous when he'd dropped her at the airport curb in September with a casual kiss on the cheek, a "see ya," and a reminder to try to eat something while waiting for her flight. He'd even stuffed a few hundreds in her hand like she was a child heading off to college and he the parent. She'd felt a little bit like a paid escort.

Sky had watched him walk away, tears spilling down her face as she willed him to turn around and he hadn't. The pain of it. Standing there feeling abandoned and rejected like she had been so many times before by her parents. She'd wanted him to beg her to leave school and stay with him. Instead she'd stared at the long line of his back, straight and strong, wide shoulders tapering to narrow waist and fluid hips walking as fast and far away from her as he could get, one hand placing his Stetson back on his head, his tumble of dark curls barely visible under the brim.

That image of him leaving had been branded into her brain. It had been her first sculpture in her series 'Out West.' Kane Wilder walking away. God, he'd moved like water. His body hadn't seemed to adhere to the same laws of physics that most of the rest of the world were stuck with. He was a bull rider. An unforgettable man and just to add to her torture, she'd sketched that walk away over and over using charcoal then pastels.

Five months pregnant and barely starting to show, she

made her first bronze casting as a sculpture class project. She still had the final version in her studio only she'd added chaps—fringe flaring, his protective vest and his bull rope dangling in his hand. Back to her.

And that same night while she'd flown east sobbing and terrified—the future feeling like a gaping howl without Kane in it—he'd been photographed with two spray-tanned blondes, tits spilling out of their tight tops, garish frozen cocktails in their hands and Kane between them grinning like it was Christmas.

"Now's not the time to talk about it," she whispered and stared at the desert blurring by.

"You're right. The time to talk was when you suspected. At the latest when you got a positive pregnancy test." Each word was a rock hurled at her chest.

Yeah, well, if you hadn't been Kane Wilder I would have.

But she didn't want to say that. Too honest. Vulnerable. Kane had had women throwing themselves seriously in his path since he'd been fourteen, and now that he was famous, hordes of women lined up for his autograph and more. He wore confidence like his Stetson—sexy, stylish, natural. She was a mass of insecurity around that man and she wasn't going back to living and feeling like that.

"I had my reasons," she said stiffly, totally unable to meet the searching gaze he kept lasering her with. "And I'd prefer you keep your eyes on the road."

The truck accelerated, pressing her deeper into the cushy

black leather seat, but just as quickly he slowed back to a leisurely seventy-eight. Did he do everything fast? Duh. He was a bull rider.

"I can't think of a single reason to justify keeping a child from her father."

"I could name ten," she said flippantly, hating feeling so vulnerable and exposed.

Kane's fingers flexed on the steering wheel. His cheeks hollowed. She heard him swallow.

"Not another word, Sky. Not one more."

"Or what? I get a time out?"

Oh God, he was making her bitchy. Her emotions swung wildly. It was like she'd kept them on such a tight leash the past four years to make a new and stable life for her and her child, but now she'd let go and they were galloping off without her. And why was she antagonizing him? It wasn't her way at all. She was quiet. The pleaser. The one who hung back desperate for approval and acceptance, but wary of the attention.

But every time she looked at all his physical perfection, and felt his confidence and certainty and sexual potency engulf her like a sandstorm, she wanted to slap him. And then she wanted to slap herself harder for being so stupid and falling in love with him at first sight and not having the brains or the willpower or the self-preservation to get over him years ago.

Even now every nerve in her body was clamoring to

touch him. She felt primitive, like a wild animal captive.

It was just lust. Just lust. Just lust she mentally chanted to herself. Nothing else. She was pathetic. Kane had probably forgotten about her the first night. She needed to hook up with a man and wipe the taste and feel of Kane Wilder from her mouth, body and memory forever.

Yeah right.

"It's just lust," she chanted again for good measure.

"I wish to hell it were," he growled startling her from her throes of self-recrimination, "but you'll just have to wait for that part of the solution when we don't have a captive audience." He glanced in the rearview mirror at the little girl who still stared out the window singing.

Sky slapped her hand over her mouth and nearly curled up in embarrassment. She felt the flush roll over her face and down to her collarbone.

"I didn't say that word, did I?" she whispered mortified.

"Sky, you blurted your thoughts all the time around me."

"I did not," she objected. "I've always been quiet. Shy. I let you have your own way in everything."

His quick, narrow-eyed glare scorched her.

"How the hell do you figure that?" he demanded. His normally low, smooth voice was rough. Tension poured off him in waves. It should have been terrifying. Her parents had been volatile and she'd spent her childhood tiptoeing around them unless Bennington was home, so why wasn't she scared now?

"Everything was about you," she said trying to keep some dignity and not let him know how deeply she'd loved him and how badly he'd hurt her without even trying.

"Are we even having the same conversation? Were we even in the same relationship?" he demanded. "One look in the back seat proves nothing was about me. Nothing. If it had been about me, I would have *chosen* to do the *right* thing by you and our child. We'd be married."

The last word sounded like a curse, and it would have been. His self-righteous declaration was like a stab wound to her heart. She'd known he would have married her if she'd told him she was pregnant. But even at nineteen and completely consumed by her love for Kane, she hadn't wanted him to do the *right thing*. She'd wanted him to love her, even without the baby.

The minute she'd suspected she was pregnant, she'd felt sick imagining telling Kane. Oh she knew he'd suck in a deep breath, school his features into bland acceptance and take responsibility, but he was a bull rider fast rising in the ranks. Twenty-two. Fearless. Different city every week. How would he have been a dad? How could she have asked him to give up the career and life he loved? She hadn't been able to stomach the idea of being someone else's burden again, of having her child grow up unwanted, but tolerated, the cause of two people's deep unhappiness, a reminder of lost dreams.

She'd vowed to keep her mouth shut so that her daughter wouldn't grow up with the same snarling resentment she had.

"If it had been all about me—" Kane growled interrupting her churning memories. He broke off. Sucked in a deep breath and seemed to gather his thoughts. Then his eyes flicked over her with heat though his mouth was grim. His voice deepened, and he drawled the next part. "We'd probably have another booster seat back there and we'd be getting ready to install one of those rear-facing infant seats and my hand would be resting on your swollen belly right now."

It was so visual her heart stalled.

"Not funny," she breathed.

"Not laughing, Sky. You lied to me."

How was he turning this all back on her? She'd let him keep his life, his freedom. She hadn't saddled him with a wife and kid he didn't want.

"Take us home." She had to get out of this truck. He was scrambling her mind and her body and weaving a fantasy of them becoming a family, and the craving for the family she'd never had—a real family that was not just a public façade—was starting to edge out reason. And there were a lot of reasons she and Kane would be a disaster.

"I want to go home. I have a whole life, and I don't want to walk away from it."

"Too bad. You stole my child. Without a thought." His voice sounded ripped from his throat like Velcro separating. "Even now you don't regret what you did to our child or to me."

"Why would I?" she shot back. The clawing tension clashed with the memories—him holding her in the Pacific Ocean, the sun dazzling her as they kissed, her teaching him yoga and sitting on his back while he did pushups, him making love to her in the shower, in his truck, in a field, in a pool. They made her reckless and desperate to escape. The visuals of them together kept rolling through her head like a car wreck. "I'm not a genius like you with numbers and everything else, but I can add and subtract and there were more negatives in why you'd be a bad bet for a father than positives."

The minute she spit out the words that she hadn't even consciously formed, she regretted them. Each one. She'd wanted to hurt him because she'd loved him so much, probably still did and always would. But he was making her crazy. Kane hadn't wanted to be a dad at twenty-two when he was consistently ranking in the top five of bull riders on the acknowledged most intense and competitive tour in the world. Still she didn't need to rub his face in it.

It was something that her mother—fueled by drink—would have yelled.

Cruel. Sky stared at her hands in her lap. She'd never deliberately tried to hurt someone before. Her mouth felt metallic. Bile mixed with chai burned her throat. She couldn't look at him. She wanted to say something. Form the right words this time. Kinder words.

He had been her brother's best friend. Her lover. The

father of her child. She'd known him since she was eleven and he fourteen. Kane had never been anything but kind and tender to her. Respectful. When her brother had been critically injured by a bull, Kane had sat with her in the emergency room all night at the hospital waiting while her parents had flown back from Paris. He'd held her when she'd heard the grim news, and she'd soaked his shirt with her tears.

It wasn't his fault that he hadn't fallen in love with her. Kane never would have slept with her if she hadn't made it so easy. She'd practically stalked him, invented an art series she was working on. She'd pretended to be a sophisticated siren with an artistic vision when instead she'd been a naïve, lust-addled, seriously crushing nineteen-year-old with nothing more on her mind than being Kane Wilder's girlfriend.

Sorry.

She thought the word. It was an anvil on her heart. Kane's hurt rolled off him in waves, and she felt like she was drowning. Sorry wasn't going to cut it.

"I didn't mean it like that," she whispered.

She waited. Nothing. Just the engine. And Montana singing and talking to herself. And Kane staring blankly at a straight line of asphalt stretching to the horizon. God, was he even aware he was still driving? Sky gulped in air, panicked for all three of them. Her rioting emotions and finally unearthed resentment were going to kill all of them.

"I'm sorry. I'm sorry. I'm sorry."

Kane made a strangled sound and veered off the highway to the shoulder, and then out into the desert for a dozen or so yards. He killed the engine. And sat there. His shoulders trembled. She could hear him breathe like it was hard.

"Kane," she said after she counted to ten. Then twenty. Thirty. She reached out to touch him. He shook her off. Palmed the keys, opened and slammed the door and stalked off into the desert.

"Where's Daddy going?" Montana asked softly, after a few beats of silence where she and Sky watched Kane create more distance between them. Sky wanted to reassure Montana, but she didn't know what to say. Story of her life.

"Ah…I think for a little walk." She managed to push the words out of her throat.

How was her child coping with this so beautifully whereas she was a mess? Montana's daddy had always been a man in pictures smiling or in a video in some crazy contortion on a bull. She'd never let Montana watch the competitions live because anything could happen and a lot of it was bad, but she'd let her watch the winning rides on YouTube. And she'd shown her child pictures of her daddy as a teen with her uncle who was in heaven. And with her mama hiking, swimming in rivers, hanging on him like he was her entire life because he had been.

But she'd never met him until this morning and Montana was acting like seeing her daddy smile and swoop her out of a gallery and into a truck and away on a long ribbon of unknown asphalt was normal.

But stopping the truck and striding into the desert was not normal. Sky didn't want to think about what that meant because Kane had always been crazy disciplined and controlled.

"What's Daddy doing now?" Montana asked, and her voice quavered.

That snapped Sky to attention. She had to make this right. Somehow. She'd left Kane because she didn't want to live with resentment and disappointment that would turn to hate and hurt like her parents' marriage had. She'd vowed she wouldn't live like that. She turned back to Montana and forced a smile, but Montana was having none of it. Her fingers fumbled uselessly with the childproof harness buckles.

"Montana. No." Sky was stern. That was a hard-and-fast rule. "Don't even try it. Only Mama or another adult unbuckles."

"I want to go with Daddy."

Her heart sunk. It was going to hurt Montana when her daddy rode back into reality on the back of a bull, his secret family out of sight and mostly out of mind. Had Kane even thought of that? He thought of everything else. Planned out and analyzed everything—his bull rides, the routes to the city, his nutritional and exercise requirements, his investments. And he'd burned through online classes like they were matches. He'd been wicked smart and most people probably thought all that intellect was wasted on the back of a bull, but oh, he was a thing of incandescent athletic and physical beauty when he rode.

"We'll go get Daddy, okay?" Sky said snapping herself mentally and emotionally back into the truck. She watched Kane drop down into a small arroyo. Venturing out in the desert with no shoes was stupid, but it was her fault for speaking without thinking. Not like she didn't know how much the wrong words could hurt. She'd grown up in a minefield of verbal grenades.

Sky bunched up the length of her silky skirt in her hand, trying not to think about the wrinkles she'd be creating and the deposit that Jonas had paid for the dress and the shoes despite her continued objections. She swung herself carefully out of the truck.

It was an embarrassingly long drop. The truck was big and the tires massive.

"I want Daddy."

"Let's go get him." Sky infused her voice with false enthusiasm. Her brilliant daughter wasn't fooled.

"I go get Daddy," she said climbing out of the truck after Sky released her.

It would probably go better, Sky thought, wincing inside because in half an hour, Kane had already taken center stage in Montana's life. And what would happen when he walked off again busy with the tour, his sponsor functions? Another busty blonde buckle bunny? Just the thought was a blow.

Worried about Cholla cactus and scorpions, Sky swung Montana up on her hip. She was probably using her daughter as armor. She winced as the hot sandy gravel ground into the soles of her feet. Damn Kane for flinging off her shoes and hurling them at the gallery. Not that they would have done her any good in the soft sand. She probably would have broken her ankle.

"Kane?"

No answer.

Calm down, she cautioned. He wouldn't walk forever. Sky took a few tentative steps. Forget it. The pain if she stepped on sharp rocks or cactus would be her penance. And if she got a cut on the sole of her foot, at least it would be a reminder to keep her tongue controlled and to not lash out at Kane when she was really dealing with her own pain.

And then she saw him a short distance down a gentle slope. He was bent over like he'd been punched hard in the solar plexus and was struggling to suck in air. Hands on his knees, head down. Sky hesitated on the lip of the arroyo. She looked back at the truck and then at Kane. Indecision clawed.

"Are you hurt?" she called out nervously, not wanting to panic Montana.

No answer.

"Are you okay?"

Stupid question from a stupid girl who'd never known how to handle people well and Kane least of all.

She had done this. Hurt this beautiful, perfect man, and his pain seemed to manifest exponentially in her chest.

"Hey, do you see any wild flowers underneath the acacia tree?" she asked Montana and pointed to a tree only a few yards from Kane. "Maybe you could pick Daddy a flower to cheer him up?" she said, her worried gaze bounding between Kane and their child. She rushed down into the arroyo, sliding in the warm, almost hot sandy soil.

"Why Daddy sad?" Montana asked quietly.

She really was the worst mother in the world. So determined to protect her child's delicate heart, and face it, her own, that she'd just torched all three.

"Mommy was mean," she whispered, surprising herself with her honesty although the understatement choked in her throat.

Holding Montana's hand, they walked down the gentle slope.

"Find a flower," she whispered, seeing a few, but wanting to give Montana something to do and to give Kane time to pull himself together again.

"Kane." She put her hand out. Touched his back. It was like touching one of her sculptures when she was working with them. Hot. Hard. Detailed. She could feel the delineation of each muscle group without even pressing hard with her fingers.

He'd be an exquisite model for an artist's anatomy class. She'd certainly done an obsessive amount of sketching him while they'd been together. And she'd taken a lot of pictures.

All that strength trembled beneath her tentative fingers, which scared the heck out of her. Yelling she'd grown up with. Broken dishes, slammed doors and sometimes more. As a child, she'd been terrified. She'd hidden under her bed and later had curled up in her closet, but at least that was familiar. Kane's tight control fraying was something scarier because she didn't know what to expect. What if he couldn't piece himself back together?

"Tell me what's wrong," she whispered, not sure if he was still dealing with what she'd said or if he'd been bitten by a scorpion or a rattler or a…

He sucked in a ragged breath, and then another. Then jerked up and spun to face her. She jumped back and cringed. He stepped closer, the tension pouring off his body in waves. Sky wanted to run, but her body had short-circuited. She was numb. Useless. His face was pale and tight.

"How can you ask that?"

"I'm sorry." Her voice broke, and she was aware of the utter inadequacy of the words. "I'm sorry," she repeated. "I need to know." She brushed a trickle of sweat off her hairline with the back of her hand. It was getting hot as the sun climbed higher. And Montana's life depended on Kane pulling himself together. She needed to suck up her own pain and not cause him more. "Are you okay?"

Stupid question. He was a long way from okay. Neither

of them could even see okay in their rearview mirror. But she meant to drive. His eyes shimmered. He looked agonized.

"Why?" he asked taking two steps toward her, lurching in the sand a little. It was the first time she'd seen him move awkwardly in the twelve years she'd known him. "Why?" he asked, eyes and face stark and bleak.

"Why what?" Her voice trembled more than his.

"Why did you think I'm unfit to be a father?"

She hadn't said that, exactly, had she?

"I..." She took a step back. And another, her feet sinking in the gravelly sand that poked the soles of her feet. "I...you and I are so...different." The sun, rising higher in the sky, now felt like needles in her eyes. She had to squint against the brightness and the morning breeze whipped her long, dark hair sideways across her face making Kane blur in and out of her vision.

"Bullshit." He knocked away that excuse. "Why did you keep me apart from my child?"

"I don't want to talk about this now," she said nervous about what might pop out of her mouth and reveal just how desperately she'd been in love with him, and how much fear and insecurity had once ruled her life. Once, she reminded herself. Not now.

"We're going to talk about it until I can wrap my head around how you could do something so cruel."

"Cruel?" she echoed. She'd loved him. She'd wanted him to pursue his dream. She'd wanted him to be free, not to saddle him with a wife and kid he didn't want. And she didn't want to go from one cold, dysfunctional family to another with snarling tension and broken hearts. She'd wanted better for her child, better than she'd gotten.

"How could you do that?" he demanded, his voice a lash. "How can you not understand what the fuck you did by keeping our child a secret from me?" His breath sawed in and out.

The barely restrained anger in his voice sent panic rocketing through her. Her breath reduced to tiny puffs as if by every part of her getting smaller she could escape the growling fury that was battling to get out of Kane. She'd always sucked at confrontation and was completely unable to deal with Kane like this.

"I…I…" It struck her now how appropriate that pronoun was and had been. She hadn't even thought about Kane's feelings. Not really. She'd been protecting their child. And honestly herself as well. "I didn't…" She was so bad at this. Thinking under pressure. Everything just froze up and shut down. Fight or flight. What a joke. She just froze when she panicked. She would have been the first person in her evolutionary tribe to be gobbled down by the saber tooth or whatever wild animal stalked her ancient ancestors.

"I knew you wouldn't want a baby," she finally whispered. "It was so obvious."

He'd always used a condom. Always. And he'd suggested she go on the pill "just to be extra safe."

Extra safe hadn't been safe enough. Kane should come with a potency warning. She forced herself to meet his angry glare.

The sparks that had been practically shooting out of his eyes went out like a dead battery and something invisible inside seeped out. Kane fell to his knees in front of her.

Kane Wilder on his knees in the dirt.

Her mind just spun like the Apple icon with too many open tabs. Kane was so proud. So vividly alive and on fire and now he had crumpled to the sand like a discarded shirt.

She took the long, hard three steps toward him, and her fingers gently threaded in his curls. This time he let her touch him. She stroked her fingers once, twice, letting the dark silk curl through her fingers.

"Daddy." Sky had been so absorbed in the seething family drama all of her own selfish making according to Kane, she thought bitterly, that she had forgotten she'd sent her daughter on a mission. Montana clutched a fistful of white flowers. "These will make you happy," she said, so sweet and innocent, Sky felt like she needed a whip or one of Kane's spurs to flagellate herself.

He looked at his daughter, his face and his eyes softer, some of the tension drained out of his body. He took the flowers.

"Mommy's sorry, Daddy." She looked so serious. "Mommy won't be mean again. She promises." Montana's eyes swiveled toward her clearly worried. Of the few times she'd allowed herself to imagine a reunion with Kane, it had always been joyful, never this awfully painful and awkward. She didn't know who hurt more. Him or her, and Sky had thought she was done being hurt by Kane a long time ago.

His eyes closed. He sucked in a breath. Sky couldn't breathe. At. All. She felt like a criminal. Worse—all the reasons she'd kept her pregnancy and her child a secret seemed all wrong. But she knew, absolutely knew that the reality of Kane's life would not make her reasons stand out so starkly black or white. Daddy a hero. Mommy a villain.

"She's not mean, baby girl." He leaned forward and kissed his daughter's sweet curls. "She's just… just…" And it seemed like for the first time since she'd known him, Kane Wilder was out of words.

Chapter Five

"NOW THAT'S A walk of shame worth getting to the arena early for." The voice was low and amused and drawled like warm honey but with enough of an edge that Kane—walking into a side door of the arena in Santa Fe, his duffel bag slung over a wide shoulder, a garment bag dangling from his fingers and his free hand holding his daughter's tiny hand—paused.

Sky, bare feet burning from the hot asphalt even though Kane had parked as close as he could to the arena, struggled behind him. One hand bunched up the flared lace dress that was too long without the heels. She also held Montana's backpack and clutched at the front of the dress that was embarrassingly low now that the body tape she'd used to hold the halter dress in place on the sides had lost its stick.

The cowboy, who'd been looking at videos of bulls on his phone, while he stretched in an isolated area of the arena, casually arched into another stretch, but his eyes were sharp on Sky and then her child. His gaze lingered, lit with knowledge and then homed in on Kane. Sky had a feeling he had cool indifference down to an art form.

She struggled to control her blush. She shouldn't care what some random cowboy thought. But no, full bright pink washed over her, but she did force herself to hold the cowboy's gaze for all of two seconds. Damn Kane again.

"Prom date?" He smirked.

Kane's eyes said 'fuck you,' while his trademark smile that sold enough products to fill a house, slid easily into place, and the other rider clearly didn't like it, or him, at all.

"Cody, this is my fiancée Sky Gordon, and I'd thank you to keep your hands and your attitude, and your speculations to yourself."

Sky was so shocked at the F word he dropped so casually, Montana's backpack slid to the floor, and as she bent to retrieve it, her foot landed on the skirt, tugging her bodice down precariously low. She clutched at it as if it were the only thing between her and a fiery doom.

The cowboy laughed. "Guess we won't shake hands," he said, his eyes briefly lit with amusement, and despite the situation, Sky suddenly had the urge to smile. The whole day was absurd. Her in this glamorous dress at four in the afternoon hundreds of miles from the artist pre-auction brunch she'd been attending. Now she was skulking barefoot through a side door of the arena that in a few hours would be packed with fans and families and buckle bunnies all wanting to watch a bull rider give his all to make history.

"So I guess hanging tight for eight seconds isn't your entire skill set." Cody went into another stretch. "Who's the kid?"

"This is my daughter…" And then Kane's face shut down like a computer screen. He was pale under his tan, and a muscle ticked in his jaw.

Sky felt his tension like an icy hand sliding down her spine. When would all this unbearable awkwardness and the questions and the doubt and the worry ease? How had Kane, who'd demanded answers to everything she hadn't wanted to tell him, not asked the one question she'd have been willing to answer?

"Montana." Sky slid the name into the conversation, but her voice barely hit a whisper. Kane's eyes swiveled toward hers. They were hot with accusation and again the tremble woke and rumbled deep in the pit of her stomach.

"I'm watching Daddy ride bulls," Montana told Cody.

Sky winced, worried what the bull rider who clearly was amused by Kane's predicament would say. Something cynical and sarcastic no doubt.

"Then you're in for some fun tonight, Montana." He stressed the name. His eyes narrowed and sparked when he looked at Kane. "Your daddy…" again the word had exaggerated emphasis "…has a reputation…" his gaze seemed to laugh at Kane "…of being pretty good sticking on the back of a bull."

Montana nodded her head. "He's the best!"

A small smile might have twitched the corners of Cody's

mouth. "Not everyone would agree with that, but yeah he does okay."

Definitely not a friend. Sky was so tired of the tension between her and Kane and now there was barely veiled hostility between Kane and the other rider.

"I watch Daddy ride on Mama's computer on Sundays."

Kane jerked a little next to her, and without thinking, she ran her hand soothingly down his arm, tracing the corded muscles. A ghost memory of her fingers digging into those muscles so she could angle herself up and he could slam into her harder, deeper slapped her memory without warning.

She jerked her hand away.

Stupid. Don't touch. Don't get caught up in him again.

It had been four years away from all that masculine energy and animal charisma, and she had to fight the urge to not touch him, to not fall under his spell. She should not fall victim to the desperate need for love and attention that had plagued her during her childhood, nor would she languish in the guilt trap where she'd spent her teen years, sorry for her existence. Sorry for everything far beyond her control. And she wasn't going to put Montana in that situation—ever. Kane Wilder and his questions and demands could go to hell.

Stay strong.

Cody's expression slid back to cold as he eyed Kane. "Alicia will be pleased with the news," he drawled.

Kane didn't react. His hard body and harder attitude already out-harded the damn sculpture that had landed them both in this mess.

"She's heading out late tonight for a family wedding if you want to keep a low profile." He jammed back in his earbuds. "Like you ever would."

Then the side of his mouth kicked up slightly, and Sky realized this man would be devastatingly attractive if he ever made the effort. "Sky." His voice sounded like a taunt. "Like the name." He looked up at Kane, his gaze definitely indicating this wasn't over.

Cody turned his attention back to his phone and another video, but Kane was already striding away.

"Um…bye," Sky said and walked after Kane, forcing herself and her short legs not to run. She already looked ridiculous enough.

He slowed a little, clearly impatient.

"What was that about?" she asked.

"Nothing." His face and voice were tighter than ever. He swung Montana up on his shoulders, and she laughed reached above her head as if she could stretch and touch the ceiling. Again his strides ate up the long, cement hallway.

"Stop rushing." She had to rush to catch up.

"Can't be late. I have two interviews scheduled at four and four ten with local radio stations and a TV sportscast at four twenty-five. Then a meet and greet with some local sponsors and their families."

"Great, this again," she huffed, pissed to have to chase after him when she didn't want to even be in the same state, and frustrated that she kept stepping on the fragile stretch lace hem of the dress. She was going to trip again. Or rip the dress and lose her deposit.

"This being my job?" Kane's jaw was so tight and tense he could pulverize walnuts.

He didn't stop walking.

"Yeah," Sky said. "You used to always stash me away when you went to your meet and greets and interviews and even most of the shows like I was a secret."

It had hurt how he'd hidden her away for the most part, leaving her in the trailer waiting for him to come back.

"Is that why you left?" Kane stopped walking. "You wanted to punish me for my career?"

"I wanted you to be happy," Sky burst out, tired of being the only one in the wrong. She quickly smiled up at Montana to cover the lapse and then lowered her voice. "I wanted you to live the life you wanted."

Couldn't he see? It had been about him. All about him. Keeping him happy. If he'd loved her, it would have been different. She would have been thrilled about the baby, excited to share the news. But he hadn't. Not once had he said he'd loved her. Never. And she'd blurted it out their first time together like the immature and sappy idiot she'd been.

"You and Montana are my life." His voice and frustrated expression dismissed her motivation. His fingers around

Montana's ankles tightened fractionally. "How was I supposed to be happy without my child?"

Before she could fully register that Kane had listed her importance first, and his heartfelt question, he turned around and started walking quickly away. Sky had no idea where he was going. And she was tired of being in this stupid dress, and looking like a hookup that had gone badly. Cody had been right. She probably did look like a lost high school girl who'd escaped a really bad prom. With a baby. The visual she presented was funny, or would have been if it had been someone else.

"Kane, just stop for a moment. Just stop."

He didn't.

"You're acting irrationally. You can't keep us..." She paused, hesitant to use the word 'prisoner.' Would Montana know what that meant? Plus it sounded more than a little melodramatic. What she wouldn't give for five minutes with him without her overly curious and sometimes disturbingly brilliant little girl listening.

"I don't even have shoes."

Or proper underwear.

"My dress is about to go pull a full wardrobe malfunction. I am supposed to be at a party tonight."

He stopped.

Icy gray eyes locked on to her.

"You are going to miss it. I didn't even know her name." His voice was a tensely whispered accusation, and again, Sky felt herself flush. She hated this. She'd tried so hard to hold her feelings at bay for so long, protect herself from this man she'd loved whole-heartedly nearly half her life, telling herself that she was protecting her daughter as well, but every moment was a slap in her face that she hadn't considered Kane's feelings. Not. At. All.

"My own child's name."

'I'm sorry' wouldn't cut it. And she wasn't sure she could have done it differently even if she had thought about Kane's feelings, but she'd been nineteen. Scared. Hurt. And really self-absorbed.

"Why?"

"Kane, I can't…" She shook her head. She couldn't explain. Open herself up like that. Just split herself down the middle and let her heart and guts spill out for his disdainful perusal. He'd admired her parents so much. Loved them. He wouldn't understand. Wouldn't believe her. "Please stop asking that," she said, so exhausted that if she could have sat down she probably would have fallen into a stupor.

"You're like a dog with a bone," Sky said, looking up at Montana, who smiled down, blissfully unaware of the tension her presence was causing, and Sky would do anything, *anything* to keep it that way. "Let's just have this discussion later."

"Already four years too late."

"I can't do this here." She looked around at the bowels of the arena. A few people were coming and going, mostly workers with boxes on hand carts.

"Here is where we are. You could have shared the exciting news over dinner or breakfast four years ago."

"Exciting?"

The way his eyes narrowed and sparked she shut up her mouth. Of course she loved Montana and had never once regretted having a baby after she'd been born. She'd been very conflicted in the months before her birth. So did that also make her a monster? Easy for Kane to be judgey. And if Montana had not been perched on his shoulders playing with his hat and hair, she would have called him on his self-righteous attitude.

Did he somehow not comprehend the concept of privacy when it wasn't swirling around him? For being such a public figure on the AEBR circuit, Kane Wilder had been intensely private—staying in a trailer far from the arena, usually keeping her far from his profession and rarely talking about his family except his older brother Luke.

"The gallery owner," he suddenly barked. "Are you involved with him?"

Where had that come from?

"None of your business."

Like he hadn't been with dozens, no hundreds, maybe thousands of women since her.

"You're upset to miss the party."

"I'm upset because having my sculpture chosen to be a part of the art auction for the hospital guild was an incredible career opportunity."

He watched her, clearly thinking. "Who picked the sculpture?"

"Dr. Austen Sheridan met me at an art fair where I was a juried artist." She couldn't help the note of pride that had crept into her voice. Many artists had to try for years to get into that show last Christmas. "He came to my studio and saw all my sculptures. He loved the western bull-riding theme." She felt a little embarrassed now, not wanting Kane to read too much into her subject matter. "He chose that one."

"I bet he did."

"It was a great honor." Sky's temper notched up.

"You're being played, Sky."

If he hadn't been holding her child, no their child, she would have kicked him.

"How so?" she challenged. "You think my art doesn't belong there?" Her voice rose. She couldn't help it. She'd been dismissed for most of her life. Did Kane think he was the only one worthy of a stellar career?

"You are insanely talented, Sky. Truly gifted. I am awed by you and your work. It's powerful and emblematic, but Dr. Sheridan…" he sneered the name "…chose that piece for a reason."

"Why?" She was momentarily deflected from her anger as Kane's admiration rang true in his voice.

He made an irritated sound. "I need to get you more

practical clothes." He glanced at his watch and then pushed open the double doors at the end of the hallway.

Sky followed, her head swirling from the change of subject. They had so much seething between them it was like neither of them could focus on what they really needed to resolve. But she would feel better in normal clothes.

KANE WALKED DOWN the outer circle of the arena where all the merchandise and food vendors were restocking for tonight's show. He felt dizzy, a little out of his body, as if he were slightly out of phase with reality. He couldn't even remember why he had brought Sky and Montana to the public areas. The doors weren't open for another hour at least, and he had eight minutes forty-nine seconds to get to the broadcast area for two interviews. In nineteen minutes eleven seconds he had a meet and greet at a whiskey sponsor's tent. He still needed to check his rope. Stretch. Get focused. He felt like he was underwater. Drowning.

Betrayed. On all sides.

How had he not thought to ask his child's name in the last six hours?

What was wrong with him? He should have thought of that. Obvious. Why Montana?

Sky had kept so many secrets from him, and a whole life that should have been theirs. Stolen, and she wouldn't tell him why.

Liar.

The word tasted metallic on his tongue.

He'd trusted her. They'd been friends long before lovers. Sky had been the only woman he'd let travel with him, stay with him and actually sleep with him after they had done so many other things. Sky had given him a glimpse of what his life could be. And he'd craved it. Unconditional love. The only person who had loved him when he lost. When he hurt. Her love had been the one pure and perfect thing in his life. Or so he'd thought.

So many lies. So many questions. Alicia and management were going to want answers he didn't have. The AEBR prided itself on its family-friendly image and one of its biggest stars couldn't just show up holding a three-year-old who looked so much like him it was eerie, without an explanation.

A deadbeat dad. He felt it like a blow. Everything he was, everything he believed in just dropkicked, discarded. Sky had made him into a deadbeat dad. Herself a single mother. That shit ended today. Now. That was the only thing that made sense in all the shit running through his head.

Clothes. She needed clothes. No way in hell was he letting Sky parade around in that dress. Fucking Cody. What wasn't threatening to slip indecently low, clung to her like a beautiful blue, lacy skin making her look like a character in *Avatar*, even more ethereal and otherworldly than she did already with her huge, heavily fringed deep blue, nearly violet eyes that he'd always drowned in.

His heart burned, but his lungs seemed frozen. He couldn't get enough air. Couldn't focus his thoughts. Everything spun and flew and raced dizzyingly around and around, his brain on fire like it used to be before he'd learned to meditate, focus, control, maintain balance through strenuous mental and physical discipline.

And all his famed control had been felled when a little girl with his eyes, his hair and his smile ran across a gallery floor and stopped and looked up at him.

Daddy.

There was his life before.

And now after.

Montana.

And he needed to stop. Focus. Think. Plan. Only no time.

Eight minutes.

Shoes. Clothes. A place to wait until after the show.

Hotel.

Rollaway bed. What kind of bed did a three-year-old sleep in?

His will. Attorney. Financial planner. College plan. Was he even on her birth certificate? He didn't dare ask until he had himself under control. Christ was he going to have to adopt his own daughter?

His one vow to himself shattered.

He felt sucker punched.

Life insurance. He had it for his mother although she didn't need money now. He'd have to change the beneficiary. Get Montana and Sky on his health insurance. Passport. Marriage license. The list kept growing in his mind. Blurred at the edges.

He'd sort the legal issues tomorrow when he drove them back to Scottsdale for the Phoenix show. Pack up her apartment or wherever she lived because Sky was not going back to her old life. This morning had been her first day of *after* too.

Seven minutes forty-nine seconds.

"YOU'RE NOT SERIOUS." Sky was mortified. "I can't wear this." She tugged at the frayed hems of the Daisy Duke shorts emblazoned with AEBR in pink bull-horn-shaped bling on the butt. The tight deep V of the white T-shirt with AEBR Tour '17 and a bucking bull with a cowboy on her chest was almost as bad. She didn't have a bra, which she felt was screamingly obvious with the thin, stretchy, white cotton T. Slut much? The look was completed by pair of red cowboy boots. Great. Red, white and blue. Kane was probably secretly laughing his ass off. He knew she was modest, well, when not bouncing with him. She looked like a...buckle bunny.

"Not a lot of wardrobe options at the arena," Kane said sounding so practical that Sky wanted once again to smack him. She did not like this new, emerging violent side of herself.

"If you hadn't over-reacted…" she objected and crossed her arms over her chest thinking of her phone and purse and change of clothes back at the gallery.

If I hadn't panicked like always. If I'd have been able to think.

"Over-reacted," he echoed in disbelief. "If you hadn't been so secretive you would currently have a sprawling house in the town or city of your choice and a walk-in closet full of clothes. Yours and mine." He emphasized the last word as if she'd somehow forgotten that he had declared his intention to keep her.

Like she was a tea set he didn't really want but felt he should keep as a gesture of family respect. And a beautiful house wouldn't have prevented all the rifts that would have driven them apart.

"You're trying to humiliate me. You're enjoying this."

Sky noticed the salesperson, whose booth wasn't yet officially open, but who had been stocking up her small, colorful display, and who was studiously trying to look like she wasn't listening.

Kane smiled. "Darlin'." He leaned toward her with the famous dimpled smile easy on his beautiful mouth that she wanted to slap. The worst part was that even as his mouth claimed hers, she forgot that she wasn't ever going to kiss him again. Her lips parted, and her breath feathered. She felt like he was pouring fire down her throat and she swayed into him, one hand coming up to hold his arm to steady herself. A sound escaped, and she sighed into his mouth.

"I'm enjoying nothing. You've ensured this is the worst day in my entire goddamn life," he whispered against her mouth, his lips still feathering hers apart. "I'm finding nothing enjoyable in the fact that my child is a stranger to me—as is her mother."

He winked and straightened, his eyes hard as metal. "We'll discuss all the details later, baby."

Sky felt like he'd dumped an ice bucket on her head. He hated her and he could still light her up. Her breath was embarrassingly ragged, and she couldn't look at him. Not. Ever. Again. He was so much better at pretending than she could ever be. One more strike against Kane Wilder. And, oh God, now her nipples were getting in on the action.

"Mama pretty." Montana tugged on her hand.

Montana now sported a pleather fringe jacket, cowgirl hat and cowboy boots and cuddled a bull stuffed toy.

Kane made a bit of small talk with the girl who had sold them the clothes. Another woman had found Sky and Montana the boots. Both of the vendors had probably been burning with curiosity, but they'd tried hard to hide it. Kane had handed out hundreds like they were candy to pay for the boots and clothes.

Show-off.

"Kane, the T-shirts for the 4-H group you sponsor in Phoenix are back and ready for me to distribute. You usually sign them before the kids get here. He has so many groups he sponsors." The young girl, sweetly crushing on Kane, turned to smile at Sky.

"Thank you, Janie, I will." Again Kane glanced at the massive watch that looked like it did a heck of a lot more than tell time. "Once I finish a couple of interviews, I will come sign all the shirts. Let's roll."

They walked toward a large cordoned-off area marked 'press' with lots of people, lights, equipment and a buzz of activity. Sky slowed, feeling massively uncomfortable. She'd always felt bad that he left her out of this part but now that there were more people moving about, most of them with a strong sense of purpose, Sky balked.

"What?" Kane waited. "You wanted to experience my job, all of it, the whole tour." His voice had a definite edge.

"We'll just wait…" She looked around for somewhere to sit or something to do. Montana had books in her bag. And now a stuffed bull. And blanket. She might take a nap.

"You're going to be busy," she said looking at the press area, nervousness making her voice husky. "Really busy."

She didn't like crowds on a normal day. Walking the gauntlet of press with an AEBR celebrity while she was wearing a buckle bunny outfit was not in her plans. She knew her parents didn't watch anything that covered the

AEBR or rodeos since Bennington had died, but they still owned a huge ranch and other properties in Scottsdale. Some of their friends might catch a glimpse of her and Montana and Kane and put two and two together. She'd already ruined their lives enough. She didn't need to rub their noses in their grief by hanging on the arm of the man they blamed for their son getting into bull riding instead of heading off to college to study business and law like they'd expected. She didn't need to add one more insult.

"I am not hiding my daughter away like a secret," he hissed.

"There you are, Mr. Wilder." A man with a headset walked out of the press area. "Right on time as usual."

He shook Kane's hand, glanced at Sky and kept staring. His eyes lit with interest and Kane frowned.

"This way," he said motioning for Kane to follow. "Ma'am, you can come too. Tom Davis." His voice oozed charm and he held out a hand. "It's lovely to see Mr. Wilder bring a guest."

Sky barely restrained an eye roll. Kane Wilder probably squired busty, blonde beauties to interviews on a daily basis. With her slim body, barely there breasts and long black hair she definitely didn't fit Kane's dance card.

"Welcome to the AEBR," he gushed, still holding her hand. "You are in for a great show. I can let you sit in the press area if you'd like. I can give you some pointers on what to look for with the bulls and the cowboys during the rides if you are new to the tour."

Sky dredged up a smile, and gently tugged back her hand. "Aaaah, thank you." She hated how she looked to Kane for the answer. Already she was reverting to her teenaged self or worse, her mother. Apologetic. Submissive. Looking for direction.

"Thanks, Tom," Kane said easily. "But I have Sky and Montana in the family section." Two bull riders walked by, greeted Kane and stared at Sky, glances clearly taking in the view. They spoke in a language she didn't speak, probably Portuguese. They gave Kane a thumbs-up.

"I'll wait for you outside the press area," Sky said stiffly, arms crossed high on her chest. She'd always been small breasted, but with the T-shirt, she felt like she was flaunting the small gifts nature had given her in bright lights.

"Hold up a sec," Kane said unzipping his garment bag.

The way he'd been checking his watch, Sky didn't think he had a second to spare, but even time cooperated with Kane Wilder.

He pulled out a light blue silky western-style shirt with black snaps and fed her arms through the sleeves.

"Kane, I can do it," she said conscious that some of the din of the press area had quieted. She could feel the looks and smirks even though she kept her eyes glued to his hands as they moved up the shirt. Snap. Snap.

"More fun this way."

She quickly looked up to discern his mood. Could he be

forgiving, letting go of some of the tension that had ridden him so hard the last six hours? His eyes were hooded, his face intent, but his hands were gentle.

The shirt was silky against her skin, and she had to fight the urge to hug the fabric close to her body. He cuffed the sleeves four times, and they stood toe-to-toe, and for a moment, his gaze dropped to her mouth. She held her breath. Was he going to kiss her again? Did she want him to?

"It's like a dress," Kane said, amusement tingeing his voice. Then he slid a belt off the hanger and from a separate sealed compartment he pulled out a buckle.

He wrapped the belt around her waist, and worked on fastening the buckle. Sky held her breath when his knuckles brushed against her. His hands were warm, and she could feel goose bumps rise along her arms and her tummy as they tingled with awareness. She gasped and his sandalwood and cedar scent teased her senses, making her feel a little dizzy.

"Won't you need this to ride?" she whispered, recognizing the buckle for what it was—the AEBR World Championship buckle from last year.

He finally met her gaze, seeking something Sky thought with a sinking heart that wasn't there. Once again she was coming up short. Her breath squeezed in her lungs. This close, she could see his long, spiky lashes that framed his beautiful eyes so dramatically. His pale blue irises that seemed to go silver when he when he was angry or aroused darkened to turbulent gray. She'd never seen him angry close up until today, but she remembered the color when he was aroused. She'd mixed pigments trying to match that mercurial silver shot through with a little blue.

His eyes were spectacular. But so were his dark brows, his bones, his sensuous mouth that still managed to shout masculine. "You're so beautiful," she said helplessly, unable to censor her thoughts.

He let go of the belt and straightened up slowly, his gaze not wavering, and Sky realized with a thud of her heart that she could see forever when she looked at Kane. She had no idea how she'd found the strength to push him away four years ago. Her fear had been more powerful than her love, which was truly pathetic to admit, but she didn't think she'd be able to do it again.

Somehow, in one day and one mad dash across the southwest desert, her life had once again changed.

"I'll wait," she said, meaning it, hating it, but knowing with despair that it was true.

Chapter Six

SIX HOURS LATER Sky's life had spun around in another one-eighty. And feeling punch drunk she curled up on an ugly blue and lilac vinyl cushioned waiting room seat and watched Montana play "tea party with Daddy." Her heart wrenched because Daddy, after a perfect high-scoring, jaw-dropping ride in tonight's final, had ended up on a stretcher behind the closed doors in the ER.

Sky hadn't seen it happen. She'd seen the ride—and the slam of amazement, thrill, pride, fear and love that he could actually do that had stolen her breath; but Montana had dropped her bull and then her cowgirl hat, and while Sky had crawled on the disgusting kettle corn and soda splashed cement to retrieve both, the crowd, standing up and cheering had suddenly groaned, screamed and then gone eerily silent.

By the time she'd scrambled to her feet, Kane was flat in the dirt, and the clowns were distracting the bull and the cowboy on his horse had even galloped forward, lasso whirling. Kane got up, after what seemed like an agonizingly long time, but then he staggered, nearly going down again before someone from the medical team helped him to walk off. Sky was sick with worry. For all she knew Daddy might never get a chance to actually play tea party with Montana.

What if today—six hours in his truck with one stop, incongruously for pancakes at one-thirty in the afternoon—was all the normal Kane got with his child?

Stop.

Sky jumped to her feet too agitated to try to contain the fear and doubt and guilt assailing her mind and her body. Twelve hours ago Kane hadn't even known he had a child. She should have been winding down from her splashy evening event at the gallery. Montana's daddy should still have been limited to pictures and images on YouTube. Now what?

What if he were like Bennington? Her brother had gone down, been trampled by a bull, and when he'd been rolling away from it, a hoof had caught his head. Her brother, the golden one, the beloved son and brother, had never gotten up. Never spoken again. What if today were her last memory of Kane—him angry, bewildered, closed off and feeling betrayed but still driven to fix the situation. As if that were possible, but Kane, ever the optimist, was determined to try.

God, she could use some of his optimism now. She'd been four years without him, and now, even though she'd dragged her feet, protested all day, and wrapped herself in a defensive cloak, all she wanted to do was curl herself around him. Promise him that she would try to surmount her doubts and salvage something of their relationship so that Montana had a shot at having her mom and dad in her life.

Together?

Did she have the nerve to actually go for that? Had he really been serious or just reacting? Maybe once he settled down, he'd realize how improbable the idea was. If he could think at all. She mentally shook off the fear. She had to be strong for herself and their child.

Theirs. It was the first time the thought had come naturally all day.

And now it might be too late. Agony shot through her like a flaming arrow. Why wouldn't anyone tell her anything? Her fault because she wasn't family. Because they didn't know her. When she'd finally gathered her wits enough to try to find the medical staging area at the arena, Montana trailing quiet and exhausted behind her, the only thing she'd been given had been an eviction order, and when she'd tried to push past the security guard, she and Montana had been escorted out of the arena and into the night.

No keys to the truck. No money. The buckle bunny style clothes.

She'd convinced an off-duty cop who'd been helping with security to drop her off at the hospital. He'd been skeptical, but Sky thought that Montana had swayed him. She'd asked him if he knew her daddy. It had been pretty much the only thing that had gone right all day.

How many times had he been hurt in four years?

Sky really didn't want to know. She paced by a fish tank of tropical, brightly colored fish. Weren't they supposed to soothe you and lower your blood pressure? Not working.

Should she try to find his brother Luke somehow? His mother? Sky didn't even know if either of them lived in Scottsdale anymore. She knew Luke rode the professional rodeo circuit. Kane had told her. He'd watched his brother's stats and tapes obsessively. He'd been so proud of Luke.

"Mama, I want Daddy." Montana was playing pretend tea party with her bull in a toy area in the emergency waiting room.

"Me too. Soon, baby. I hope soon," Sky said automatically—not wanting to lie, but wanting to reassure her daughter. She couldn't imagine a world where Kane wasn't striding through it so confidently, so sure he was right.

A large group of people surged into the emergency room. Three suits, but also several cowboys, which made Sky think they must be from the AEBR. About time. One woman, tall, slim and dark, wearing a dark business suit with a red blouse who was perhaps late thirties or early forties seemed to be in charge. She was talking into a cell phone, but also clearly directing the others in the suits who were typing out something on iPads.

Sky bit her lip. Her instinct was to hide. But she'd been doing that for four years. Bennington used to say 'ball up' when he had to do something difficult that he didn't want to do. The unexpected memory made her smile. What was the female equivalent: ovary up? Womb up? Somehow it seemed sexist that there wasn't a cool phrase that she could toss out to get her butt in gear and quiet her always-clamoring nerves.

She was tired of being afraid.

"Montana, I'm going to go talk to those people for a moment," she said softly.

Montana looked up from where she and her stuffed bull were having tea.

"Then we see Daddy?"

"I hope so. I'll be right over there." Montana stood up, looked with interest at the knot of people and then resumed pouring out more tea and asking her bull if he wanted cookies.

Sky shuddered to think about the germs in the emergency room waiting area toys. She normally would have wiped everything down but Brandy hadn't packed any antibacterial wipes in Montana's backpack. Sucking in a deep breath for courage, Sky touched her hair that she'd twisted up in a messy bun that she'd done and redone reflexively on the way to the hospital. Kane always liked her hair down, specifically he'd liked to take it down, run his fingers through it, his beautiful blue-gray eyes darkening as he became aroused. Would she ever see those beautiful eyes open and focused on her again?

She needed to find out how Kane was even though she was terrified of the information.

If she'd married Kane, she'd be in there now. Or at least

people wouldn't have treated her like she had a disease. If she'd married Kane she would have had to go through this waiting routine many times now. God, how many times had he been hurt the past four years? She hadn't wanted to know. If she married Kane she wouldn't be meeting his colleagues in this skimpy outfit. No wonder no one took her seriously. She was going to kill Kane for this after he was better.

And he would get better, she vowed and with shoulders back and chin up a little because she could pretend she had it together for a few minutes, Sky walked toward the group wondering when they'd notice her. Being small and shy meant that you could really sneak up on people and often when you were there, they didn't notice you right away.

No one missed or ignored Kane. He'd open a door and everyone would instantly look up, stop talking, approach him.

Damn charisma.

It wasn't helping him now.

Small, shy and stealthy did not work on this crew.

The cowboys were open with their curiosity.

The businesspeople looked on with cool disdain.

"Yes?" the woman in charge asked, guarded. Did she ever smile?

"I'm wondering if you have news on Kane, please."

She hated herself for adding that last word. *Please* would not work on that armor.

"No," the woman said all succinct confidence as her eyes swept down Sky, clearly unimpressed. "And you need to go home, honey."

"I can't."

That was true on many levels.

"Honey." The woman's voice expressed patience and dismissal at the same time. "I have been down this road with y'all."

That brought Sky up short. Like she was part of a group. Of what? Groupies? Buckle bunnies? Did Kane have so many women following him they could form a band? Why was he trying to drag her around if he had his own band of women?

"Just head on home. Kane's going to need his rest tonight. Besides, sweet cheeks, ever heard of HIPPA?"

Sky drew herself up to her full height of maybe five-two with the boots. Five-three with good posture. Maybe.

"I am not a…" She could barely bring herself to say the word.

"Buckle bunny." The dark-haired woman laughed. "Nothing wrong with the bunnies," she said, her voice not unkind. "But you are definitely not his type."

Tall. Blonde. Or honey brown. Sometimes two at a time she'd read more than once when she was making a scrapbook for Montana. She'd had to cut out almost as much as she'd kept. Beautiful women who were stacked and eager to tug off his buckle with no more provocation from him than a wink or a quirk of his dimpled smile if rumor wasn't exaggerated. And it likely wasn't. Still Sky held her ground, tilted her chin up, as much to hold eye contact as an act of defiance. The emergency room was not AEBR domain.

"Mama." Sky had been so focused on taking a stand, she hadn't noticed her daughter tugging on the shirt Kane had given her to wear. Montana's fingers traced the buckle and then she pulled at it.

"I want Daddy to give me one of these to wear too. Shiny."

Montana pulled at the shirt Sky had bloused over the massive buckle, not wanting to stand out and scream bull rider's girl. Montana traced the large letters and poster image of a rider atop a bull, hand held high.

"I want it now." She pulled harder.

Sky recognized the signs of a building tantrum and no wonder. Montana been cooped up in a truck most of the day and was completely off her schedule with no familiar reference points other than an overwhelmed mother who was barely holding it together. She tried to pick up her daughter, but Montana kicked at her, still clutching the material.

"I want to see Daddy now." Montana was seriously agitated, stomping her feet and pulling at Sky, who struggled to hold on to her daughter.

"Soon, sweetie, soon." Sky finally managed to haul the squirming girl into her arms and slung her to the side of her body, locking her in tight. That's when she noticed everyone was staring at her. Well, not her exactly her but at her very exposed pale as milk midriff and the glaringly shiny and huge buckle that took up a lot of real estate.

Chapter Seven

THE WOMAN IN the suit sucked in a breath and then her gaze riveted on Montana who stared back at her, eyes suspicious, tiny fists grabbing handfuls of her mother's hair and pulling. Everyone else stared too. Sky felt like she was holding her breath, for what, she didn't know, but the woman exhaled on a long, long fffff…and then she looked at the man who had hovered next to her the entire time.

"When Kane is vertical again I'm going to knock him back on his prime ass for this curveball."

"Stand in line," Sky muttered, because the curveball was also a cutter, slider, knuckleball and changeup all in one wicked fast pitch, and Sky didn't even play baseball but she'd cheered during hundreds of her brother's games.

She noticed more than a few eyes still staring at her stomach and the giant buckle Kane had insisted she wear, and she felt herself flush. "Eyes up, cowboys."

"Ma'am," one of them said with a cocky smile.

"Is that the real…" One of the men reached out, and Sky took a step back. The cowboy flushed. "Sorry," he said straightening and stepping back himself.

"Always told Kane he'd a make a beautiful woman." Another smirking cowboy stepped forward and touched Montana's bull. "That's a mighty fine animal, young lady. What's her name?"

"Bulls are boys," Montana said scornfully, building temper tantrum forgotten.

There was a hoot of collective laughter from the cowboys, and Sky's heart lurched because no one seemed concerned about Kane, whereas her tension continued to ramp up.

"And his name is Bennington."

Sky's heart pinched. Bennington. Her brother.

"Hmmmm." The woman in the suit looked her over, even walking a half circle around her. Sky felt summed up. "I usually don't come to the hospital," she said softly. "But it was on the way to the airport, and I wanted to give last-minute instructions. Bad luck for Kane. He's really been hiding a lot."

That caught Sky's attention. Kane hadn't been hiding anything. She had, but his friends and colleagues and fans would think that he had been hiding her and his child. Like he was ashamed of them. Again, Sky's decisions four years ago rose up to taunt her. She had never once considered Kane's feelings. She'd assumed. And everyone knew what that got you.

"It's not what you think," Sky said, not wanting to explain herself to this stranger, but not wanting Kane to be seen in a bad light either.

"Oh it's exactly what I think and more. You're the artist, and..." her eyes flicked to Montana "...so much more. That's why Kane assured me that he would handle the trademarked art issue."

"And why he busted ass to get out of the dressing room and on the road," one of the cowboys said. "He skipped the autograph line. Hasn't done that before. Not hard to see why now."

Sky wasn't sure if she was being insulted or compliment-ed, and she didn't have the energy to find out which one. "I want to see Kane and then get out of here."

Even without keys or a wallet or cell, Sky wasn't sure how true that was anymore. Did she really want to leave Kane? Could she even do it again? And what about Mon-tana? Even in the twelve hours, she'd bonded with her daddy.

"Do you have any news on him? How badly was he hurt?"

"Still waiting, same as you. Alicia Flores." The woman smiled, reminding Sky of a sleekly beautiful but calculating cat, maybe one of those Egyptian statue cats left in the pharaohs' tombs. "Head of PR for AEBR. Image crafter..." again the disparaging walk around Sky "...crisis handler and storyteller. And you look like Snow White."

Haven't heard that before. Not.

"Not in the mood for a story. I want to see Kane. And Snow White was stupid about the apple."

"Good. You have some spine. You'll need it for Kane, but ditch the attitude with me. Damn. I have to fly out in another couple of hours." Alicia pursed her lips and looked at her assistant. "No one sees her, talks to her until we write up her background."

Sky's eyes widened in surprise, not sure she fully understood what this woman thought she could create and why she imagined Sky would go along with any of it. What kind of people had Kane surrounded himself with? No one even seemed that concerned about him.

"Maybe we should shelve this conversation until we know more." Another cowboy limped up to join the group. He had a flank rope in his hand that he held delicately, as if it were precious.

"Shelve it? Rory, really. That's not my skill set. I don't shelve things. I've got one of the top riders in the AEBR for the past four years flat out in the ER, combative and rambling and some random woman shows up with a kid the spitting image of him and Kane has said nothing, absolutely nothing about either of them to me. I can't have secrets like that sauntering up to take a bite out of AEBR's ass. Ironic, really when you think about what legal's had to deal with over the years with some of our boys, and one of my cleanest has been more than a little naughty."

"My daughter is here," Sky said.

"My point. This needs to be contained and crafted."

Before she could burst Alicia Flores's bubble about containing or crafting an image, the ER exam room doors slid open and a man walked out in a western-style shirt and jeans. He didn't look like a doctor but everyone in the knot of bull riders turned toward him.

"Doc Freeman. Finally," Alicia said.

"The scan is clear."

Everyone breathed a sigh of relief and the cowboys spoke quietly and seemed like they were about to leave.

"So where is he?" Alicia asked.

"They're keeping him overnight. I've asked for an MRI because he's combative as hell and rambling about the Montana Sky, which is concerning. I thought he was from Phoenix so the doctor and I aren't sure what's wrong at this point."

Sky was pissed she'd been the good girl cooling her heels in the ER so long when Kane had needed them. He wouldn't have sat politely in the waiting room if his daughter had been in the ER just because he didn't have permission.

"Done with this." She grabbed Montana's small hand and pushed past Alicia to get closer to the doctor. "I'm Sky. This is his daughter Montana. We're going to see him."

She didn't even wait; she just swished through the sliding doors.

She wasn't sure what she expected. A curtained-off area? Several medical professionals around Kane? But no, the curtains in his bay were wide open so anyone walking in could see him. He was in a medical gown and alone in a metal bed flat on his back, jerking his arms, but they weren't moving off the bed. He was swearing loudly. One young man in pale blue scrubs was entering something in a computer next to Kane, and he asked him to rate his pain on a scale of one to ten.

"Fuck my pain. I want the fuck out of here."

Sky winced. Kane was always so cool under pressure. Controlled. He'd hate this.

She rushed forward. "Hey, baby," she gushed like the biggest fan girl buckle bunny ever. "How are you?"

Stupid question. He was a wreck. What if he didn't recognize her? The familiar doubt assailed her, but still she kept moving forward, squatted by his bed so he could see her. She picked up Montana and in a dim part of her brain hoped he had the ability to cool it with the language. She really didn't need her three-year-old to start regularly pulling out the F word from her enormous vocabulary repertoire.

His beautiful gray eyes were clear, but angry and frustrated, and she could also see pain. His body relaxed as if some air had oozed out of it.

"You're here."

The words were so simple, but the wonder behind them made tears prick her eyes. One day. That's all it had taken to turn her world upside down.

"Yes."

Montana gripped her bull and stared down at Kane. What did she see? Sky wondered. The bruise on his forehead and cheek and the bloody line dissecting his eyebrow made her feel nauseous. Was Montana scared? This was not a life for a little girl, seeing her daddy get hurt in front of thousands of people whose first question was 'what was his score?' since he'd stuck the ride and the second was 'could he compete next week?' and who said 'Phoenix is his hometown' like they knew him.

When his eyes met his daughter's, Sky could see regret and sorrow chase across his face. Pain crawled around his edges. Slowly she lowered Montana to the floor again, and her fingers slid along his raw wrists. Holy cow they'd actually restrained him. Like a criminal. She remembered the doctor's word: combative.

"I want these off," he said tersely. "Get Doc Freeman. Tell him."

"Hold on there, cowboy," the man in scrubs said in the patronizing 'the patient is a child' tone Sky hated.

She winced and let her fingers lightly soothe his wrists. Then she whispered to Montana: "Hold Daddy's hand. Tell him about your tea party."

Sky strode back to the door. It swished open.

"Kane wants you," she said to Doc Freeman. "You got a knife?"

A rumble went around the knot of people, and she thought she heard an "I like her."

Boys.

"Hey, Sky." She recognized Cody from earlier. "I brought Kane's gear." He piled the duffel bag, chaps and Stetson in her arms. "His keys, wallet and cell are in the bag—I checked. I drove his truck and parked on level A. He good?"

"Think so," she said, starting to shake now that her fear was turning to relief that seemed to be translating into exhaustion. Hella twelve hours.

She took Kane's things, surprised that Alicia and her two assistants were heading out before checking in with Kane. The cowboys were leaving too, Cody cadging a ride from someone named Casey.

Didn't they want to see Kane? What kind of friends were they? Even the AEBR woman after advising her to keep her mouth shut and a low profile was striding away, talking into her cell phone, her stilettos clicking on the bland hospital floor. Sky turned back to Doc, who looked set to leave too after also asking the bull rider Casey for a ride. "He wants the restraints off," she said. "Can you do that?"

"Not sure if it's a good idea."

"That wasn't my question."

His eyebrows rose, but he followed her back into the emergency bay.

"Hey, Kane. The neurosurgeon says you look good. He'll be back in thirty minutes to check you again," the doctor said.

"I want to be released. Driving back to Phoenix tonight."

"I know you don't think you're human." Doc laughed. "But you are staying overnight for observation." Doc Freeman did not seem intimidated by Kane's tension or his glare that practically shot sparks.

"Can he have the restraints cut off at least?" Sky demanded.

The nurse shook his head. "Doctor said to wait until he returned. If Mr. Wilder is calm that long, we'll cut the restraints. So far I haven't started the timer. He kicked a medic and knocked away two of the nursing staff and they are pretty big men like me. Oh, and a member of the security team. I think he got a little confused about his career and thought instead he was the bull."

The idiot actually smiled at his own 'joke.'

"He was injured and worried about his family," Sky said.

Kane pulled hard again and again. "I am not waiting thirty minutes."

"Shshsh," she breathed against his ear. "Are you good if I cut them? Montana's here? Can you keep it together?" she whispered and then levered back a little to see his expression. Could she trust him? Kane was a big man. And fiercely strong. He'd never once hurt her or frightened her, but he was definitely capable of damaging something or someone if he was not thinking clearly or felt threatened.

His eyes narrowed to slits. "If you ask me the day or the name of the god d… of the dang president I am going to lose my mind." He looked at Montana, who plunked her bull on and off Kane's bed like it was an animal trampoline. She started to climb up using the thin blanket like a vine. Sky caught her and lifted her up. She curled up beside Kane, tucking her bull next to him.

Sky's fingers tangled with his.

"Maybe I should ask you to tell me Euler's Identity," she teased.

"$e^{i\pi} + 1 = 0$"

Sky sighed in relief and barely resisted laying her head on his broad chest.

Yeah. He was definitely fine. Censoring himself. Spouting off some equation. She didn't know what it meant only that Kane absolutely loved math and numbers and what he termed the beautiful certainty of equations.

"Okay," she whispered. "You're good."

"Baby, I'm better than good."

Sky spied the doctor's western-style belt and his leather case for his pocketknife. Cowboys and their knives. They couldn't help the habit even when they became doctors for bull riders. She snagged the knife, popped the blade and keeping her body low over Kane's quickly cut the plastic restraints.

"I want to take you back to Phoenix," he said sitting up. His face went white and he swayed sideways. "Pack up your things. You and Montana..."

"You are not driving anywhere tonight." Sky was outraged. Kane's face took on a green tinge, and she didn't think that was all hospital lighting. "Montana needs to sleep and not in her booster seat. She's not a package you can haul around on a whim."

"Not a whim. I've planned it out."

Of course he had.

"Kane, give it a rest." Doc Freeman frowned as Sky tucked the plastic zip tie restraints in her back pocket, closed the knife and handed it back to him. "Stay for observation tonight. Then you can slay your dragons tomorrow."

"Leaving." Kane swung his legs off the bed, holding Montana in place against his side. He winced but quickly schooled his expression.

"Calling security," the nurse said giving Kane a lot of space like he was afraid he was going to go all Hulk on him.

"Please, Kane, please." Sky put her hands on either side of him so they were face to face, so close that she could see just where the light blue bled into gray. She laid her forehead against his.

"Please." Her voice broke. "Bennington had a head injury too." She knew it was different. Her brother hadn't been wearing a helmet. He had been conscious at the arena but by the time the ambulance had headed out, sirens screaming, he'd gone quiet, and then unconscious, never to speak or wake again. "Just stay. You're exhausted. We're exhausted. Montana needs to sleep."

She needed to sleep. Preferably in a plush bed with silky

sheets. Ha! Like that was in her future tonight. And if it were in her future tomorrow, she'd be in even more trouble than she thought.

"Please," she whispered and somehow ended up kissing his bruise, just lightly brushing her lips across it, and then the cut on his eyebrow. "I'm tired. Scared," she admitted, scared of so much more than his injury but scared of the rest of her life—their lives. "You scared me tonight. Stay. We'll stay with you here. I can't cope with any more tonight, Kane. Please."

His arms snaked around her, pulled her half onto the bed, half on his lap.

She could feel his heartbeat slow and steady under her palm pressed on his chest. The hard flex of muscle brought back so many memories. Tears flooded her eyes and she let them fall, too tired to keep a grip on what felt like her brief show of strength and confidence.

"You won't leave?"

She shook her head. With his thumb, he caught one of her tears, and holding her gaze, he tasted it with his tongue.

"Okay," he said. "We'll stay."

One battle won, Sky thought. Thousands ahead, but she was done with hiding. No more running. And no more pleasing others unless it pleased herself. She knew it was easier thought than done, but she had to start somewhere so why not tonight. In…where was she? God, she felt wrung out. Santa Fe. Yes. Tonight in Santa Fe. Sky Gordon 2.0.

Chapter Eight

KANE EASED IN and out of sleep. Despite his assurances to everyone, who hadn't listened to him that he was fine, he had a mother of a headache. Before he could begin a full body mental assessment, which would definitely include his ribs and his left hip, he breathed in Sky—lemon verbena and something sweeter, floral. His heart wrenched. He remembered her smell more vividly than her face and touch. Her hair fell around his body and face, covering him like a shroud.

Even through his pain and general pissed off attitude toward Sky and his idiot younger self who had taken no for an answer when she'd sent him away four years ago, Kane found himself fighting a smile. Sometime during the last couple of hours, she had climbed onto the bed with him and wrapped herself around him, sprawling across his body just like she used to.

He had loved sleeping with her. Not just the sex although that had been way over the top amazing and he'd never come close to duplicating the intensity or intimacy before or since with another woman. Hadn't even tried.

But now she was here.

And he was so close to getting back everything he'd lost before he realized what he'd let slip through his hands. His child slept on a small window seat couch wrapped in his shirt and Sky was in his arms, her breath warm on his neck, her hair silky on his skin and her legs straddling him, which reminded him that part of him was wide awake. The nurse was not going to like that, but since the doctor had talked to him over an hour ago and signed the discharge form, he figured no one would bother them. So he'd let Sky and Montana sleep.

He tangled his hands in her long, silky black hair, and she murmured and snuggled closer.

He wasn't sure what hurt more: his head, his ribs, their past or his dick.

Four years.

He still couldn't comprehend why Sky would have kept their child a secret. It was like a bad movie or a book with a glowering asshole hero doing the heroine wrong. Had he been a jerk? Too controlling? That wasn't hard to picture. Shit. Had he made Sky think she couldn't have long-term with him? Was it the danger his career posed?

Four years. He'd missed so much.

Last night when she'd woken him up every two hours, instead of letting her ask him stupid questions advised in medical texts, he'd asked her questions. What was Montana's first word? When had she taken her first step? Had Sky breastfed? What was Montana's favorite food? Had she ever been sick or hurt? What was her favorite thing to do? So many questions filled his brain.

And Sky had answered the questions, her voice tentative and apologetic at first. Then, after she'd made a bed for Montana on a built-in couch in the room, and wrapped their child in the shirt he'd given Sky to wear, she'd sat beside him, run her fingers along his scalp, which had soothed him from his pain and the anger and bewilderment that continued to course through him.

"She's smart like you," Sky had whispered. "Wicked smart. I was already starting to worry about schools."

And he wanted to throw something. Rage. But he'd done none of those things. He'd held it in, held it together like he had for so long, feeling the fury roar through his blood, sizzle his nerve endings, pound at his brain like a storm—demands and recriminations dammed back for now. His goal for the past seven years he'd been a bull rider was going to have to change. He couldn't be focused on helping his mother reconstruct her dream of purchasing her family ranch that had fallen into bankruptcy and ruin and restoring it for all of his brothers and their growing families. Now he had a little girl, and Monday he'd have a wife. He had to build something for them and build a life with them.

It sounded good. Fucked up now. But he'd fix it. Make a family with Sky and Montana. It just took will.

SKY WOKE UP realizing she and Kane were not alone in the room. She listened, intently, but could hear nothing except the gentle exhalations of Kane's warm breath on her hair. Montana stirred in her sleep. The alarm hadn't gone off again so it hadn't been two hours. How had she ended up sprawled across Kane like they were still a couple? And the tiny shorts and thin T-shirt were not nearly enough protection from his potent masculinity. Her nipples were peaked and she was wet. She was a perve! Kane was injured. What was wrong with her?

Grayish light was filtering in from behind the curtains.

It was a new day. Sky couldn't begin to imagine what this day would bring when compared to yesterday.

So who was in the room? A nurse or tech would have done something. A fan? So what should she do: jump up and confront the person? Stay still and hope they went away?

"I know you're awake." The deep voice was a whisper of sound and Sky rolled off the bed to standing. Balls of her feet, arms away from her body, fists lightly clenched, joints loose, muscles tense, ready.

"You really want to take me on?" No expression crossed the hard, fallen angel face, but the low voice edged toward amusement.

Her heart slammed. He was one of the biggest men she'd ever seen. Taller than Kane by a couple of inches at least and way broader. Muscled in a way that said serious, and he didn't even react to her sudden movement. He couldn't have looked less like medical personnel if he'd been practicing.

"Who are you?" she demanded, keeping her voice low.

His eyes looked almost gold in the early morning light beginning to filter in through the shade she'd closed, knowing that light might bother Kane in the morning.

"Who the fuck are you?" he challenged right back.

He was as still as a mountain. All the self-defense moves she knew would be laughable against this man. Everything she'd learned from classes and training as she'd studied yoga and Pilates and spin and kickboxing to teach to college students and professors, and then wealthy professionals to support herself and Montana while she began to build her reputation in the Scottsdale art scene.

Her eyes skidded to Montana—still asleep—then back to the man. Everything about him screamed danger. Even though he was physically so handsome women would spin around and stare if he walked by. And if he approached, their breathing and pulse would be as controlled as a shaken and then opened can of Coke. Just like Kane.

She tried to moisten her dry lips but her mouth was cottony with fear.

"Why are you here?" she whispered, hating the familiar fear and despising her tendency to freeze up even more. Evolutionarily speaking her cowardly genes should have died out millennia ago with one snap of sharp teeth.

"To check on Kane. Give him a ride home if he needs it."

How the heck did he make that sound threatening? His voice was like liquid honey poured over gravel, and Sky found herself backing up a little until her butt touched the bed, and her arms went out as if the man planned to grab Kane, heft him effortlessly over his shoulder and run.

Was he a friend of Kane's? He screamed military or something even darker. Why would Kane have a friend like this?

"I'm his brother." His eyes narrowed at her protective stance. "Move over. I want see him."

"You're not Luke."

"So you know Luke?"

He whipped out a cell phone and took her picture. Then texted something.

"What are you doing?"

"Checking your story."

"I'm not giving you my story." His words reminded her of the AEBR public relations director telling her that on the next stop the team would work with her on creating her story with Kane.

"Name?"

"You tell me your name first," she pushed still holding out hope that she could be different. Stronger.

He surprised her. "Colt."

Like a gun. Fabulous.

And then he moved toward the bed. Her breath hitched. He froze.

His phone buzzed. He looked at it.

"Luke says 'hi, Sky.'"

No expression. That rocked her even more, and she was practically sitting on the bed. She eyed the call button, but what would she say? And it would take them a long time to arrive. And some young nurse wasn't going to be able to handle that man.

"You need to back off," Sky said, her voice not nearly as strong as she wanted it. Maybe he could call Luke and she could talk to him even though she hadn't seen him for four years. And she'd only met him a handful of times.

Kane's hand snaked out and splayed across her stomach, pulling her to the cradle of his hips even as he tried to sit up. He bit back a groan, squeezed his eyes shut, and Sky was torn between soothing Kane and facing the threat.

"Shshshsh," he whispered in her ear. "It's okay. You're okay."

He was awake. Talking. Remembering. And even though everything was wrong between them, he still tried to comfort her. Sky squeezed her eyes shut on the spurt of tears. She didn't have the time to cry, but she hadn't had anyone help her or stand up for her since her brother had died—except Kane, but she'd run from him.

"You should lie down." She pushed at his muscled shoulders, but of course he didn't budge. "You're still hurt."

"I'm fine."

"Yeah, right."

Her hands soothed down his arms, her fingers tracing his corded muscles.

And now a whole different set of sensations danced down her nerve endings and played with her breathing and heart rate. Kane was injured. Everything was wrong between them and yet she still went liquid when Kane touched her. The huge man with the honey-colored eyes that were so cold watched it all. Sky swallowed hard as Kane's hand heated her flesh and his lips skittered sensation from her neck to her nipples. Kane Wilder wasn't even trying to seduce her.

What would happen when he did?

What if he didn't?

"Colt." Kane sucked in a deep breath and swung his legs over the side of the bed.

He lurched, and Sky tried to block his fall, but stronger hands were faster, steadying Kane. Sky's gaze darted from a glittering golden glare to a cool gray, pain-filled stare. The guy was hot but intimidating as hell, and Sky had to fight the urge to press closer to Kane. She was supposed to be protecting him.

Ignoring the intense giant, she feathered her fingers through Kane's curls that brushed his shoulders.

"Do you have a headache? Are you dizzy? You should lie down longer, Kane," she urged. "At least take the Ibuprofen. The nurse said you can have pain pills. She left two last night." Sky reached for the paper cup that held the meds on the side table.

"I'm fine."

Of course he was.

"You didn't need to come out for this." Kane sat all the way up, his hand clenched on the rail of the bed. He clearly made an effort to let go of the railing and sit all the way up. "Luke acts like I'm his younger brother," Kane groused.

"You are, but he's still a dick that way," the man said expressionless.

"Don't want him worried. His wife, Tanner has her scan early tomorrow," Kane practically growled.

Sky didn't understand who Colt was. How he could be a brother? And who was Tanner and what scan was she having? She felt a pang because she didn't belong in this room or this conversation, but she felt left out, which was stupid and would get her into trouble. She'd left Kane Wilder for a reason. A lot of reasons. And every minute in his presence reminded her that all of them had been solid even though she kept forgetting them and now felt guilty about her decision.

A ghost of a smile lit Kane's lips. "Luke's as fired up about twins as he was on his wedding day."

"He's an idiot. I love being married, but would have skipped the shit involved in the actual day if it wouldn't have burned Talon's ass."

More people she didn't know. What had Kane been doing the past four years? Collecting strangers and making them family? And what woman had whatever the cool feminine word for balls was to marry that man? She needed some of that mojo in a serious way.

"That's romantic." Sky slapped her hand over her mouth. Had she said that? Sarcasm directed at a giant she still wasn't sure wouldn't eat her seemed like a bad idea. Although the fact he was married did inspire a little more confidence.

"I'd recommend Vegas." Colt tilted his head toward the bundle sleeping on the couch, and Sky felt the blood drain from her brain, leaving her light-headed. "Without the Elvis—although you're such a pretty and popular boy you probably want a tux, the girl in a white frilly dress, champagne and the horse and carriage for your big day."

He stalked over, flicked the shirt aside to reveal Montana curled up around her bull, her rosebud lips pursed and her curls haloing around her head. Sky jumped protectively to her feet, but Kane linked his fingers with hers.

"Beautiful," he pronounced. "My niece?"

"Hell yeah."

Colt looked down at the sleeping child then back at Kane. His eyes were unfathomable.

"Everyone will be thrilled except Luke. One more thing you beat him at, you smug little bastard."

"Didn't think of that. He will be pissed." Kane stood up, his face stoic, but his posture off enough that Sky could tell he hurt. "Colt, this is Sky and my daughter, Montana. Sky, this is my older brother Colt. I have another brother—Laird, his twin."

Holy cow there were two of them?

Hopefully they lived in different states to mitigate the over the top testosterone and badass vibe.

"Ummmm you only mentioned Luke before," she said. "I only met Luke when we were..." Well Kane had never seemed like a kid. "When we were..." Friends didn't sound right either.

"Didn't mention them because I didn't know I had them." Kane sucked in a deep breath, his features creased as he reached for his jeans Sky had folded on a table. "Collected Colt at last year's Copper Mountain Rodeo, and got Laird at Christmas. Luke and I didn't know our mom had been so busy."

Sky couldn't tell if Kane was serious or not. She looked from Kane to Colt and decided she didn't need to know this now, especially when Colt picked up Montana and cradled her in his arms.

"I can hold her." Sky reached out quickly, still pretty sure she didn't trust him.

"I got her. Got some catching up to do with my niece." He picked up Kane's duffel bag, stuffed the flank strap and the chaps in it and slung it over his shoulder. Then he caught up the garment bag with one finger.

"You can help Kane. He still looks a bit green—like he

might puke. Last guy who did that on me I put in a coma."

She really hoped he was joking.

Kane pulled on his jeans, while Sky tried not to notice because she knew for a fact he was not wearing underwear. Then he pulled on his boots, trying and failing to hide his wince. Then he shrugged off the hospital gown. Sky gaped at the purple bruising on one side and a lot of medical tape wrapped around his ribs.

"You good for tape?" Colt asked critically.

"For now."

Kane took the T-shirt Colt handed him. Then he caught up his Stetson and settled it on his head. All masculine, tough, don't-mess-with-me cowboy. If she hadn't seen him ass down in the dirt last night she wouldn't know he'd been injured. Well except for the bruising near his forehead and the cut through his eyebrow, which somehow made him even more devilishly attractive.

"I don't understand you," she said, thinking he really should stay in the hospital, "either of you," she included Colt.

"That's because we're Wilders. An acquired taste."

"And, baby…" Kane put his hand on the small of her back "…this time you're eating the whole gourmet meal."

Chapter Nine

HIGH NOON.

Okay, that was poetic license since it was a quarter to one by time they'd reached her apartment in a former bunkhouse on the outskirts of Scottsdale out near Camel-back Mountain. She'd lived here for the past year while her friend from high school, who'd inherited the property figured out what she wanted to do with it. Over the years parts of the former ranch had been sold off and whittled down to the remaining ten acres with a ranch house, empty barn, shop and bunkhouse.

Sky had loosely converted the shop into her studio. She loved the arrangement, but knew it was very temporary because already developers were contacting her friend, who was trying to get the zoning changed.

And now she was going to have another change. She knew she had to adjust. She wanted Kane and Montana to have a relationship. She did. She just wished she didn't feel so pressured. Railroaded. He wasn't giving her any time to process. She was trying to find the words to tell him that she wanted to slow down when he followed her up to the narrow porch that ran the length of the four-room former bunkhouse. He wore sunglasses and had his Stetson pulled low, but Sky had a feeling his head was still hurting, and the bright afternoon sunlight probably felt like an ice pick to his skull.

"Pack a suitcase for yourself and Montana for a couple of weeks," Kane said low in her ear as she struggled to unlock the door. "I'll get someone to pack up the rest of your things and move it temporarily to the ranch in Montana."

She fumbled the keys, but his hand snaked around and unlocked the door effortlessly as if he hadn't just dropped a bombshell.

"Home sweet home!" Montana sang out imitating what Sky often said when they arrived back at their quiet, isolated haven. She darted around Sky and disappeared inside. Colt had gotten out of the truck but made no move to follow them, while Kane seemed to feel he had every right to make himself at home. He walked in, not much more than a few inches behind her.

He looked around. Sky forced herself to stay relaxed. She knew Kane had grown up fairly poor until his mom had become a lawyer when he was in middle school, but who knew how he lived now? He said nothing as he took in the galley kitchen that ran along one wall and the small living area with a love seat and a rocking chair that she had found at Habitat for Humanity and sanded down and stained and made new cushions for. There was a small round bistro table she'd also refinished along with mismatched wooden chairs she'd painted a festive color where she and Montana ate and sketched.

The bedroom and bath were next door in the second bunk bedroom—long ago a wide doorway had been cut and framed with pinyon and a rough door made with reclaimed wood from some long derelict building. Sky had created an ocotillo design out of metal that she'd mounted on the door to make the rustic look just a little bit more artsy instead of slapdash.

"Daddy." Montana stood in the doorway holding her stuffed bull, and a handmade rag doll Sky had made for her one Christmas. "Come see my room. I share with Mommy."

Kane immediately followed Montana through the door. Sky automatically followed, but paused. She should give them some time alone. She looked at the empty doorway. She could hear Montana's high voice talking fast, and Kane's lower one, but he was mostly quiet, soaking it all in.

Sky looked around the small living area, feeling the need to do something, clean something or bake something. She didn't want to pack. Packing would mean she was leaving, and she'd worked hard for this life. Reality was starting to set in that Kane was back in her life. She had the idea that he was still operating on adrenaline and hadn't yet worked out the fine details of actually keeping them with him.

Dragging them around with him on tour would be hard

on Montana, and hell on her trying to establish an art career. She had a lot of tools and equipment and supplies and required a lot of space. She also needed access to a large enough college or university where she could do her casting for her bronze sculptures. And that didn't even count finding other teachers to sub in her exercise classes.

Too on edge to sit, Sky made a pot of coffee. She could still hear Montana talking. What was she showing Kane? Curiosity burned, but she wanted to let Kane know she trusted him alone with Montana. She looked through a window and watched Colt lean against his truck and talk on his phone. He made several quick calls, speaking briefly, listening a lot more. Not surprisingly, he wasn't much of a talker. He hadn't said much during the six-hour drive back, and Sky, sitting in the back seat with Montana, had been too intimidated and emotionally wrung out to attempt to fill the silence.

Kane hadn't helped the awkwardness. He'd stared straight ahead, probably in pain, and eventually, he'd lowered the seat back and had closed his eyes. His features had been tight, and Sky couldn't tell if it was pain or just the emotions that had been clawing at him and at her for the past twenty-four hours. God, was that all it had been?

When he'd winced and barely bitten back a moan, Sky hadn't been able to handle it anymore. She'd slid her hands under his shoulders and began to massage his shoulders, neck and then lightly stroke his forehead and scalp. Kane sighed and settled into her hands. Sky had watched his face, trying to decide if he were awake, but then decided it didn't matter. She couldn't help how she touched him: care was in every stroke.

Memories crowded in of their summer together. How many different ways she'd touched him—massage, icing, taping, arousing, comforting, love. Sky knew she was doing it again, opening the door to her heart wide and letting him in. She'd tried to tell herself it was just kindness. He was hurt. They had a history. But truthfully, she loved to touch him, and she'd always loved his careless hair—the way it tumbled like night over his forehead, and he'd brush it back out of his face with his large, rough, but beautifully shaped hands. He had a widow's peak hairline, like his mother, like Luke, and the new brother, Colt. She'd loved to trace it when they'd lain in bed together. She'd traced it in the truck, let the silky soft curls slide across her palm and through her fingers.

Memories were harpies swooping in to dine off her soul.

"Coffee?" she called out to Colt and then wished she hadn't when he looked up at her. Even through his aviators she felt the burn of his gaze. She felt like an idiot fifties housewife or something. "If you want any," she added because apparently she could be an even bigger idiot.

This was dumb. She was letting Kane take over because she felt guilty. She was guilty, but she needed to figure out a way to work with him. To have him work with her. She walked quietly to her bedroom door.

Kane sat on the white, wrought-iron twin-sized bed she had pushed against one wall and heaped with colorful cushions embroidered with flowers. His boots were kicked off, and his legs were crossed. Montana sat on his lap, one finger in her mouth, as she pointed to pictures and told stories about them.

Sky's heart sank. Of course Montana would pull out the daddy book. Sky kept a scrapbook of articles and pictures of Kane—interviews from local media, articles printed from the AEBR website, cutouts from ads he'd been in, even some stills from the documentary about bull riders that had come out last year that he'd been featured in. She'd made a separate scrapbook about Kane as a teenager—pictures she'd taken of Bennington and Kane swimming, hiking or horseback riding.

She also had pictures from later, a few selfies she'd taken when he'd met her for lunch or dinner or to catch a movie or a round of mini golf when he was on tour break. Then there was the book she'd made of their summer together. A few of those pictures had made it into the regular daddy book, but the book of her and Kane was more private, intimate, not sexual exactly but it had all centered on her and Kane or shots she'd taken of him when he hadn't been posing—taping his ribs or shoulder, smoothing on arnica for his bruises, holding her hand while the tattoo artist added to his bull tat using the artwork she'd created, putting rosin on his rope, watching bull tapes, reading, swimming in the river, him paining her toenails. Their life in real time.

"There's another book Mommy hides under her mattress," Montana startled the snot out of Sky by saying. She slid off the bed and slipped her small hands under the quilted comforter on the opposite full-size bed and pulled out the third scrapbook where Sky had tucked it when they'd moved in. Sometimes she'd take it out and look at it. Usually at Kane in happier times, but also at the few pictures she'd included of herself pregnant and just after Montana's birth before she switched over to making Montana her own baby book and daddy book.

"This is my favorite. Mama looks so pretty and happy. You too, Daddy."

Carrying the book in both hands like it was something that could spill, and it could—all her secrets—Montana returned to her throne on Kane's lap. Sky stared at the book and the shining eagerness on her daughter's face. She had to get the book away from them. Kane would take one look at that book and know the truth. That she'd loved him with her whole heart. That she'd never stopped. For a moment Sky froze even though her brain screamed at her to grab the scrapbook and run.

Kane was slow to respond to Montana's eagerness. He seemed to be in a dream, and as Kane reached for the book, Sky managed to unlock her muscles. She tried to snatch the book mid handoff. Kane held tight.

"Ahhhh…" Sky paused, trying to think of the right words. "Kane, those are private."

Those words were definitely not the right ones.

Twin pale blue, nearly gray eyes sparked. "No more secrets," he said. "Not one more."

"Kane." She didn't let go of the book either. Words were like space junk pummeling her from all sides. She wanted to run, give herself time to think, but she'd created this situation, inadvertently—she'd had no idea Kane would have been so angry, so hurt that she hadn't confided in him about her pregnancy. She still couldn't reconcile what she'd thought with reality.

"Nothing off limits," he said.

"Does that go both ways?"

Silence. Sky let go of the book. Typical. She'd done everything but drain a vein for him to prove her love but he kept his thoughts and feelings and history locked up tight.

No thanks.

"Do you want to see the book, Daddy? It's my favorite."

Trapped. Stuck. Everything Kane's way and she had no time to think.

"Maybe later, Montana," Sky said. "Daddy wants us to pack some clothes. We're going to take a little trip." Sky spoke each word slowly and carefully.

As a distraction, it didn't work. Kane had already opened the book. The first picture was of Kane, Sky and Bennington in her parents' back courtyard. They'd been swimming and were wrapped in towels. The sun was setting so everything was pink, gold. They were squished in a giant pool chair, a bonfire blazing before them, and they'd clearly been roasting marshmallows for s'mores. Bennington and Kane wielded their sticks like swords, marshmallows flaming. Sky's attention in the photo had been wholly focused on Kane.

Obsess much?

Sky wanted to grab the book and run far, far away. Kane's head was bent over the book. He turned the page, lingered, turned again. Montana's eyes sparkled but Kane's gaze was shuttered. She could see the brewing storm clouds barely contained. He was angry. Angrier than he'd been when he'd pulled over in the desert. He should have been having a sweet moment with his daughter as she shared her treasurers, but instead he was furious.

Sky had never known how to deal with anger. Her father had been coldly critical and cutting. Dismissive. Her mother had yelled and screamed and cried. And thrown things. Sky knew she needed to step up and say or do something to ease the tension, but she always froze. Shut down. Became so exhausted that she could lie down and sleep like a turned-off computer.

Montana broke through her fugue by taking her hand.

"Mommy sit," Montana said. "Sit here." She slid off the bed and pushed Sky down next to Kane. She perched lightly, trying not to touch him. "Sit with Daddy."

Montana stepped back as if surveying her work. Sky stifled a sob. It was so sweet and painful and such a perfect blend of them both—bossy and artistic, going for the emotional heart of the visual. Montana climbed back up on the bed and knelt beside Kane. She whispered something in his ear and then sat down beside him. Impatiently because he still hadn't moved, she turned the page. Then another.

"That's me," Montana said importantly and pointing to a picture of Sky in a long skirt and form-fitting T-shirt. "I was in Mommy's tummy," Montana said. "I was this little." She curled up in a ball and then rolled off the bed. She stood up and stretched her arms up. "And now I'm this big."

Kane's gaze slid helplessly toward his daughter. From his profile, she couldn't tell what he was thinking, but he looked to be holding so much in—emotions rattling around his caged heart—that Sky felt like something had just dropped on her head. Kane really did want to be in his daughter's life. He really would have welcomed a baby. And as Montana stood on her tiptoes and stretched higher, and Kane stared at his little girl being playful, his finger unconsciously traced the rounded lines of Sky's stomach in the photo.

She really, really had misread him four years ago.

As Kane had driven her and Montana to Santa Fe, she'd still convinced herself she had made the correct decision. She'd had all her rationalizations lined up, polished and ready to show off. One by one. Only they hadn't worked for him. And she didn't think they were working for her anymore.

She hadn't wanted to be in a loveless marriage like her mother had been. She hadn't wanted her child to be rejected by its father like she had been. So she hadn't given Kane a chance to hurt her or his child. Only Kane wasn't her father. And she could stand to see him hurting.

So now what?

"Mommy, I'm hungry." Montana tugged at her fingers. She needed to move. To say something, the but weight of the mistake she'd made four years ago pressed down on her, made her feel like she was underwater, drowning.

Montana bolted away toward the kitchen and relief washed through her when she heard Montana talking to Colt and his deep voice answering something about grilled cheese. Then she heard the fridge open and the water turn on. Montana started singing the alphabet song. It sounded so normal when everything had gone to hell that Sky pressed her hand hard against her mouth the hold in the sobs.

Kane seemed in his own personal stupor. His head was lowered, and the book slipped a little down his legs so she wasn't sure if he was still looking at it or…

And here they were—a family. And she was going to have to meet Kane in the middle to form some kind of custody arrangement or… She could barely even think about what Kane seemed to want—being a family. No way could that work. It was impractical. He traveled to a different city and risked his life on a weekly basis, and he hated her. He was angry and bitter, and she couldn't blame him. She was loaded down with guilt and fired up with suspicion. She couldn't trust him. He didn't seem likely to forgive her.

Not exactly anyone's idea of a happy ever after.

"Kane, I didn't…I never intended to hurt you," she whispered.

She'd loved him. Had been so crazy in love with him and if he'd stop glaring and accusing and ordering her around for five minutes, she'd probably find herself head over heels again.

"I was…" Scared. Confused. Wrong? How did she explain her teenage fears to a man who'd never had a doubt in his mind? "You were always so sure of yourself, of your place in the world." She had craved that certainty and strength. "You had everything planned out—your career, how long you'd ride, the money you needed, the ranch you were going to have with Luke, and it was all going according to plan for you."

He met her worried gaze. His eyes had gone silver, and Sky had to resist burrowing into him for comfort. She didn't deserve it. She twisted her hands together.

"I thought you'd be upset about the baby."

She'd been terrified that he'd suggest an abortion and even though she hadn't wanted to be pregnant or have a baby at nineteen, she could never have destroyed anything that was part of Kane. And she'd known she could never give up his child. She thought the baby would be the only thing she'd ever have to love, or the only person who would love her.

"I know you don't understand my reasoning."

"I don't accept it," he said flatly.

"I thought I was protecting you," she forced herself to continue in the face of his strong denial. "I did think that," she repeated when his eyes flashed. "But yes, I was protecting myself and my baby too."

"Our baby. Ours," he whispered, but the words held more power than if he'd shouted. "Why did you need to protect our baby from me?" His voice hummed in anger.

"I didn't think you'd want her," she defended.

He reared away from her. Catching up the photo scrapbook before it hit the ground.

"Did you tell her that?" he demanded, his face pale and a muscle ticking in his jaw.

"No, of course not."

"Didn't she ask about me? Wonder why she didn't have her dad?"

Hard to explain that one. The answer would probably hurt more, but maybe they just needed to unload all their personal crap, put their personal history on the table and sort through it.

"She's three, Kane."

"She'll be eight one day. Ten. Not a stretch to think she would have wondered then. She would have felt that I had rejected her. It would have clawed at her heart and her confidence."

"Kane?" He sounded like he spoke from experience. Sky realized then that she knew nothing about his father. He'd talked a lot about growing up with Luke, always trying to be faster, stronger, smarter than his big brother. He'd spoken fondly of his mother, but there had always been something in his voice that revealed there was something hidden, and she'd lacked the confidence to ever push him for more than he was willing to give her.

"What if she sought me out on her own later?" Kane paced in front of her now. Fluidly and crackling with energy. He stopped in front of her, and Sky, who'd found herself watching him helplessly, the now familiar guilt choking her, stared at the floor.

"Imagine all the wasted years then, Sky." He tipped her chin up so that she was forced to face him—see his anger, but it was his pain that hit her hardest.

She would have seen that same pain on Montana's face.

"I tried," Sky whispered, gesturing vaguely to the two scrapbooks, suddenly realizing the total inadequacy of her effort.

"You turned me into a character in a book," he accused, his voice echoing in disbelief. "Do you realize how insane that is? How stupid? Cruel? I can't believe we made a baby and you relegated me to a goddamn book."

She winced and scrunched her eyes closed waiting for…something…she didn't know. Him to hurl the book, knock something over. Throw something against the wall.

"I'm sorry, Kane. I'm sorry." How many times would she have to say it before he knew that she hadn't hidden her pregnancy to hurt him? Her throat felt squeezed, and burned with everything she was suppressing, but she got the next bit out. "I did what I thought right."

He held her by her shoulders, his grip firm, but not tight.

"You fucking knew it was not right to run away from me." He spit out that word like it tasted bad. "You knew it wasn't fucking right to not tell me we'd made a baby. A child who would grow up thinking her dad didn't give a fuck about her." Sky flinched at all the profanity. Kane hardly ever swore around her and now it was like a storm brewing over her head, hurling lightning bolts. "Do you know what that does to a kid to know they weren't wanted? Do you?"

Yes.

But she couldn't speak. Share more of her shame.

"You look me in the eye and you tell me you think Montana will have a better life, grow into a happy and independent young woman, be more confident, more financially stable and secure without knowing that her father cherishes her and loves her and will put her first. You tell me that, Sky." He used the word 'you,' like a curse and started backing her across the room as he spoke as if the words generated so much energy, he couldn't hold it in. He backed her against the wall and her head bounced a little. "You look me in the eye and tell me you really believe that you did the right thing."

"Hey." The deep voice was like a gunshot. "Think you need a break."

Sky jumped. Colt stood in the doorway, massive, nearly taking up the whole thing, tall, broad and looking a little mean.

"I'm not done," Kane said, his voice and breathing harsh.

"Done for now," Colt said and took a step into the room.

Kane looked at Sky and then took a step back, ran an agitated hand through his hair. He turned away from her.

"It's okay. We're okay," she said to Colt although she couldn't think of anything less okay than where she and Kane were at the moment. "Kane and I have a lot to discuss and work out, and that's my fault," she said firmly, forcing her body to stay relaxed so Colt would stand down—not think she needed help.

She could feel Kane's hot stare burning through the back of her head.

She slowly turned around. She'd wanted to protect her daughter and her heart, but she'd ended up hurting all three of them so much more. She had to stop running away. Today would be the first step back on the path she should have taken so long ago. Kane was right.

"Kane." She wanted him to turn around so he'd know she was sincere, but she was not sure of her reception. She still didn't feel ready to tell him everything—about her family history and all the secrets and resentments—but still, she needed him to know that she was going to try for Montana's sake to meet him halfway, to co-parent although how that would work was beyond her. One step at a time.

She took one more step to close the distance, and after hesitating a moment, she stroked one finger down the back of his hand. He didn't pull away. Trying to hold on to her faltering nerve, she lightly laced her fingers with his. Something in her calmed. She'd always loved to touch him, and she admitted to herself that she'd missed this, missed him.

"Kane, I can't say that Montana's life would be better without you in it. She has been with you only a day." Half of which he was on his back in the hospital. Her stomach lurched. It could happen again. He could get hurt worse next time. And then what?

One step at a time.

"She's already so attached to you," she whispered. "I was wrong to not tell you. I was just so scared," she said.

He turned around. She expected anger. Derision. Fired-off questions. Instead his silvery eyes searched hers, curious, wary.

"I was scared that we'd hold you back and you'd resent us." She sucked in a breath, but kept her gaze glued to his. "I was scared that I couldn't handle your lifestyle—the danger and the traveling and the celebrity part." She swallowed hard. "I still don't know how I am going to do it, how we will parent Montana together, but I am willing to…and I want to try."

What was he thinking? It took all her nerve to stand there and wait.

"Not try," he said flatly, giving her nothing. "We succeed. We win. There can be no doubt in your mind."

So much for meeting halfway. Kane did nothing by halves.

"Not so easy," she said softly.

"We just commit," he said. "And you can start by packing up a suitcase."

Sky nodded. "You are in Phoenix for a week, Kane. I have exercise classes to teach, subs to find since I'm only giving a week's notice," she said quickly seeing that he was about to speak. "I can stay here with Montana and start sorting things out, and you can stay in a…"

He cut off the rest of her sentence with his mouth. Hard. Aggressive. Sky whimpered, not shocked so much as she was overwhelmed by the wave of instant hot and drugging pleasure that rolled over her and tumbled her head over heels, dizzy. She hadn't felt this alive and intense for four years, and her inadvertent noise gave him his opening. His tongue delved inside her sensitive lips, traced her inner heat and then tangled with her tongue.

Kane Wilder could kiss. It was like he ate her alive. Possessed her. And she jumped in, fell three hundred feet into his liquid fire.

"Kane, we were supposed to be talking. Arranging

things," she said breathlessly when he finally broke the kiss.

"Done talking. Tomorrow," he said his voice dark with promise, and she was helpless to not look at his mouth. "I'd do it now, but it's Sunday."

When the heck had Kane cared about keeping it G rated on Sunday? He'd loved Sundays because he had a reprieve from thinking about his next draw for the day, and if he hadn't been too banged up, Sundays had been their lazy day just spending with each other in bed and out.

"Monday morning, first thing," he promised. "No waiting period. No residency requirement. ID and seventy-six dollars buys the license I already checked."

"What?"

"We can get a judge or a justice of the peace to do it the same day."

"Wait. You're not serious," she said. "We are not getting married tomorrow."

"Yes, Sky. You. Will. Marry. Me. Tomorrow."

Not a proposal. A demand.

"What is the rush?" she breathed.

"Rush. Four years late is not a rush."

"We have to stop focusing on the past," she said even though she certainly wouldn't win any awards for her forward thinking. "We need to think about a future, building a stable life for Montana. We need to be thoughtful. Plan. Feel our way."

Kane was not impressed.

"I've given it more than enough thought. Marriage. Pack a suitcase—enough for a week or two for you and Montana. At my next break we'll go to my brothers' ranch in Montana and decide where we want to have our home base."

She sighed. "Kane, you still want to make up for lost time, but marriage isn't going to do that. It won't solve all that is wrong between us."

"It's a beginning." Kane leaned forward and framed her face with his rough hands. She inhaled his scent. She had very little armor against him, and she wasn't sure she really wanted to anymore. She was tired of fighting. One day and he'd worn her down. How did that bode for her future? "And marriage is only the beginning of what you owe me, Sky."

KANE WALKED AGAIN through the tiny two-room house, rough plank floorboards creaking, unable to settle. Sky had pulled out two large canvas totes and a small suitcase to pack up some clothes, but she wanted to check on her studio first. He'd let her go. They both needed a breather. Colt was playing Candy Land with Montana, and he'd made her a grilled cheese sandwich. So normal.

He should be the one making her a snack and playing a game, but instead he was losing his mind. He had three years to catch up on, but he couldn't wrap his head around any of it. He had a daughter he didn't know. Sky, the one woman he'd trusted, the one woman he'd begun to let inside his paranoid and padlocked heart, had betrayed him on the most primal level.

She'd grown up with a loving mother and father in a sprawling, hacienda-style house in one of Scottsdale's most prestigious neighborhoods with two acres of landscaped desert surrounding the house. She'd been cherished and safe. She'd always known who she was and that she was wanted. How could she deny his daughter that same security?

He still didn't understand why she hadn't come to him. She'd told him she'd loved him over and over and even he had started to believe it. He'd started making plans, but forced himself to wait because he wanted Sky to have the opportunity to finish school. Traveling on the tour with him would have been grueling, and he'd wanted to have enough money so that they could have a home base so she could choose—travel with him or pursue her art—and he'd come home during breaks.

But she'd left. Lied. He knew he had to get a grip. Accept. Forgive. Move on, but Kane didn't think he could forgive this. Taking his child from him was too big a betrayal. He always believed he could do anything if he set his mind to it. It was just will. Determination. But forgiving Sky was like a huge wall between them. Three years. Three goddamn years. Lost. Stolen. Taken.

He'd faced a few paternity claims since he'd risen in the

rankings, all totally baseless—three of the women he'd never even met. One he had, but she'd been drunk so he'd done what he always did when the woman hitting on him drank too much—taxi to her apartment or condo, help her inside and make sure she locked the door behind him, before he caught the taxi back to his hotel alone. Fucking ironic. The one woman he'd actually knocked up had done a runner.

He didn't even remember the last bull ride in Santa Fe. Or dismounting. Hadn't checked his score. He'd wanted to get it done. Get Sky and his daughter out of the arena and back to Phoenix to figure out the rest of their lives. But he did remember glancing up and not seeing Sky where he'd put her.

He pinched his nose hard. Usually he could climb above the pain that was nearly always there in his body, ride it like a wave, skimming across its surface, use it to focus himself. Now it was another wall he kept crashing into. Pain from the bull muscling him into the gate, wrestled with the pain of discovering he had a beautiful daughter who thought of him as character in her daddy book. Was she going to expect him to climb back in that goddamn thing once the novelty wore off?

Fuck the pain and fuck the past. That was the best he could muster for the moment. Sky hadn't started packing. She'd gone to her studio to see if she had a larger suitcase, but she had pulled out a small carry-on and two large bright floral canvas totes that hurt his eyes to look at. He'd pack for her. He wanted to be clear. She and Montana were coming with him.

There wasn't a closet in the small bedroom with two beds, but there were two small, clearly banged-up vintage dressers and a garment rack filled with pretty patterned sundresses in a see-through plastic garment bag. Kane unzipped it and reached for one strapless sapphire blue dress. Memories crashed—Portland, Oregon—Sky in his truck, holding his hand, sucking on his finger, the moist heat of her mouth jacking him up so crazy fast he'd veered off the main road onto an unpaved and unmarked dirt road and drove cursing while she'd worked his finger in a rhythm and style that left little doubt about what she intended next.

And when he'd finally found a turnoff and driven down that, ending up at a feeder stream to the Yamhill River, she'd unbuttoned his jeans and stared at him as if he were holy, then she'd looked into his eyes, one finger lightly stroking the moisture already leaking, and spreading it around his sensitive tip and down the underside that always made his body shiver and had said, "I love you, Kane."

She'd meant it. He'd been able to tell by the deep purple of her eyes, the way they'd glowed, and the way her beautiful face was so serious and her touch so sensuous and reverent. She'd said it many other times, in many other places, but that had been the first time he'd started to believe it, and this had been the dress she'd been wearing. Kane let the soft material slip through his fingers. He leaned in and inhaled.

Lemon and verbena. His head settled a little. Same for his gut.

He was back in his old truck, the blue one that had reminded him of her eyes, pulling Sky onto his lap, her skirt hiked up, the top of her dress pulled down so that his hands could palm her beautiful small breasts that had so obsessed him.

He'd wanted to say the words back to her. They were true although new and terrifying. She'd become his world so fast, so unexpectedly, but his heart had swollen so full he'd choked, and his eyes had pricked and burned, so instead he'd buried his face in her neck and had inhaled her scent and fought back stupid tears and did what he always did: talked with his body.

Kane heard a car. He re-zipped the bag of about ten sundresses and with one finger through the hangers, dangled it over his shoulder and strode out of Sky's apartment. He unlocked his truck, hung the dresses next to his shirts on the custom bar and turned toward the other building that Sky had disappeared into a few minutes ago.

Of course the gallery prick would drive a silver Audi. Kane wasn't sure why that irritated him so much. Maybe because if he didn't usually haul a trailer or drive around his family's Montana ranch helping out during his time off, he might have bought one himself. He didn't want to have anything in common with Jonas, and he definitely didn't want him alone with Sky. Slamming the door of the truck, he loped into the large, long metal building, but paused at the entrance as his eyes adjusted to the light. He couldn't see Sky, but he saw Jonas walking across the cement floor with purpose.

He heard Sky's soft musical voice. "Jonas, I wasn't expecting you." She didn't sound tense, or apologetic or nervous like she'd sounded with him the past day and night.

Dammit.

"You should have been," Jonas said looking preppy and smooth in his starched, white button-down and navy chinos. His sleeves were buttoned at the wrist with jeweled cuff links. Seriously. On a Sunday late morning. "You promised me a sculpture and you left your whole life in the gallery. Here's your phone and your purse and...well I don't know what's in this bag."

"Thank you," she said, her voice soft and prim, not aching with emotion and defensiveness like how she'd sounded to him the last twenty-four plus hours.

Sky couldn't like this guy. She absolutely couldn't. She'd been raised in wealth and casual elegance, but she'd always been so sweet and down to earth. She'd liked to sew her own sundresses for Chrissakes. She'd even designed and tailored several shirts for him to wear during competition. He'd had them saved, and sealed in a garment bag with cedar balls. She deserved a man who would cherish her, not let her fall on her face in front of a bunch of strangers and leave her there for Chrissakes.

"So where's the cowboy?"

"In the house. I needed a moment."

Jonas laughed. "You and me both. Dr. Sheridan's personal assistant, and I didn't know doctors had those even if they are considered world class—" he put the last two words in air quotes, and finally Kane could get on board with Jonas's snide attitude "—has been ringing me hourly about the damn sculpture and your disappearance. The press has been a boon both for the gallery and for the auction. I'm opening up early today. My sister's already there, and she says there's quite a crowd. The other artists are thrilled with the press and extra viewing hours so all in all your cowboy didn't create a total cluster fuck. Even missing last night made you more mysterious."

"That was not my intention," Sky said.

Kane knew eavesdropping should probably have gone out of his repertoire when he'd been eight and spying on his eleven-and-a-half-year-old brother Luke, chatting to a girl from school who'd ridden by their apartment on a Razor scooter that Kane had coveted.

"Snow White and the Thieving Cowboy—one blogger posted the video of that idiot striding out with my art and you chasing after him like he was Justin Bieber. It has over ten thousand views already. Can you believe that?"

Damn.

Good thing Alicia would be busy with a family wedding. Not that she wouldn't be looped in tighter than a bull rope within seconds of landing. Justin Bieber, his ass.

"And then that smoking hot kiss in the spotlight has definitely not gone unnoticed," Jonas said, sounding peeved. "You had ample opportunity to tell me you were involved with someone over the past few weeks."

"I wasn't, but…" Sky sighed. "I am sorry, Jonas. I did say I wanted to keep things professional between us. My relationship with Kane is complicated."

"Love always is," Jonas said. "Or so I'm told, and I imagine cowboys are especially complicated. Never mind. I want to talk to you about something else. I am here hoping to talk you into giving me something."

"You'd better be talking about art." Kane walked fully into the building. His boots clicked on the cement with deadly intent. Yeah he was feeling more than a little mean right about now. "And I have a name. Kane Wilder."

Jonas rolled his eyes. "Yippeekaiyay."

"I don't believe this." Sky looked from Kane to Jonas. "You are men. Not boys." She had her arms out and palms up in the international 'stop' pose and stood between them.

Kane had to fight the urge to circle around her to get in the rich and prissy gallery owner's face.

"Kane, Jonas is here to return my phone, purse and clothes, and he is going to look at the other sculptures in the same series. Jonas, this is Kane, Montana's father. He and I are planning on getting married."

Immediately he calmed. She was admitting it. Accepting

it. Still she looked pissed and adorable. Sky had never once been pissed off at him that he'd known. She'd always been calm and loving, which had soothed him, but Sky standing up to him was new and turned him on. But he had to remain focused on the plan—getting married, getting his financials in order to include her and Montana. Hell, he still hadn't found out whether her was on her birth certificate. That questioned burned hot. If the father line was blank or said 'unknown', he really didn't know what he was going to do.

For a moment he couldn't breathe. Rage swirled around him. Taunts. Powerlessness. Fury.

Focus.

He breathed in to a count of seven, held for seven, breathed out for seven. Seven times. If it were blank he'd get his name added. Montana was only three. She wouldn't know. Probably wouldn't remember much of her life without him in it.

Unless he died in the arena.

That brought him up short. Hell, it was always a possibility. Every bull rider knew that. He'd seen it fucking happen. He'd seen riders go down and not get up and live but never ride again. He'd seen them die. His best friend had died by the hoof of a bull. He could be doing that to Montana. Here today, memory tomorrow.

For the first time, seriously the first time, his determination to ride to age thirty had a big fat question mark. Did he still need to do that? He knew his savings amount to the penny. His retirement. His investments in Phoenix, Portland, Seattle and LA apartment buildings. The largest amount of money set aside for purchasing the Wild Wind Ranch in Marietta back for his family, his much larger family now since Luke had married Tanner McTavish this past Christmas, and he and his sister-in-law were expecting twins, and also in the past year he'd discovered two more brothers that his mother had birthed at age fifteen after being seriously injured in a car accident. Her father had set up two separate adoptions for the twin boys before his mother had recovered enough to leave the hospital or know that she'd given birth to twins, not just one baby. One brother, Colt was married now and had adopted his wife, Talon's, son, Parker. Laird, his other brother was engaged to Tucker McTavish.

Seeing his brothers settled and happy had been a mixed blessing. He'd been relieved to see them so in love, but he'd never felt more alone. Wrestling the Wild Wind ranch back from her ailing and estranged father's nearly bankrupt hands had been his mother's dream, not his although it had made sense. They had ranching in their blood. Luke had ridden the rodeo circuit for ten years. He and his wife Tanner bred bucking bulls for the AEBR and pro circuit. Tucker had been a winning barrel racer and now helped breed bulls but also she wanted to breed and train horses. But was ranch life right for him and Sky now?

"Do you still want a cowboy-themed sculpture for the

donation, Jonas?"

"Yes. I'd love the one you took." His thoughtful gaze settled on Kane.

"Not going to happen."

"It is a trademarked pose, I'm afraid," Sky said. "I did sell the rights to that image, not just the picture. I didn't realize what I was signing away. But I had…" she broke off and blushed and Kane found himself fascinated by the convulsive swallow of her delicate throat and her pink-stained cheeks "…thousands…um…a lot of pictures that I took while researching bull riders. I mean bull riding. I can show you more sculptures from that series."

"Researching," Kane said, surprised to find himself amused. "Is that what you were doing?"

Her blush deepened, and for the first time since yesterday at nine thirty-seven a.m., the roaring in his head stopped, and his gut stopped burning.

"Yes. For my masters in fine arts," Sky said primly. "Follow me, Jonas." She hesitated and looked at Kane, uncertainty clouding her eyes. He preferred the blush. "Do you want to see them?" she hesitantly asked him.

"Of course." Kane frowned. Why the hell wouldn't he?

She nodded. "Then behave," she whispered. She jumped when he linked fingers with her.

"Depends on what your definition of behaving is."

Sky nibbled on her lip and then a hint of a smile chased across her face.

"Jonas." Sky walked across the concrete toward the back of the converted shop or barn. "I hope you find one of these an acceptable substitute for me to donate for the guild auction next weekend."

Her voice caught, and he hated that. She didn't need Jonas's approval on anything.

"I'll buy the sculptures, Sky," he said, wanting to be gone from the reminder of their years apart and start his life with Sky and his daughter. What had her parents been thinking letting her raise their only grandchild in a former bunkhouse when they had a hacienda-style mansion a few miles away?

"Like hell!" Jonas burst out, stopping. "You can't buy all of her sculptures."

Kane longed to pull out his black Amex just to shut Jonas up and show him that yes, he most definitely could. And would, but Sky would not define that as behaving.

"How will Sky establish her career if you take an entire series off the market in a private collection?" Jonas breathed, like Kane had just suggested giving everyone Hep C. "She's getting incredible buzz. She needs to build on that, not disappear."

Kane didn't want anything of Sky's going to the cheating and lying squirt of sperm's hospital wing named in his exalted family name. But he didn't want to hurt her career when she had so much talent and had worked so hard.

"Kane, maybe wait in the house," she suggested gently. "You really don't have a say in this part of my life."

"Is that so?" he drawled, furious again she was dismissing him. "No say," he repeated even though he hadn't intended to have a say about her art, but now he walked toward her full of purpose. Saw her swallow and clench her fingers. Her eyes widened, pupils dilated and the beautiful blue deepened to smoky purple. "Not even if it's a sculpture of me?"

He stopped toe-to-toe. Her breathing was shallow and ragged. Finally something he could control. Sky's reaction to him. She still lit up like a Christmas tree. He'd been handling her all wrong. Fuck talking, being practical and trying to comprehend her twisted illogic and childish reactions. He should have just tossed her delectable small handful of an ass in his truck and taken her to a hotel and fucked her blind and stupid to remind her of what they'd had and what they'd have again when she finally got on board that Montana was his child, and he intended to raise her all the way to walk her down the aisle, and he wasn't going to be a single dad, divorced or married to a woman not Montana's mother when he did it.

"Not everything is about you." Her whisper fractured, and he could see the blush that stained her cheekbones flush down to her collarbone that he'd so loved to trace with his fingertips and then his tongue because it had caused her to moan and shiver and beg.

For a man who'd always been highly sexed, Sky had been his perfect match—scorching hot and ready to burn within every time he even started to think about sex, which with her had been a lot. But it had been her sweet and her total acceptance of him, win or lose, good or bad, that had stormed his heart.

"Really?" He let his voice go deep and leaned in closer to her, allowing his body to brush against her so she could feel his monster hard-on. Her eyes fluttered shut, but then she opened them again as if gathering up her tattered willpower. His Sky had been so sweet and giving and totally his. Whatever he'd wanted. Always. This Sky was new. More of a fighter, and he would never have guessed that that would have turned him on.

"I'm going to make you prove that later, Sky," he said, leaning even further into her space, and curling his finger under her chin to tilt her face up so that she could see his intent. He leaned closer slowly so she had plenty of time to move away, but no, not his girl. She held her own. "I'm going to make you beg." His lips feathered along her ear.

"You can try." She trembled, but didn't push him away, nor did her midnight blue eyes look away. "I won't," she promised.

God, he'd forgotten how utterly beautiful she was, how she just looked at him and it was like she could climb inside him and wrap around his soul, warm all the parts that were ice cold and rigid.

His hand spanned her throat, and he felt her swallow in his palm. Desire pierced. He knew she would. He wanted her to beg. He'd string her out as long as he could stand it.

"You remember what I do for a living?"

Rhetorical question, and she didn't answer it.

"That I live and breathe challenge, right?" His mouth descended toward hers. Her lips parted.

"Kane," she whispered, more of an invitation than a protest.

He huffed a laugh and stepped back.

Sky blinked. Spell broken. He felt like a torch ignited in his belly. Sky still wanted him as much as she ever had. They'd been good together. Too good. That summer with her was the only time in his entire life he'd come close to wavering from his goal. Make more money than his so-called biological father's family had. Get his mother's birthright Montana ranch back for her, him and Luke. But during the summer with Sky for the first time he'd tasted peace. He'd experienced happiness. He'd felt normal. A regular man, and he'd wondered what it would be like to be that man with a wife and a house and a regular job and to not be driven by things set in motion before he'd been born.

"Later," he said, the word as much of a promise as it was a dare.

Her eyes flared. She looked at Jonas who was standing further into Sky's studio in a shaft of light coming in through the windows up high near the roof line. He stood still, staring, mouth slightly open.

"Stay," Sky told Kane. "Behave." She hurried after Jonas.

Kane was not a dog. He followed.

Sky switched on a light and a semicircle of six bronze sculptures shimmered in the golden light from the small halogen spot lights mounted on a dropped beam. Each sculpture, four of a bull and rider, and two with just a cowboy, one back to the viewer, walking away, rope in hand, the uneven tilt of his shoulders indicating pain and loss. One hand dangled loose at his side, and Kane felt a lump in his throat. It was him. He'd been tossed at the seven-second mark. It had been the last time Sky had watched him ride, and when he looked at the empty hand, he couldn't stop the thought that he should have been holding on to something—his wife and child. Instead nothing. The invisible family.

The final sculpture was of a cowboy climbing up out of the dirt. Each sculpture had its own pedestal of a different size and height, and the way the light hit the metal created shadows and a shimmer as if the image were alive.

Kane's breath seized in his lungs. He'd never seen anything more beautiful. More powerful. The images were so immediate, raw, still yet pulsing with energy, tension. His heart thumped hard. He swore the sculptures breathed. Moved. Sky had created these with her hands and her mind and her imagination and her heart. While he'd been riding for money and the win, she'd been watching, analyzing, remembering.

He felt awed.

The images captured a split second in time, but so much

more. Each sculpture was a dance between the fury of the bull and the will of the rider. They were also a taunt to nature, gravity and balance. And how did she create the shape and color of the metal? He felt mesmerized and humbled.

While he'd been playing the short game and challenging death and the laws of physics, Sky had been creating something eternal. She'd been memorializing her lover, her child's father, while he'd been trying to forget the only woman he'd loved existed by burying himself mindlessly in the bodies of other women until he couldn't take the boredom and loneliness of it anymore. Lately his life had felt like a black hole monk stage he hadn't had the stomach to crawl out of.

He felt tired. He felt worn down.

"Amazing, Sky," he said unable to stay in her presence another moment until he could wrap his head around what an idiot he'd been and how much time he'd wasted. He'd failed her on an elemental level. He'd kept his feelings close and secret. He hadn't understood her. Hadn't even tried. He'd let himself get lost in her body and what she did to his.

She'd left him because she hadn't trusted him.

And he hadn't deserved her or her trust, but he sure as hell was going to work hard to win it this time. No failure.

He took her cool hands in his and rubbed them briefly to warm them and then brought them to his mouth. He kissed one then the other.

"I have no words." It was a confession. Her talent and

vision humbled him. "Sort out what you need with Jonas."

He walked out of the studio and back to the house before the protest clawing for supremacy, the one that didn't want a piece of him or Sky's to help out anything associated with the hated name Sheridan, burst out like an unleashed, unmuzzled id. His shit was his own to keep a tight lid on. He couldn't hinder Sky's career. She had too much talent and had worked too hard. So she could donate a sculpture, get the buzz, lay her foundation, continue her work. He'd build her a studio wherever they landed, but he was still going to change her life.

Chapter Ten

KANE UNLOCKED THE door to a suite at the Phoenix, one of Scottsdale's premier resorts. Sky'd only driven past it in all the years of living here. The pleasure she felt at settling with Jonas, not only with the donation of one of her largest sculptures of a bull rider mid-ride, but also that he was going to show the other pieces in his gallery. Being featured in a gallery of that size one year out of her MFA program was truly an accomplishment, but she was so tied up in knots over Kane that she couldn't even enjoy the moment. She wasn't really sure yet what she'd agreed to.

"Certainly moving up in the world," she breathed out, a little intimidated, frustrated, and impressed all at once. Her emotions and thoughts had been all over the place since Kane had walked back into her life, and she still had no idea which one to settle with. "No more trailer?"

"My brother, Laird and his fiancée are using it at the moment."

"This can't be the tour hotel," she said thinking that the Phoenix was astronomical. They'd come to dinner here once for Bennington's sixteenth birthday. Sky, who'd grown up in what most people would think of as luxury, had been intimidated.

"I don't want to discuss money now," he said coldly, and opened the door.

Money. Obviously another minefield they'd need to walk across. Sky was almost relieved that Colt was still with them. He held the sculpture—the one that had kicked off the drama and reunited her with Kane and brought his daughter into his life. Permanently.

The new normal. Sky felt like she needed to pinch herself. She also needed a few days—make that weeks—to come to terms with the changes. Kane wasn't offering her any time to process anything, and his continued nearness was awakening too many memories that she wanted to keep locked away until she could deal with the present.

The bellman brought the rest of their luggage—Kane's large suitcase and his leather duffel and her smaller one that he had packed while she'd been meeting with Jonas as well as a box of toys, games and books Montana had packed up with Colt earlier. Montana carried her owl backpack and wore another, larger one on her back that she declared made her a turtle because she now carried "my home on my back."

Their daughter had held Kane's hand the entire time they'd checked in and had danced in excitement beside him. Probably a lot like she had, Sky remembered disparagingly. When they'd hooked up she'd been so thrilled to be with

Kane, too blissed out to ask any questions and she sure as hell hadn't made any demands.

Montana ran to the wall of windows that looked out over Camelback Mountain and the natural red rock sculptures tumbling across the sweeping desert view.

The minute the bellman had left, large tip in hand, Colt put the sculpture down in the center of the large, round, reclaimed wood dining table.

"You two have a lot to discuss," he said.

"You should stay at the hotel," Kane repeated. He'd tried to reserve a room for his brother as well.

Colt looked around at the studied, rustic elegance that gleamed with money and shook his head. "Laird's flying out with Tucker. He'll help me settle up Sky's place, and Tucker's going to take over for Tanner supervising the Triple T's Team with the AEBR bulls."

The hits kept coming, Sky thought. A whole family of Kane's she had to meet. More people to judge her. Take Kane's side and shut her out. Tell her how she'd royally screwed up. Go big or go home, she mocked herself bleakly.

"Colt," Kane said taking a compulsive step forward. "Thank you."

"You need us we come." Colt wasn't looking at Kane; instead he watched Montana at the window.

"Montana, I'm out. See you tomorrow."

She ran across the room and hugged Colt around his knees. She was always so comfortable with people. Like

Kane.

He smiled. "Your cousin Parker's coming to meet you tomorrow," he said, and the way his face momentarily softened warmed Sky on the inside. Her daughter was going to have cousins. More soon since Luke and his wife were expecting. Guilt settled more heavily around her shoulders. She'd denied Montana a lot more than her father. She'd denied her an entire family—aunts, uncles, now cousins, and a perhaps a grandmother, though she wasn't sure how close Kane was to his mom.

Her parents hadn't been a presence in Montana's life. The tense estrangement that had kicked in after Bennington died had only grown with the years, and she hadn't wanted to subject Montana to the coldness and critical indifference she'd experienced growing up. Besides, they would have known who the father of their grandchild was on sight, and since they wrongly blamed Kane for Bennington's obsession with being a bull rider and all things cowboy instead of becoming an attorney, that knowledge would have cut them deep.

"You good?" Colt looked piercingly at his brother.

"Fine."

A lie. Colt didn't let him off the hook and drilled him with that strange golden stare like a bird of prey.

"Getting there," Kane grit out through his teeth.

Colt nodded to her. "Sky." And then was gone.

So much to discuss. The silence seemed electric as if by

leaving Colt had flipped a switch.

"Daddy, when are we going swimming?" Montana looked up at Kane expectantly.

"Now." Kane roused himself and tried for a smile.

"Wait. What?" Sky said. "Montana, it's time for a nap, and we don't have suits. Maybe tomorrow."

"Daddy said he'd take me swimming. Today." Her lower lip pursed. "He promised."

Great. Already different pages for parenting although that was a problem she should have seen coming from a long way off.

"Just a quick swim," Kane said this time finding his smile. "Some fun after such a long ride in the truck. Then a nap."

The grin Montana shot her dad matched his, and once again, Sky felt on the outside looking in.

"We don't even have swimsuits," she said in a low voice, one more thing he could judge. She'd managed the basics only.

"I know. I looked." Kane kicked off his cowboy boots and shucked off his jeans while Sky gawked. Kane held her gaze as he unbuttoned his shirt, snap by snap. "You gonna help me, baby, or just stare?"

Apparently she was going to stare. Kane shrugged fluidly out of his shirt and kicked the pile of clothes into the closet. Her mouth dried. He was perfect. Defined shoulders, muscled ridges on his arms, especially his forearms, strong tendons. Six-pack abs didn't begin to cover it and when he turned to pull out black and gray swim trunks from his leather duffel bag, she could see the flex of his obliques. Her fingers ached to trace the bull tattoo that leaped across his upper back.

"Daddy has a picture on him, Mommy," Montana said as Kane went to the bathroom to change into his suit. "I want one too."

Great.

"Should have thought of that before you told me tats turned you on and created your stylized version of Berserker." Kane loped back instantly, trunks on. He looked like he belonged in a magazine. He was in magazines. He'd been one of a celebrity magazine's most handsome man two times running. He'd been one of the featured bull riders in a documentary a couple years ago and attendance at AEBR events had soared and had shown no signs of dropping off.

Kane tugged on a snowy white T-shirt and slipped on flip-flops.

"Ready for a swim?" Montana nodded, her arms wrapped tight about her bull.

"Bennington goes too," she said.

"Bennington can watch," Kane said easily, pocketing the room key, "but he can't swim."

"Neither can Montana," Sky whispered miserably, following him out of the room.

The look he shot her was a fierce WTF? But Sky ignored

it. It hadn't really been an issue. They lived in the desert. No pool. No rivers. Instead she focused on Montana's pleasure as she ran down the wide sandstone hallway broken up by woven Turkish rugs.

"You didn't think it was dangerous not teaching her to swim when your parents have a giant pool in their center courtyard?" Kane asked after a beat of simmering silence.

"I just moved back to Scottsdale, well, Phoenix, technically last year."

His eyes searched hers in the hallway. Sky sucked in a breath. He saw too much. Always too much.

"Your parents didn't help you?" Kane sounded outraged, watching Montana as she darted ahead and then circled back. "And why didn't your father ever find me? Demand I do the right thing."

Sky winced. The last thing she'd wanted at the time from Kane was an offer 'to do the right thing.'

"I'm easy to find. My schedule is published a year in advance. My stats are online. Sponsor events are publicized weeks before we hit each city."

"I didn't want him to find you," she said quietly.

"Why not?"

She couldn't tell him that. It would kill him. He'd loved her brother as much as she had. And Kane had been so close with her parents. He'd be so hurt, stoic, but hurt to know that they blamed him for Bennington's death, but he'd been doing what he loved. Kane hadn't even been in the country for a year prior to Bennington being injured. Bennington had started on the lower rungs of the rodeo circuit determined to move himself up to the AEBR. Kane had started on the professional circuit, but further from the hype—honing his skills in Australia and Brazil where it seemed like a lot of the top talent was coming from.

Montana ran back toward them and then hopped on one foot then the other.

"Swimming." She took off down the hall again.

"Can't we go into all this later?" she asked, miserable. She couldn't even have a normal conversation with Kane without one of them stepping on a land mine from their past.

He nodded, and then called out Montana's name. She turned back again and ran toward Kane who caught her and tossed her up in the air. Montana shrieked in joy.

"Again," she demanded. Kane complied, all the way to the elevator.

"New workout routine." He put his daughter down and looked at Sky. For the first time, no shadows flickered in his eyes or across his face. She smiled tentatively back, remembering how he'd incorporated her into his workouts—sitting on his back when he did push-ups or doing some yoga poses together. She'd also walked on his back when it was sore and massaged him.

She'd been so in love with him. Had felt so happy in his presence. What would they be like now together? What were

Kane's expectations? What were hers?

"JOIN US." KANE'S voice was pure sin as he stood in the waist-deep water at the edge of the pool where they'd had three lounges set up with towels in a cabana Kane had rented for the week. It was absurdly expensive and Sky hovered between resentment—feeling like Kane seemed intent on pointing out the financial advantages for Montana—and the ever-present guilt that she'd been too afraid to seek him out.

She hadn't trusted his feelings for her. She hadn't trusted her ability to handle his lifestyle—the time on the road, the obligations, the ever-present danger and all the women. Between the danger to his health and the temptation of the women, Sky had no idea how she was supposed to negotiate that with a smile. Last time Kane had kept their relationship mostly separate from his work. She didn't know what he planned this time. He probably didn't either.

"Mama swim." Montana, tucked into her father's chest, slapped the water.

She sat up and regarded them. She propped her new TOMS sunglasses up on her head, where they perched in the messy bun she'd twisted up.

"How's the water?"

"Perfect," Kane said, his gaze not wavering from hers.

Were they flirting?

Kane was definitely trying to make some sort of connection between them. The resort hotel, the cabana and when he went shopping, he seriously shopped. A pile of pool toys had been tumbled in a basket—water toys, water wings, a life vest and four swim suits for Montana, and then without hesitation, he'd stalked over to the women's section and chose three stylish and beautiful but very skimpy bikinis for her and two suit cover-ups that exposed more than they covered.

Sky clutched the swim wrap closer to her, a little embarrassed by how sexy the suit was.

"You used to love the water, even when wearing less," Kane said, his mouth curved in challenge, or was it memory of how she'd skinny-dipped with him in more than one hotel pool long after hours.

Where had that brave girl gone?

"I'm afraid I'll blind everyone."

Kane laughed. "Go for it."

"Easy for you to say—you are still wearing your sunglasses."

A thought hit her, and she sat up, worried.

"Is the light bothering your eyes?"

"A little," he acknowledged. His honesty surprised her. "Join us, Sky, please."

She slipped off the Oka-B silver flip-flops that matched her silver bandeau bikini top and black and silver crochet bottoms and then shred the wrap. She slipped into the water.

"Chilly," she said, conscious that her nipples beaded tightly and were obvious through the thin material.

"Not chilly enough apparently," he said self-deprecatingly, reeling her in closer and she caught her breath when the hard length of him brushed her exposed tummy.

It was suddenly hard to swallow. And she kept forgetting to breathe. The pool wasn't crowded. Most of the guests were poolside stretched out on pool lounges shaded by wide blue umbrellas. Sky didn't miss the very interested looks more than a few women were casting his way. She'd winced when two women had made a big show of sitting up on their lounges and reapplying sunscreen and lipstick.

Even though she knew she shouldn't care, she'd been comforted that Kane had focused solely on playing with Montana and teaching her to swim, and now he was focused on her.

"Kane," she whispered. The worries about money faded; the guilt faded. It was weird. For a moment she felt like she used to—when it was just them, and she'd made him her world. "I don't know what to do."

He surprised her. He leaned forward, kissed the corner of her mouth and then stepped back, a playful smile touching his lips, and his dimple danced into sight.

"Get ready to catch a fish," he said, holding Montana, his hand splayed across her tummy. He let her go and Montana splashed and rolled and kicked up a tsunami of waves as she thrashed her way across the few feet of water separating her parents.

Sky caught Montana and lifted her up above her head, the memories easing a little and her heart soaring with pride for her little girl.

"You did it!" She hugged Montana tightly to her.

"Again, again!" Montana squirmed, and Sky lowered her into the water, whispered encouragement and watched as her daughter swam away from her, full of life and confidence.

If only bridging the emotional gap between her parents could be so easy.

LATER SKY SAT up on the chaise and even though they were in a cabana, she smoothed sunscreen over her legs and arms and her chest. She was just stroking it on her shoulders and back when Kane and Montana returned from watching a collection of exotic birds get fed. They had ordered food—a Sunrise acai bowl for her, chicken Caesar salad for Kane and a fish taco for Montana—and Kane had taken Montana to see the birds when she started getting restless for her snack.

She was off her schedule. It was almost too late for a nap and too early for bed, but she couldn't begrudge Montana this time with Kane. The pool had been magical. It reminded Sky that the last three years had been a lot of work and not enough fun. Kane had always worked hard, but boy-oh-boy had he known how to have fun. They had done a lot of sightseeing when they'd traveled, taking small detours to see beautiful views and go hiking.

Kane took the sunscreen from her hand, sprawled out beside her on the same lounger and squirted some sunscreen in his palm, and then he warmed it by rubbing his hands together. Sky caught her breath as his hands, warm and sure, began to stroke down her skin.

"Kane," she protested, but didn't move away.

Desire pierced her low in her core and radiated out in waves of liquid heat. Her legs stirred restlessly, and she tried not to remember how he had done this many, many times before. She closed her eyes and just for this moment allowed the indulgence. Pretended that she hadn't ruined everything through fear and lack of confidence. Those two bitches had ruled her life, and when she'd left home for art college, she'd thought she'd left them behind. And now, here they were again.

"Kane." She finally stirred even though his hands continued to stroke her body, and she felt so decadent and relaxed even though she knew she had to get a grip and take charge. Not easy when facing Kane Wilder. Montana relaxed on another chaise singing softly to her bull. Perhaps if Montana weren't taking Kane's sudden appearance in her life so easily, it would be easier to push him away.

But seeing her little girl so happy made her realize how much Montana and Kane had missed, and heck, why lie? She'd missed out too. Being with Kane made her feel happy and alive in a way she hadn't been in four years. She'd been building a life for herself and Montana. She was finally gaining confidence in herself, no longer always hearing the disparaging voice of her father or feeling the chilly reception her parents gave her, which had gone frigid after Bennington had died.

But she hadn't one felt even a tenth of the emotions or attraction that she'd experienced in the past day and night with Kane. It was thrilling and exhausting.

"Kane." She spoke softly, barely restraining herself from leaning back into his body. "We really need to talk, make a plan to co-parent and what that will look like, how it will work."

He rubbed more sunscreen into his palm and now his hands were stroking low on her back, his fingers brushing just slightly under the hip-hugging bikini.

"We have a plan, baby: we get married tomorrow. I've already put calls in to my financial advisor and attorney. They are flying out on the first flight from LA to expedite all the paperwork for us so we can get it done."

It?

He was summing up their future in a couple of sentences.

"You sure kill it with the romance," she said and immediately regretted it.

He stiffened behind her.

"There's nothing romantic about this situation."

She didn't deserve romance. Not that he had been romantic before, not really. No grand gestures. No flowers. No flowery words. Not a lot of compliments. But he'd never let her pay for dinner or even one chai latte if he were within shouting distance. And he'd liked to do things with her—it hadn't just been sex, although they'd had a lot of sex. He'd listened to her, asked about her art and her day. "I know. That was a stupid thing to say."

Silence.

Okay, really stupid.

"What paperwork?" she asked curiously, not wanting her girlish wish to hang awkwardly in the air between them.

"Will. Life insurance beneficiary. College fund." His hands had slipped down to span her waist, which sent darts of heat pooling low in her middle. "Sky." His voice went tense. "Am I on her birth certificate?"

She shivered. How could she explain that to him? At that point she'd still been hoping to have some support or relationship with her parents. Knowing Kane was the father would have infuriated and devastated them, and she'd been skating on ice so thin she'd been poised to fall in. She'd had no idea Montana would look so much like her daddy.

"No," she whispered.

"Why the hell not? What did you tell your parents? Lorenzo?"

She closed her eyes. When he put it like that it sounded awful. She was awful.

"You were never going to tell me. Never."

She tried to swallow but her throat wouldn't work.

"You were going to deny me my child forever." He whispered the words, and they sounded broken, and Sky felt her own heart, wounded so many times so long ago, crack again on familiar fault lines. She just felt so hollow.

Instead of pulling away, she turned into him, pressed her face against his pec. She squeezed her eyes shut, but could still feel the hot spurt of tears. She held on hard to his muscled shoulders.

She didn't have to answer. He knew.

"Why? What did I do that made you think I would be a terrible father?"

"I never thought that." She pulled away and touched his mouth with gentle fingers. "Never that. It was me. I knew we were having a good time and all, and it was fun, but never permanent for you." She felt like she was ripping off a Band-Aid from a wound that needed a tourniquet, but this was all on her. Not Kane. "You kept saying it was just for the summer so at the end…" She gulped a breath. "I had a shelf life. I knew that."

"You were going back to school. You said that in June when you approached me." He cupped her face; his thumbs traced her cheekbones. "Didn't you want to go back to school?"

Of course he'd cut to the matter. Now she'd sound like the biggest idiot in love ever.

"No," she whispered, anguished. "I kept hoping that you'd ask me to stay on tour with you, and I was so ashamed because you were so focused on your career, and I was so focused on you."

"You never said anything," he breathed out.

"Kane, I don't want to talk about it. It's humiliating. I drove you away because I kept telling you over and over how much I loved you and you never once… Not that I blame you," she said quickly, dashing her tears away. "I still should have told you about the baby, let it be our decision instead of mine. I was immature and…and…"

He looked stricken.

"I was nineteen but still I should have put on my big girl panties as my roommate from college always said and sucked it up. So it's on me. Not you, Kane. My fault. I didn't doubt your parenting skills. I didn't know how our life would work, and I wanted you to have freedom to pursue your dream. Still I should have done the right thing," Sky said fiercely in a total mea culpa.

Kane pulled her to him. Held her so tightly she could barely breathe, and she didn't care.

"There's so much past," she said softly. "But we have to find our future."

"We will," Kane said and his voice was adamant. "We will."

"Fish taco?"

Total moment slayer. Sky scrambled out of Kane's hold

and realized that she hadn't put her cover-up on yet so she was quite exposed in her bikini. The waiter handed out the food, smiling at Montana and handing her a mango smoothie along with her fish taco. She kept herself busy helping their daughter until Kane held out a spoonful from her acai bowl.

"You need to eat, Sky," Kane said. She paused and then leaned forward, letting the spoon slide between her lips. He'd liked to feed her. She'd forgotten that. He'd hold a fork of something he was eating or she should have been eating and then watch her eat it, so much pleasure shining on his face that her hunger would take a different path. Some nights they hadn't been able to get horizontal fast enough.

He spooned a second bite into her mouth and followed it with a quick, light kiss. "Let's focus on the present," he told her. "No more blame."

"ONE BED?" SKY stopped on the threshold of the suite's bedroom. She'd just finished giving Montana a bath in a tub that was practically a Jacuzzi and then she'd tucked her into in a sleeper sofa bed with pillows all around her.

Kane had just sauntered out of the massive marble bathroom, towel very low around his narrow hips. The large purpling bruise on his ribs didn't detract one bit from his masculine attraction.

Sky needed a shower, a nap and a few days to process the changes in her life. Unfortunately, she had none of those.

"We're not sleeping together," she said, immediately picturing his tanned body sprawled on the pristine down white comforter.

Yet.

It was not how she'd intended to start the difficult conversation of shared custody and what that could realistically look like because jumping into a quickie marriage was not on her agenda, but seeing the plush California king bed screeched her brain to a dead stop.

He ignored her and instead opened his large leather duffel bag and pulled out a pair of workout shorts.

"Montana and I need our own room, Kane," she said taking another step into the room and then another so that she stood between him and the massive bed she was trying to ignore. "Or I can sleep with her." She thought of how expensive a room must be here. "Or we can stay at my…"

"No," was all he said. His eyes flicked over her, and she gulped in a breath redolent with the scent of man and citrus shampoo.

She felt her blush bloom over her fair skin. So much for trying to meet him halfway.

Kane held another towel in his hand and ran it over his wet hair, drying it enough so that the loose curls began to form, nearly brushing his shoulders.

"I know we need to talk," she sighed. "And it's going to

take time to sort through all our…issues." She settled on a word that sounded rather stupid to her. "We always jumped to sex before," she admitted, and she'd been just as guilty as he had been. "But time and discussion is going to help us decide what the future will look like, not sex."

"I didn't say anything about sex." He held the pair of gray workout shorts in his hand and turned to face her. A drop of water chased down his pec and clung to his nipple briefly before falling onto the towel that hung precariously low on his hips, stark white against his olive skin. Kane laughed. "That was you."

"I said no to sex." She tried to breathe without dragging his scent into her lungs. Where was the air in the room? Even with the air conditioner cranking, her skin prickled with heat. "And I'm not sleeping with you."

"I didn't say anything about sleep." His voice went low and rough and another flash of heat lodged between her thighs.

"This isn't…I'm not going to…you know," she whispered backing up as he stalked toward her.

"What? Sex?" She could tell he repeated the word deliberately. "We always communicated with sex. We had our best communication naked and having sex."

Her heart thudded. That was true but that type of communication was what got them in trouble.

"We didn't talk enough."

"You certainly held back vital info," Kane dismissed. "So

maybe we should start with sex."

She held her hand up as if to stop his advance, but he dropped the towel and Sky's arms dropped to her side and her eyes strayed south. Stayed. Her mouth dried. Her heart thundered. Her body went liquid.

"I'll talk now," she whispered each word distinctly even as the backs of her legs hit the bed and she sat down and was now eye level with his fierce erection. "I promise." She was distracted as a drop of moisture beaded on the tip of his erection and without thinking her finger smoothed over the tip, stealing the moisture, and she brought her finger to her lips, already plumping with desire for him. "This is not a good idea, Kane." She tried to think of all the reasons sex was a bad idea. Brain fail.

"It's a fucking brilliant idea. I just look at you and think about sex and you get wet for me."

"That's not true," Sky lied.

"Baby, you were always ready to burn, and I was right there in flames with you."

"Things are different now," she said a little desperately.

"Prove it." He laughed and grabbed the front of her swim cover-up and ripped it down the front. Kane flung the material over his shoulder.

"I can't believe you just did that," she gasped. "You spent a stupid amount of money on that cover-up."

"The cover-up was a dumb idea," he conceded. "I like looking at you."

"And I don't like how you keep throwing money around," she said, trying to focus on something that didn't involve Kane naked and determined to revisit their sexual past when their emotional past was still a minefield. "You don't need to prove anything to me, and I don't want Montana to think she can instantly get anything she sets her heart on, which with little girls is a lot and often."

He pushed her flat on the bed, his arms caging her in, her legs wide as he stood between them.

"Fuck the money," he said. "Do you know how much I earned the month you left me—September 2013?"

"Not relevant," she said, mesmerized by the way he held himself above her, his body parallel to hers, none of it touching but she felt on fire. Her nerve endings remembered, and they wanted all that glorious sensation his mouth and hands and cock could deliver. It took all her willpower not to reach up and drag him down on top of her.

"Relevant as hell. Seventy-eight thousand four hundred fifty dollars, and that was just for two wins and a new sponsor. Not even residuals on ads or earnings from investments. And that was four years ago, when I was just starting to regularly place top ten a lot more. Hell of a lot's changed since then."

Sky stared. So much? She had no idea he could earn that much in a month.

"Did you not ever look at my stats online?" he demanded.

"No." She'd been too busy looking at him. "Seemed a little stalkerish. And your draw was never the money for me."

"Probably the only woman I'd believe saying that considering where and how you were living," he muttered. Then his hot gaze skewered hers. "I wish to God you'd been more mercenary."

"No. I'd hate that—staying with someone for money. It's disgusting."

Her dad had always flung his money and power in her mom's face. Used it to intimidate her. To get his way. She was not walking down that path. She wanted them to be equals.

"Your money is your money. You work so hard and risk so much. I know you have financial and life goals that you want to meet. Montana and I are fine financially. You don't need to make up for the years we were apart."

Kane's expression went tight again. "You really don't get it do you?" He sounded equally pissed and astonished. "You really don't understand where this is going."

"Co-parenting," she whispered, wanting him to know that she wasn't going to shut him out and that when he was available on a break, he would have full access to his daughter. "But you don't need to buy her love."

"I'm not going to buy it. But I am going to fully support you and our daughter, and it's not going to be in a falling-down bunkhouse with jury-rigged electrical."

"It's up to code," Sky denied and glared at him. "Get off

me."

"You really want that, baby?"

"Yes."

"Prove it."

Before she could process that request, he pulled off the black bikini bottoms with his thumb and forefinger and dropped it on the floor. Still levered above her and naked, he leaned forward and breathed warm air on her tummy. Sky shivered as he pressed tiny kisses around her belly button. His tongue traced the path he kissed and dipped inside her navel. Sky nearly shot off the bed.

"You were always so sensitive," he breathed against her skin. "You always got so slick, baby. All I had to do was look at you. All I had to do was start thinking about sex and you'd be ready."

He caressed her tender and quivering flesh with the slight stubble of his chin and then kissed over the pink he created.

"Kane, we're supposed to be talking, working things out." As a protest, it failed utterly.

"This is another method of us talking," he murmured, licking along her collarbone. Her breathing fractured. "I remember once I almost made you come just looking at you and talking about what I wanted to do to your breasts. Are you still so sensitive?"

She tangled one hand in his hair to pull him closer to her. And her legs wrapped around his narrow hips to pull him down to her. She sighed.

"Kane." Her voice ached with desire.

With his teeth he pulled down her bandeau silver bikini top and sucked her nipple deep into his mouth. Sky pressed the back of her hand over her mouth to keep from screaming and maybe waking Montana. She arched into his mouth.

"Please," she begged as his tongue laved her nipple into a tight, aching peak. After four years, her body came alive and burned like a flame.

"So, yes or no to sex, baby?"

She should say no. She tried to find the word in her vocabulary, but this was Kane, who'd routinely made her forget her own name.

"Yes," she whispered, her orgasm already building, making her insides feel hot and achy. Deep inside the trembling started, and her breath sawed in and out. He kissed his way down her body, and then his hands gripped her hips.

"I wonder if you taste the same."

But he didn't move.

"Kane, hurry," she urged.

"Say please." He breathed warm air on her hot core. "Say now." He kissed her dead center.

Her legs shook. It had been so long. She was melting when she'd thought she was done with hot sex. Since she'd left Kane and then had Montana, she hadn't once desired sex with any men she'd met. She'd felt sexually dead. Still she made a grab for sanity.

"Not hearing what I want to hear, baby." Kane kissed

along the insides of her thighs. He traced something high on her inner thigh with his tongue. And then again over her glistening mound.

"Do you remember when I shaved you here in the shape of a heart?" He traced a heart so close to her clit that she whimpered. "All of your silky tight curls gone but a little heart. That turned me on so much."

His fingers were along the folds of her slick lips and then he looked up at her, his body still between her legs. He licked his finger. "Your scent and taste always drove me crazy. Could never get enough."

"Stop playing around." She grabbed his head to anchor him where she wanted him to be.

He laughed. "You really should make me work for it a little more, Sky," he said.

The words were a slap in the face by reality. She jerked away and scrambled to the head of the bed. That quickly Kane sat in front of her. His hand spanned her throat and tilted her face up to his.

"You stole my child. You took three years of her life from me, and I can never, never get that back. You can never give me that time back."

His eyes glittered with an expression she'd never seen before, but it was so intense, she felt like he'd seared her with a welding torch.

"I know," she said, taking his hand and curling her much smaller one around it. She brought his hand to her cheek and pressed it there. "I know. But you said that we had to move on from that."

She kissed one knuckle, and then each one after.

"I don't know if I can," Kane admitted. His voice sounded tortured, and Sky felt like her heart started to bleed all over again. "I know I have to, but I'm not sure I can."

"It will take time," Sky said, feeling a stab of disappointment even as she told herself she should feel relief. "We should take our time getting to know each other again and figuring out what is the best course of action."

"No. We get married. We raise her together."

"Kane." Sky stroked her fingers gently down his tortured face. "I know you think you want that, and I'm not saying no. I just think that you need time to come to terms with having a child, and I need time to…"

"What can you possibly need time for? You've had four years. Four years when I missed learning about our child, hearing our baby's heartbeat at the first appointment, feeling her kick, watching her grow inside you, and then holding her when she was born. You had all of that without me."

And she'd been terrified. But she couldn't tell him that. He was tortured enough, but still his constant reminders stung.

"You need time to wrap your head around this," she said knowing it was true. "And I need time to feel like I can trust you." She felt the need to push back.

"Trust me?" he demanded, outraged. He practically

launched himself off the bed. "What the fuck does that mean?"

He dragged on boxers and his workout shorts. Sky was not putting her wet suit back on, and the cover-up was torn and a blatant reminder that a minute ago, they were about to start something quite different than a dissection of their relationship, which seemed pretty non-existent at the moment. She tried to tell herself it was good to get everything out in the open. To not fall back into sex. Kane handed her a soft hotel robe.

"Do you think I can't keep it in my pants?" he insisted.

"I didn't say that."

"But you think it or you thought it then?" No mercy, he was back in her face again, leaning over the bed and pulling the robe closed and tying it tightly around her waist like she was going into battle. "You think I'd fuck other women even though we were married? You think I'd fuck another woman and then come home and climb into bed with you?"

"Stop saying that word." Sky winced.

"That's the word that works."

She closed her eyes and dragged in a breath for calm or strength or wisdom for dealing with a righteously pissed-off male. She sucked at confrontation, always crept away, but that wouldn't work with him. And it wouldn't work for a parent, especially co-parenting with a strong, alpha male who didn't have retreat in his vocabulary.

But her fears were valid.

"You have a lot of opportunities." She nibbled on her lip. "Women used to hit on you when I was right there. All the time. It was…" She couldn't even think of the right word, aggravating, humiliating, thrilling because he'd been momentarily hers. "Even this afternoon at the pool there was a group of three women who kept staring and whispering and watching you. You must have noticed."

Kane made a dismissive sound through his teeth.

"I was swimming with my family. Why the hell am I going to notice what other women are doing? Do you think I need other women's attention for validation?"

Put like that, it did seem ridiculous. Kane snapped, crackled and hummed with confidence. "And…and there are always so many pictures of you with women. That just got old and hard to take." She wanted to get it all out in the open now.

"I told you that's work." Kane pushed away from her and leaned against the dresser, arms crossed. "We are often scheduled for autograph signings at the arena or at a sponsor's business. We attend sponsor parties, and are expected to be friendly and pose for pictures. Part of the job," he reiterated. "I am not expected to grab a woman's tits, but they do shove them in my face sometimes, and I've had my ass felt up more times than even I can count when I have to suck it up and smile and be friendly when posing for photos. And sometimes sponsor's wives or daughters or employees make it hella-awkward when they treat me like a piece of meat or a new sex toy they want to take for a spin, and I have to think of clever and kind ways to say no, so not buyin' it, Sky. I can keep in in my pants."

It sounded awful.

"I thought you liked all the social events."

"I like meeting the kids," he said. "And the families. But I like the sponsors because that means money. This is a short career, and I want to make the most of it and still be able to walk when I'm done so I ride hard, but pace myself. Keep healthy through diet, exercise, rest and luck."

"But your reputation," Sky said, loath to admit that she had followed him online, "that you would often leave a bar with more than one woman."

He rolled his eyes. "Women get fired up and sometimes suck down one too many fruity cocktails or glasses of chardonnay at these events. I think to get their courage up. So I put them in a taxi, make sure they all get home and then catch the cab back to the hotel. Hardly going to announce to the other riders or the press that I'm a fucking Boy Scout in this business and *didn't* get laid. The other riders would eat me alive."

Sky pressed her hand against her mouth. Did she believe him? Did she dare? Somehow, thinking back about how sweet he'd been to her when they'd been kids, it sounded like something he'd do. And yet, she knew he'd been with a lot of women when he'd been younger. Her brother had bragged about how lucky Kane always got at parties even as he complained about it.

"But you've been with a lot of women."

Something crossed his face that she didn't recognize, but that made her nervous.

"What does that matter?" he dismissed. "This is about now."

She wanted to ask if he'd cheated on her that summer, but didn't quite have the nerve. She'd have to work up to that one. Would he be honest? Would she believe him? Could she trust him?

"But you prefer blondes with more…" She made a gesture with her hands. "I never knew what you were doing with me. And you would miss all that."

He stared at her. "Are you fucking serious?"

Great. Now she'd just held up a neon sign about how insecure she'd been, probably still was.

"You were gone a lot. You kept me separate from a lot of the tour. I would see pictures of you online in publicity for the AEBR and other sites with a lot of women drinking and looking…" She spread out her hands not sure what words to use—hotter than she'd ever been for sure.

"There's always an AEBR bar where a few of us are expected to show up. We take turns," Kane said. "Bull riders have a reputation with women who think we're sexy or bad boys or whatever fantasy they've got going."

"You have all the answers," she said. "So smooth and practiced."

"What's that supposed to mean?"

She wished he didn't look so absolutely beautiful and cut and masculine and like sex personified right now. It was not helping his case and made her believe he had helped himself to what had probably been offered freely and often.

"You've probably had this conversation with a lot of women."

"No, Sky. Haven't had to. This is a first." Again the muscle ticked in his jaw. Her heart sank. She was handling him so badly.

"So all your girlfriends just believed you that you were some…what…choir boy and that you were faithful while you were out on the road and having your ass grabbed and cleavage shoved in your face."

"I was out on the road riding bulls, and yeah, I was with women some nights, and no I was never faithful. There was never anyone to be faithful to except you. And…" He stalked toward her. "You. Left. Me."

"You dropped me off. You never said anything but 'see ya,'" Sky quoted bitterly. "You never said you'd call or text. You didn't say you'd see me on a break or invite me to the finals or that you'd visit when the tour was over in October. You even stopped calling and texting, checking in like you used to." She'd prayed for that, prayed for the secret to be taken away from her by force.

"I thought it was over."

Now that she'd opened up this painful door to their past,

she couldn't shut up. "And that night when I was balling my eyes out flying across the country and worried that I was pregnant, you were at a bar 'working.'" She used the hated air quotes. "Drinking shots off some woman's breasts."

She felt like her voice echoed off the walls. And then the silence hung like a dropped crystal vase just before the shatter. She couldn't even look at him, and didn't realize she was crying and making weird animal noises, until her hands came away wet. Pictures didn't lie. He might say it was work, but that hadn't looked like work, and even though he'd said the right things, she didn't feel right with him or their past at all.

"You're upset," Kane said, stating the obvious in a voice that sounded far away. "Now's probably a good time for that processing you wanted. I need to work out and a couple of hours apart will hopefully give us enough time so that we don't say something we both regret."

Too late. Sky had enough regrets for the entire city of Phoenix. Kane grabbed a T-shirt and tennis shoes, pocketed his key and left the room. She watched him go, clutching a pillow to her chest. Kane in full retreat. Never had a signal that she wasn't going to like the answers to her questions and fears been more clear.

IT WASN'T THE pounding headache after running flat out on

the treadmill for nearly an hour. And it wasn't pumping weights until the sweat dripped off him. It was fortuitously or improbably a Dixie Chicks song that sent him back to the hotel room. He'd taken out his earbuds and was stretching his hip flexors when the gym sound system played *I'm Not Ready to Make Nice*. He listened to the lyrics about forgiving but not forgetting.

That was it, wasn't it? Was he or wasn't he ready to make nice? He didn't feel ready. Not at all. He wanted to punish Sky. She'd stolen a child they'd made. She'd claimed to have loved him, and he'd counted on that love. He'd needed that unconditional love. But she hadn't trusted him. Hadn't believed the best of him. Hadn't thought he'd cut it as a father or a husband.

And as he lay back on the yoga mat and stared at the ceiling and really worked his hip flexors, he admitted it. She'd hurt him. Her lack of faith. Her frail love hurt. And the hurt had made him angry. He wanted to hold on to his anger like it was shield because it was easier than the hurt. But what would that accomplish?

What did he want?

Sky and Montana. That answer was crystal. He wanted the whole thing—the house, the damn white fence, Sky as his wife and three or four kids. Normal family. Loving. No drama. No secrets. That was the core. The ranch with his brothers would be a bonus. He'd always imagined setting up a business with Luke, and now there was Laird and Colt. He still wanted that, but Sky and Montana came first. And holding on to his anger and hurt was not going to get him what he wanted.

His anger would not give him back the time lost with Montana. Holding on to his hurt would not bring him closer to creating a family with Sky. She hadn't trusted him, but she was at least reaching out, trying to bridge the massive gap between them. And him? He'd run away clutching his anger and his hurt, and his own past secrets close to his chest.

Fuck. Time to man up.

He'd told her no more secrets. He'd told her the past was the past. And she'd been trying to reach out to him in good faith, and he'd tossed it all back in her face. Forgive. Forget. He had to. Kane stood up and wiped down the mat with a towel and faced himself in the mirror. It was a matter of will. And he'd always had an abundance of will.

Chapter Eleven

KANE YANKED ON the shower. The water was ice cold and cascaded over him, all three jets—one on the top and two on the sides—but still his blood raged. He'd come back to the room determined to apologize to Sky and to tell her why he was having so much trouble forgiving, but she'd been asleep on top of the bed. The hotel robe had been loose around her body, leaving one small, perfect breast exposed. Her dark hair had been wild across the white pillow, and he'd been seized with a lust so hot and dark that he'd barely been able to drag himself away.

Stupid. Primitive. She'd cried herself to sleep, and instead of holding her, showing her she could trust him, she could rely on him to be there for her and Montana, he'd walked away rather than expose himself. Like he'd done four years ago when he'd dropped her off at the airport instead of asking her to stay with him. He'd never once let her know what she'd meant to him all those years ago. He'd kept it casual—in his comfort zone, not hers. He kept blaming her for taking their child, but if he'd followed his heart, let himself be vulnerable, Sky would have had no reason to protect her heart and their child from what she'd perceived as sexual interest but emotional indifference.

He would have been his child's acknowledged father.

He balled his fist and barely resisted smashing it against the unforgiving shower. He welcomed the cold water. It soothed his aches and cooled the self-fury that rode him so hard.

He didn't hear Sky step into the shower until her chilled body was pressed against his back. Her hands soothed down his back and then wrapped around his waist. She stayed like that a moment, and then reached out and turned the handle to warm and then warmer. She laid her cheek against his back. He thought she pressed a kiss to his spine.

They'd often showered together in his small shower stall in his trailer. He'd loved washing her, letting his hands wander freely down her silky pale skin. He'd loved their differences. Her short to his tall. Her tender to his hard. Her full heart to his empty. Her sweet to his cynical. She had been light to his dark, and he'd been able to finally feel like he had a home when he'd been in her arms. He hadn't had to prove anything to her.

Except he should have. She'd deserved so much more than he'd given.

He didn't know what to say to her. How to apologize when he was still so raw and vulnerable to anger and the pain that sawed through his heart over and over. He did not want to be that man, a victim of his rioting emotions. His mom had been loving, but exacting and also always on the edge—happy, sad, angry, calculating, raging. She'd cycled so quickly. It had been exhausting and sometimes, terrifying. Luke had always dealt with their mom better. He'd been the calm son. Careful. Kane had been reckless and volatile, but determined to keep himself controlled. Sky had taught him how to meditate and how to find his center and stay there.

"Sky." His voice cracked.

"Shshsh," she soothed. She reached around him and snagged the shower gel. Soon fragrant suds slid down his body with her hands. She traced the lines of the bull tattoo that she had designed and drawn so many years ago. She kissed a line down his spine. He kept his back to her, head bent, ashamed.

She turned him around. Her hands strong and sure, and he didn't have the energy to stop her. She rubbed more gel in her hands, and then smoothed the suds over his shoulders, down his arms, and then across his chest, his abs and down his thighs. Her eyes stayed on her hands, her expression serious and a little shy.

He wanted to drop to his knees and beg her forgiveness, promise he could let the past go, but he didn't want to lie to her. He sucked in a fractured breath as she squatted before him, her hands spreading the gel suds up and down his thighs to his calves and feet.

Even gutted, his dumbass cock had to turn everything

into an opportunity, the arrogant bastard. Sky paused then she looked up at him, her eyes midnight blue, the water streaming off her own body, turning her hair into a dripping curtain of black silk. She kissed the tip of his cock, but before he could figure out what he should or shouldn't do about that, she kissed a scar he had on his thigh, and then the bruise on his hip and the other bruise spreading large and purple low on his side and up to his ribs.

The steam in the shower made everything seem unreal. She looked ethereal. Sky held out the gel to him. Dumbly he took it. Then she turned around, giving him the long unmarred line of her back. She flipped her hair over her shoulder. So he washed her. He couldn't see any changes Montana had made on her body. He washed her hair. When he turned her around to face him, she stepped into him, and sighed, her cheek on his chest, and something inside him broke open. Jagged.

"What did it feel like to nurse her?" he asked into the drumbeat of the water.

"Painful for the first month," she said. "The pregnancy book says it hurts for the first week or so. Total understatement. Sometimes I wanted to scream when she'd latch on and I'd pinch my leg to make something else hurt, but using chilled silicon inserts in my nursing bra helped alleviate the pain as did olive oil on my nipples."

He closed his eyes. He was an asshole because the thought of spreading olive oil on her nipples was a turn-on, but the knowledge that he hadn't had the opportunity to help her still burned.

"I should have been there to help you," he said helpless to shut up.

"I know." She kissed first one of his nipples and then his other, then she took both of his hands and led him to cup her small, perfect breasts. "You would have. I never doubted that, Kane."

His mind reeled. She was talking. She was touching him. Giving him something of herself to work with. He closed his eyes. Tried to find his center. Shove his anger and his fear of exposure aside.

"But you didn't think I would welcome a baby," he said thinking back to his twenty-two-year-old self. It had been all about him. Building his career. Building his body stronger, more flexible. The money. The image. He'd loved having the girlfriend, but he'd kept her on the sidelines deliberately. Hadn't wanted to share her with his rough world. "That's my fault."

He hadn't told her how much she meant to him. He hadn't wanted to tell himself.

Sky laced her fingers with his and brought their hands low on her body. He opened his eyes, and thought that Sky had tears mingling with the shower water. She took one of his fingers and traced a thin white line so low on her belly. "I had a C-section," she whispered, and he winced. "She was too big and breach and her legs were splayed wide. Wonder where she got that from."

Kane swallowed hard. Sky had had surgery, and he hadn't been there.

She smiled.

"But you can hardly see the scar, and I didn't get stretch marks. I gained fifteen pounds. Not enough, but I had morning sickness that definitely was not limited to morning or the first trimester." She made a face. "Montana weighed eight pounds ten ounces so I'm glad I didn't have to push her out."

"Why Montana?" Why not his last name? She should have his last name. She would have his last name. Tomorrow.

She stood on tiptoes to kiss him, but he didn't bend down and help her so she contented herself with kissing his sternum where his heart thumped.

"You'd told me once that your mom had grown up on a ranch there, that the Wilders were early settlers in the Montana territory. It was a way for her to connect with you."

He squeezed his eyes shut. Fuck. How was he going to get past this anger and pain when it continued to rear up ugly and hungry between them?

"I am so, so sorry for hurting you," she whispered. "I didn't want to hurt you. I wanted to protect her, and…and…myself."

"From me?" He felt like he was in agony.

She covered his hands with hers and linked her soapy

fingers with his.

"I was so crazy about you," she said. "So, so crazy in love, but, Kane, I'm not the girl you thought I was," she said so softly that he could barely hear her. She turned off the water and then reached for a towel. To Kane's astonishment, she began to towel him off, her movements tender. "I know you thought my family was perfect, Kane. You saw what my parents wanted people to see—members of our church, my father's law practice, our neighborhood, the country club, our private school. And when Bennington was alive it was like that. For him."

Sky bent, toweling off his legs, and he sucked in a breath wondering if she would kiss him again, take him in her mouth, bring him to paradise. Sky had always been so uninhibited and generous giving him pleasure, seeming to enjoy pleasuring him as much as he did her.

He'd missed that: the intimacy he'd felt they'd had.

She dried his calves, his feet, even his toes.

"My dad cheated," she said. "A lot. It destroyed my mother. Her confidence. Her trust. She started to drink. More and more. She hid it well for a while, but..." Sky gulped in a breath and then looked up at him quickly and then away. He wanted to hold her, to not make her relive all of the ancient history. Hers. His. "And then probably to get some kind of revenge, she cheated with the husband of a friend of hers."

Sky wrapped him in the towel. She rested her head on

his chest again, and then her hands smoothed down his arms. "She wanted to divorce my father and marry the other man, her lover. But he didn't want to leave his wife. And my mother's husband didn't want to get divorced. He was Catholic although 'marriage is forever' was the only belief he followed." She laughed but there was no humor.

"Sky." He bent to look in her eyes. "The time we were together, I never cheated on you. Never. I didn't even notice other women."

Hell. He'd not been able to stomach the thought of another woman for months after her. And afterward they had to be the opposite of her. Not surrogates.

She didn't meet his eyes. "The man stayed with his wife. They moved. Then my mom realized she was pregnant. With me."

Sky stood up like she wasn't just blasting open the world he thought she'd lived in.

"Sky?"

"My parents stayed together. My mom more miserable because I think she loved the other man, who wanted nothing to do with her." Sky swallowed hard. "Or with me."

Kane jerked. That one came too close to home.

"But they sucked it up. Pretended. For Bennington mostly. They both loved Bennington. The sun rose and set by him. He was golden. I was a shadow. I loved him. He was a great big brother, but honestly he just sucked up all the air. There was none left for me. My mom couldn't look at me without remembering her affair and feeling guilty and probably rejected, and my dad just saw another man's child he was stuck raising."

"Jesus, Sky." He pulled her close. He couldn't help it. He took the towel from her and wrapped it around her and he pressed a kiss to her sopping hair. He snagged another towel and, bending her forward, he wrapped her hair.

"You thought I was a princess, prized and pampered because Bennington took me so many places with you both, letting me tag along, but it was because I was only an apology at home. He didn't understand my parents' attitude toward me, but he tried to make up for it in any way he could."

She met his eyes, her expression sad and wry. "I didn't even know my dad wasn't really my dad until I was thirteen. I tried so hard to get my mom and dad to love me, and to treat me like they did Bennington." Her voice shook, but she steadied it quickly. "I was taken care of physically, but…" She shrugged her shoulders as if she could forget her heavy burden. "I never understood why my dad went to all of Bennington's games, award ceremonies, all of it when he never went to one school concert or play or dance recital or horse show to watch me."

"How did you find out?" Kane didn't feel right asking, but they needed to know each other.

"I heard Bennington and my dad arguing. He was yelling at my dad about the way he treated me and my dad confessed it—that I wasn't his, that I was only Bennington's half-sister. That I was only a mistake."

Kane pulled her back into his body, but both of them were chilled from the blast of the air conditioner and the rapidly cooling air in the shower. She was shaking in his arms. Or maybe he was. His stomach churned sickly.

A mistake.

Like he had been. Like he'd been made to feel his whole life by his father's continued cool rejection. Not even to his face but through a legal team. He didn't want Montana to ever feel like she was a mistake.

"I didn't want that for my child—to feel like she wasn't wanted, like she was a mistake." Sky turned a clear gaze up to him, her heart and soul radiating in her expression.

"She's wanted," he said hoarsely. "She would have been wanted from the first moment you told me."

Sky's gaze clouded and dropped. He tilted her chin up so that she was forced to look at him.

"You have to believe me, Sky. I would have been happy about the baby."

Her dark blue eyes searched his. "You say that now, and maybe you think it's true," Sky said. "But you were so careful all the time," she said. "Safety first. You even said that more than once. I thought you'd freak out when I was late."

"I would have been surprised, but we would have made the appropriate adjustments."

"How?" Sky laughed, a catch in her voice. "You were

twenty-two. Really starting to hit it big on the AEBR. No way did I think a baby would make you go to your happy place. You'd even check that I took my pill each morning. You were obsessed."

"Hell yes," Kane said. "I wanted to protect you. Of course, I was careful. You were nineteen. Still in school. Wanting to go for your MFA. I didn't want to fuck up your life with lapse in birth control."

Sky stared at him for long moments, and he wondered how she could look at him so tenderly when he'd failed her on such a fundamental level—exactly how she'd expected to be failed, he realized with insight, considering her family history.

"I was older. I was the man," Kane said. "You should have relied on me." He couldn't quite let that go, but it was now, he realized, a moot point. What man had been there for her? Not her biological father. Not the man she'd believed to be her father. Even Bennington had died on her before she'd been out of the house. Enter Kane Wilder, arrogant idiot, he thought. He'd been her first lover and had dragged her around on the tour for three months in a trailer rocking her body every chance he got, but not once had he opened up to her about his feelings. A future with her. Or discussed why he risked his life and health weekly—what drove him.

Sky took his hand and led him back to the bedroom. She kept her towel wrapped around her body as she sat down on the bed and pulled him down to sit beside her.

"You said you didn't want to dwell on the past, but maybe we need to," she said pensively. "But you can't rewrite history. You couldn't wait to drop me off at the airport to go back to school."

"I hated dropping you off," Kane admitted. "But I thought that asking you to stay was unfair. I wanted you to live your dream as I was living mine. The finals were in October. You being at school meant I could keep my focus absolute so yeah, even though I missed you, the timing was perfect. In my mind we'd be apart five or six weeks, and then we'd have almost three months together when I wouldn't be working. I thought I'd buy us a condo or something near your school so I could be with you off season and on breaks."

Her eyes searched his, and he felt he must be coming up short. If he'd asked her to stay or if he'd told her he'd spend his break with her, she probably would have thought she could count on him. The estrangement from Sky and his child had been of his own making at least halfway if not more. He hadn't bothered to find out about Sky's life other than what he'd seen superficially as a self-obsessed teenaged boy and then later as a young, horny bull-rider. She'd been fun and kind and beautiful and hot as hell and so giving.

"I just took and took and took," he admitted to himself and to her.

Kane caught up his bag and pulled out a T-shirt for her. If he didn't get her covered, he would touch her. He'd always loved touching her. Holding her in his arms, having the freedom to feel her satiny skin beneath his hands had always floored him on an elemental level.

The summer they'd spent together had been beyond any heaven he'd ever imagined. He'd been able to live out all his fantasies and create more. Sky had been so physically affectionate and so sexually responsive it had fed his needs, even as it created more and a sense of belonging to someone that had been heady. He had loved coming back to the trailer to find her waiting for him. It had been addictive and filled a hole in him that he'd never acknowledged existed until she was gone.

He helped her into the T-shirt, but couldn't help the way his fingers lingered down her neck. He breathed her in. They'd showered together, used the same shower gel, but she still exuded that elusive fragrance that was so her—and that made him hungry for her. Mentally pushing down his need, which did nothing for his monster hard-on, he pulled on a pair of boxers.

So much of their relationship had been about sex. Now it had to be about communication. And discipline. He had to forgive. She had to trust.

"I did keep you separate from the tour deliberately," he confessed, his lips against her collarbone. "I knew you were shy and didn't like crowds, but I used that to my advantage." He cupped her face. Intensity bled from him. "I told myself I was protecting you, but really I was a jealous idiot. I was afraid of all the other riders hitting on you. You'd been so innocent when we first got together, and I thought that when you met some of the other more seasoned riders..."

"Kane." She covered his hands. "There's only been you for me. Just you."

"I hated that I was jealous. It's an ugly and unacceptable trait, but I..."

"Stop." She kissed his mouth fiercely, and then withdrew, but her eyes were nearly purple with intensity. "It was always you for me. No one else. Not then. Not now. Not ever. Just you." Her voice trembled.

And this was when he should tell her the rest. His past that rode him so hard. His anger. The sorrow that yawned inside him, hungry for more of his soul. But everything bottled in his throat. Choked him. Made him weak and ashamed. Habits were hard to break, and silence was the hardest.

Fighting the tremble in his hand, Kane unwrapped the towel from her hair and it tumbled down over her shoulders. Sky stared blankly at some unseen point in front of her, and after hesitating for a moment, wrestling with his conscience, Kane got up and retrieved her hairbrush from the bathroom.

He sat cross-legged behind her and began to brush, smoothing the brush through her hair in long, gentle strokes. He continued to brush long after the thick, dark mass hung like a silky curtain down her back. She sighed her pleasure, and his fingers ached to take over. He remembered the slide of her hair through his fingers. His cock remembered how her hair would glide across him when she'd kiss her way down his body, or massage him or rub arnica into his bruises, or suck him dry.

Fuck! Why'd he think about that now? Why couldn't he brush Sky's hair without thinking about all the ways he'd had her or she'd had him? They had done a lot of other things that hadn't involved sex—hiking, dancing, swimming, visiting art galleries, concerts, even a Cajun cooking class in New Orleans. But after all of those had been mind-blowing, body-melting sweaty marathon sex that would leave him charged up and hungry for more. He needed a cool head and finesse. Not his overeager cock charged up by memories.

Sky's breathing hitched, and his cock stirred. That had always been an invitation before—the way her eyes would darken to indigo, almost glowing, and her breathing would catch in her throat. His brother Luke would have handled this situation better, although maybe not. Luke had definitely acted like a crazed drunken bear when he and his now wife Tanner had had a fight at Montana's Copper Mountain Rodeo last September, and she'd run out on him. There'd been no reasoning with his usually unflappable brother until Tanner had settled down enough to listen to Luke's explanation and forgive him.

And now they were married, expecting twins. He wanted that. Marriage. Sky pregnant. He just needed to get through this shitty part. She'd said she'd loved him that summer so many times. He just had to get her there again. Keep her there.

But how if he weren't going to use sex?

"Thank you." Sky's whisper sent a shiver down his spine that went straight to his cock. He was an animal, all instinct and lust when he had to stay in his frontal lobe. He stood up quickly to return the hairbrush, but Shy caught his hand. He didn't dare turn around. He wasn't just tenting the boxers, he pointed out of them like his dick was a compass needle. He should probably jerk off so he could let her asleep or talk more if she wanted. He needed to corral his brain to form words instead of images of him and Sky busy on the bed.

She traced the lines on his palm, and his eyes shut as he let the sensations skitter through his body. Then her palm was to his, lightly skimming in a circle, back and forth.

"Sky," he choked out, wanting to tell her that he was already at the end of his rope, and then she sucked one finger into the hot, wet paradise of her mouth.

Every cell in his body leapt toward hers, and he swore under his breath. He saw his T-shirt fall on the ground next to him. She was naked. On the bed. How the hell was he supposed to not act on that? Think pure thoughts? He hadn't had a pure thought around Sky since she'd turned sixteen. Even then he'd known it was wrong when she'd been so young. He'd told his imagination and his cock to shut the fuck up, and he'd mostly stayed away from her limiting contact to texts until her brother, his best friend, had died.

Then he'd checked in with her more often, even visiting as if to prove that he could look and talk and not touch. And he'd broken his no-touch rule the minute she'd slid across his truck seat and hooked one arm around his neck and breathed his name at a drive-in movie he'd taken her to as an old-fashioned lark. They hadn't even stayed long enough for the damn thing to start.

Sky licked the length of his finger and then around, mimicking an act far more potent, but Kane was already so aroused he was leaking. Sky's other hand reached around his hip and gripped him, and he gave up trying to pretend he could resist her.

Her thumb smeared the little bead of moisture. Heat and desire crashed through him shutting down his last struggling thoughts.

"I know we need to talk," Sky said, her grip firm as she pumped him slowly.

"Later," he growled but made a last grab for sanity. "I promise."

He covered her, caging her body with his elbows, keeping his full weight off her.

She tilted her chin for a kiss, but he held himself just out of reach.

"My way," he said letting her see that he meant it. Already her thighs had parted, cradling him like four years hadn't passed. "Everything my way."

"Kane," she whispered looping her arms around his

shoulders.

He slid down her body and she arched against him. Her gasp was music to him. He nuzzled his way across the small scar low on her abdomen that she'd showed him. He nipped the line with his lips. Sky cried out and writhed against him, trying to get closer, connect them.

"You haven't answered. My way."

He waited at her entrance, mouth close, hands on her hips.

"You. Don't. Play. Fair," she gasped grapping his hand, and trying to move it to where she wanted it most.

"Not playing here, Sky. My way. Say it."

"Your way," she agreed.

He was a dick because she sounded dazed and desperate and probably didn't know what she was agreeing to. Tough. He was beyond desperate to have her. To get past the giant, enormous roadblock she and he had erected between them. He needed to push past his anger and hurt and her distrust and fear. He just needed to hold on until the bell.

Chapter Twelve

SKY NEARLY LAUNCHED off the bed when Kane went down on her. It was like being picked up by a ten-foot wave and tossed up into the air, spinning head over heels and then plunging down into churning water. She pressed her fist against her mouth to keep from screaming. She'd always been embarrassed that she was loud during sex, but Kane had loved it. Encouraged her. He'd claim he wanted people to hit the walls and tell them to tone it down.

"Just lets everyone know how good I am in bed," he'd teased, when she'd blushed once when a hotel guest had banged on their door one night when they'd barely been able to make into the room. They hadn't been able to wait to take off clothes or get to the bed before Kane had pushed her up against the door, rolled on a condom, picked her up and sheathed himself in her body. "And out of it," he added, probably trying to make her laugh at his arrogance.

Good hadn't begun to cover Kane's skill sets, especially those of a horizontal nature, and she didn't need to think about how many women he'd done this with since, but clearly he'd had lots of additional practice or her memory had really been lax.

The first orgasm hit and Kane continued to crank her higher through to the next one.

She gripped his shoulders with her thighs as he nipped her clit and then soothed over it with his tongue, over and over, until she felt the build again. She needed him inside her now. Right now. She grabbed his hair and pulled, trying to give him the message that she needed more. A lot more.

"Get a condom," she said, trying to wiggle further under him and pull him up on her body even more. She should have known that was useless. Kane was six foot one and all honed muscle.

"My way," he reminded her, looking up at her, his middle finger circling her clit while two other fingers stroked. His eyes gleamed like hot metal. "You agreed."

Had she agreed? Being this close to his fire and not jumping in? Impossible. She would have said anything to be able to touch him again, have him. But he did kiss his way up to her breasts, and as his teeth teased them to aching attention, he scissored his fingers deep inside her slick channel.

"God, Kane, more," Sky chanted. "More, more, more."

"You feel so perfect. So tight and perfect." He groaned the words as he laved each one of her nipples while his fingers moved in and out of her.

Sky wanted faster. Harder. She needed it.

"These are so perfect Sky. Mine. Beautiful." He laved one nipple with his tongue and then sucked it deep into his mouth.

"Not sure I'm going to share them with the next baby." Sky could barely hear him through the blood racing through her body. She ground against his hand, and then let go of his hair and then his shoulders so that she could grab his ass to pull him on top of her exactly where she needed him. When had he become such a talker? She wanted action, and Kane had always been on board with hard, fast and dirty action.

He'd only talked to tell her what to do, and she'd loved how he'd been so bossy in bed or wherever they happened to be. She'd loved to make him lose control and curse and give up trying to get home and pull over wherever, whenever. It had been the only time she felt confident with him, equal.

She wrapped her legs around his narrow hips.

"We don't have forever," she whispered kissing her way along his jaw and then nipping him hard enough to get his attention.

"I want forever." He cradled her face in his palm. "Forever with you, Sky."

Sky stilled under him.

"I want you to give that to me." His eyes searched hers.

Sky felt like she stood on a precipice, a waterfall running under her feet, mist rising up to claim her, hiding how far the fall was. All this time he'd been demanding, taking. Now he asked.

"Okay," she said. She had no other choice. She couldn't imagine her life without him anymore and didn't want to.

"Please, Kane, please," she said, cupping his hard jaw and reaching up to kiss his lips. It was a tender kiss, laced with passion. "Please, now. I need you."

He bowed his head, eyes closed, and then when he looked up at her, she saw something she'd never seen before, something she didn't dare name, but she felt like for the first time since she'd watched him walk away all those years ago, they'd connected at the level she'd so desperately craved.

He angled his erection at her entrance, teased her by rubbing against her clit and her hot, wet entrance.

"Kane." She caught his hips. "Condoms."

He hung his head, breathed in deeply. "You make me forget my own name."

"Hurry," she urged. He leaned over the bed and snagged the strap of his duffel bag and dragged it to him. He pulled out a condom. Sky took it, ripped the wrapper with her teeth and rolled it on him.

Kane hissed in a breath. He sheathed himself in one deep stroke. Sky stiffened and had to bite back a yelp.

"Did I hurt you?" Kane froze in place but caught her face between his palms. "Sky?"

"Sooo perfect," she whispered finally enough in control of her body to speak. "More. Please, Kane, I need more. You have to move. Harder. Deeper," she ordered or begged, practically shaking with desire. Her hands threaded through his hair, and for a moment, they just stared at each other in the golden light heralding the pending evening.

"I missed you," she breathed shakily.

He kissed one temple and then the other. He pulled back a little so she was forced to look into his eyes.

"We're getting married, Sky. We're going to be a family."

This time, his statement shot a thrill through her. Two days with Kane and now she couldn't picture her life without him. She knew there were many things they needed to sort out, but right now she didn't care. She just wanted to burn with Kane, and when he began to move in that familiar rhythm that she matched instinctively, Sky felt she could soar. She could be anybody she wanted if she had Kane by her side.

SKY DRAPED ACROSS his chest. Her hair hid her face. His breathing had finally calmed down, and his heart rate was near normal, but he felt drained. Wasn't sure how he felt—where they went now.

Forward.

"Sky, I'm sorry." He decided that even though he wanted to take a nap—he'd had little sleep last night since Sky had woken him up every two hours, and his headache today had duked it out with his dark thoughts and churning emotions—he needed to ensure Sky was on board with the plan tomorrow.

"Why?" she asked sleepily, rolling over to prop herself up on his chest.

"I didn't know about your parents. I didn't know that you felt like you didn't belong," he said.

"Nobody knew," Sky said. "My parents were very social with their church, with my father's law firm, with the private school where my brother and I went, and I bet no one suspected."

"Still, Sky, we were friends. We were lovers. You gave your heart and your body to me. I should have taken better care of you. I should have known."

"I know you are a kick-ass bull rider," she said, tracing something on his skin, with a finger. "Are you psychic, too?"

He'd forgotten that his sweet, shy girl had teased him when they were alone.

"I should have trusted you enough to let you in all the way, but it was such a habit by then, such a way of thinking that I wasn't..." She broke off.

"Wasn't what?"

"Lovable."

"Sky." Kane gathered her close. "You are lovable." But even as he said that, he knew he'd never told her he'd loved her. She'd said it so many times to him, but never once had he looked her in the eye and committed to her beyond the next day and definitely not the future.

She'd needed something from him he'd been reluctant—damn, unable—to give her. And why? Because he had his own demons taunting him on both shoulders.

"So we start again," Kane said, determined. "Honest. Open with each other this time."

"You want to do that?" She leaned up so that she could put fists on his chest and rest her chin there. "Can you do that a real partnership?" she asked. "It's not like you talked much about your feelings or your family. You mentioned Luke, and we watched him at a few rodeos in California and in Colorado, but you rarely talked about your mother or father. If you want me to feel safe with you, you need to feel safe with me."

Kane rolled away from her and threw an arm over his eyes. He couldn't hear her breathe while the seconds tick off on his massive watch.

"Like you, I didn't know who my father was, not really until I was six or seven. I'd never had a dad. I thought Luke and I had the same dad. But when I was six and started school I was really smart and the school couldn't handle me or challenge me. That's when my mom started trying harder to get financial support from my biological father. She'd tried before. He was wealthy and connected, but as I got older, she was more motivated. She wanted to send me to a better school. He wanted to pretend I didn't exist."

Sky trailed her fingers up and down his arm, her touch soothing.

"He was from a very wealthy family, and when she'd had the affair, she hadn't known he was married and already had three daughters. He didn't want his wife to find out he'd cheated. He didn't want his daughters to realize they had a brother. He had three blonde blue-eyed princess daughters. No way would I have fit in, but my mom thought that me being a son would change his mind. A lot of my childhood was colored by my mom trying to get him to acknowledge me by stalking and ambushing him with me as co-conspirator and then later, when he got the police involved, she got help from legal aid to take him to court. He had a lot of influence so she hit a lot of walls, until later, but by then it was too late. I didn't want him, his money or his influence to pave my way."

"What about your other brothers? Where do they come in?"

"You want all the dirt?"

"Is it dirt?"

Sky pressed herself against his side. Her fingers stroked through his hair. His eyes drifted shut.

"Do you want a pain pill?"

"No. I don't like to use anything unless I really can't take it."

She kissed one of his bruises, and then kissed a trail down his body. "I'm sure that has yet to happen, tough guy."

"That feels good," he said softly for the first time feeling the years and the heartache fall away if only for a moment.

"So the dirt?"

"Not dirt. Just life. Messy. Sad. My mom had a tough father. Abusive I think. She was a bit wild. Still is. Probably is manic-depressive, but she doesn't like the medication. Tries to control everything with a naturopath. But she fell in love with a bull rider when she was fifteen. Got pregnant and ran away with him. He wanted to marry her so he was taking her back to the ranch in Marietta, Montana, to get her dad's permission to marry her since she was a minor. It was Christmas Eve. He thought he timed it right, hoping for forgiveness. Instead they hit ice, and another car plowed into them. My mom nearly died, and was unconscious for weeks. The babies were delivered and adopted out. She never knew she was carrying twins. Her boyfriend was older and was given the choice of jail for sex with a minor or being deported. It took him a year to get back to her, and they ran away again and a year later had Luke."

Sky's eyes were dark with sympathy.

"So you didn't know you had two other brothers until when?"

Kane sighed. "I met Colt and we figured it out at last year's rodeo. Then Laird, his fraternal twin, at Christmas Eve last year. A miracle."

Even he could hear the bitterness. She ran a finger over each of his eyebrows, and then down his nose. Traced his lips and he kissed the tip of her finger. He remembered this. Her sweetness. It hadn't been all desperate and hungry coupling.

"So you and your mother both missed time with their children." Her voice ached. He hadn't thought about that. Put it like that he was really a whiny jerk. His mom had missed thirty years. What was three to that?

"The plan has always been to work a ranch. Rebuild the Wilder brand stronger than before."

"The plan?" She cut to the heart of it. "Is that your plan as well?"

"It was," he said cautiously. It had made sense. He wanted to bring his mother some happiness and peace. And maintain some kind of relationship with Luke. "But now I have you and Montana to think about."

Sky ran her fingers along his scalp again, this time a little more rhythmically, and he felt his headache ease almost instantly.

"We don't have to solve everything now."

"Yes, we do."

"So you met your father?" Sky asked, her cheek against his chest and one hand still rhythmically stroking back his hair. Her voice was mildly curious.

Kane swallowed the bile that rose up. "Yeah." He tried to keep his voice neutral to keep the questions to a minimum. He knew he was going for a whole new Kane Wilder, a man of fewer secrets, but it sure as hell didn't feel comfortable.

Sky continued to stroke him. He'd felt she'd been his secret weapon when they'd been together. She'd cooked. She'd taken care of him—talking to him while he took his post-ride ice bath, soothing his bruises with arnica, massaging his aches, taping him when necessary, and biting back the fear he could feel, but they never acknowledged.

"I never met my father. I don't even have a picture," she said.

"He's a jerk." Kane rolled over and pinned her to the mattress. Night was starting to close in and Montana might or might not wake up soon. He'd tried his best to tucker her out. "And my dad's a bigger jerk. I don't want to be that guy. I swore I'd never be a man who would reject his child," he said fiercely.

"You're not," Sky yielded, her body going soft and welcoming underneath his. "You're not him at all. We'll figure this out, Kane. We've got time."

He peeled off her shirt again but kept his mouth shut. In his business, he couldn't and wouldn't count on time.

MONDAY SLIGHTLY AFTER noon, Sky walked out of her last exercise class. Kane's truck idled in front of the gym.

She was not happy she'd only had a few minutes to take a quick and cold shower after four workout classes. Her capri workout leggings that spelled out *Burn* in red/orange fiery letters up each thigh should probably have stayed in her gym bag. Kane looked amazing from what she could see.

"Did you give notice?" he asked first off.

She hadn't wanted to, but knew it was important to at least see this through until the end of the tour in six months—not that she and Montana would travel with him the whole time necessarily. She wasn't sure what would happen, but much like her pregnancy until she was handed a child, she'd decided she'd play it by ear.

"Friday's my last day teaching."

He grimaced but jumped out of the truck, took her gym bag and opened the passenger side door for her. He helped her inside the cab.

"Thank you," she said, noting his crisp dark jeans, crisp white shirt open at his throat and shiny cowboy boots.

He smiled. "Ready?"

Sky laughed. "I suppose I should say bring it on, but since I taught two spin classes back to back after a pump and a hot yoga class, I think all I'm ready for is a bucket of sun screen, kale and blueberry protein smoothie and lounging on a few noodles in the pool. You're lucky I snuck in a quick shower," she said as he drove off, rather quickly.

Bull rider. Kane did everything fast. Well, except sex. She snuck a peek at him and he navigated Scottsdale traffic and headed southwest toward downtown Phoenix. He'd definitely taken his time last night. Sky felt like her body was still liquid, and the way he'd woken her up before dawn should be illegal. She blushed. "You look nice," she said quickly trying to distract herself. Their daughter was in the car. "Do you have an interview or meet and greet today?"

"The AEBR events usually start Thursday, but since Phoenix is my hometown I have more obligations here usually. I do have two meetings with potential sponsors later this afternoon that can't be avoided."

Sky reached into the modified center console remembering Kane kept it stocked with water. Instead she saw a bottle of champagne. Real champagne from France. Not a sparkling wine or just bubbles.

"I thought your meeting was with a potential sponsor." Sky looked at him. "That seems a bit premature, but you always were confident."

"Congratulations!" Montana yelled and tossed a fistful of red petals at her. "Mommy's getting married!"

Chapter Thirteen

"I THOUGHT WE decided last night that we didn't have to rush into anything." Sky tried to keep the smile pasted on her face because Montana was still singing out the "married" word and tossing petals all over herself and the back seat of the truck with a few directed toward Sky.

"No need to wait. Already four years too late."

"Kane." Sky tried to keep her voice calm and level even though panic began to bubble in her stomach.

"Don't make me spell it out," he said in a low voice.

"Spell what out?"

"Why it's imperative to do it now."

She needed it spelled out. She'd thought with their efforts at honesty and opening up to each other last night and their concerted effort to leave the past in the past, Kane was no longer on a matrimonial tear. She sucked in a breath and then another. She hadn't been this winded after the second spin class and that had been advanced.

Meanwhile Kane held on to his calm demeanor while Montana bounced with excitement. Sky suddenly noticed

Montana had on a pale pink lacy dress and pink sandals. Even her toenails had been painted pink.

"You've been busy," she said faintly.

"Prepared."

Sky looked out the window, determined to harness her thoughts and lay out her arguments why this rush up the aisle—okay probably rush into a county clerk's line—was totally unnecessary. It wasn't as if she hadn't fantasized about getting married when she'd been younger, and if she were honest, all her dreams had featured Kane, but he'd been devastating in a tux, and she in a flowing white dress. In her dreams, she'd walked toward him carrying daisies, and he hadn't been able to take his eyes, shining with love, off her.

And there'd been guests, candles, flowers, the small church where she'd taken her first communion, music, dancing, champagne, and the reception had been under the stars with a real country music band, and Kane had danced with her all night, holding her close and telling her how much he loved her.

What a cliché!

"Thought we'd agreed to talk to each other," Kane said evenly as he pulled into the county courthouse parking lot. "What's going through your head?"

Like he really wanted to know. Talking to each other was a joke. He hadn't mentioned marriage when he'd dropped her off at the gym this morning. He'd only said he'd take Montana and meet her back at noon.

"Are you surprised, Mommy? Are you? Are you?"

"Definitely," she said through numb lips.

"So what are you thinking?" Kane asked after he parked and then unbuckled Montana from her car seat. Montana scurried over the seat, squishing the bruised petals back into the small basket that had held them.

"That when I fantasized about being a bride when I was growing up, I wasn't creative enough." Sky debated if she should even try to comb her hair and then decided the whole messy high ponytail fit with her exercise clothes. "I didn't know I'd be rocking the athletic bride look so trendily."

"You don't have to." Kane reached behind the seat and pulled out a garment bag and a shoe box.

She stared. "You bought me a dress?"

"Yes. Good or bad idea?"

"Probably better than a razor tank and Lululemon capri athletic leggings."

She wasn't sure what to make of the situation. Neither did Kane, because he looked uncomfortable for the first time she could remember.

Before she could think too much about it, Montana squealed, "Oh," and then she opened a cooler at her feet and pulled out a large bouquet of daisies.

"For Mommy. Daddy said they are your favorite. Are they, Mommy, are they?" Sky took the flowers, but kept her head down. Her eyes swam with tears. Kane had remembered her off-hand comment years ago that she loved daisies and that when she had her own yard she was going to have a border for her garden made of daisies because they were so simple and classic yet beautiful.

"Sky? Are you ready to go inside?"

No.

But she wasn't going to get a better do-over on a mistake she'd made four years ago.

She blinked back tears. "Yes," she said.

Grasping Montana's hand and her daisy bouquet, Sky followed Kane, who had slipped the champagne into a picnic basket and held her garment bag and shoes. Together they walked up the courthouse steps.

Sky slipped into a bathroom feeling like a late hired actress for a movie she didn't know the title for. Her hands shaking a little, she unzipped the dress.

"Oh." She stared at the simple strapless white dress that had some beading under the bust line—the only ornamentation. The hem was cut at an angle that looked like it would fall at the longest point mid calf. It was elegant and sophisticated while still seeming like a simple, though beautiful summer dress.

She shed her clothes and slipped on the dress. It had a hidden side zipper, and the fit was perfect. Where Kane got it at such short notice she had no idea. He'd even thought to add some white lace thong panties and a small sapphire and white lace garter. If he announced he could fly at this point she'd believe him. The shoes were silk mules with beading and low heels. She slipped them on and dared a look in the mirror.

She'd dashed on a bit of mascara and lip gloss at the gym.

Good enough, she supposed, and let down her hair and finger combed it.

She bagged up her tennis shoes and clothes and, grasping her flowers, she nervously exited the bathroom.

Kane was holding Montana, probably to keep her from showering everyone who passed with white rose petals and shouting that her mommy and daddy were getting married today.

Kane's eyes lit with admiration when he saw her, and Sky was seized with shyness, which was ridiculous after all the years she'd known him, heck after all the things they'd done last night. He had been in deep conversation with a man and a woman whom he quickly introduced.

"The judge is ready for us," Kane said, slipping his fingers into hers. "And then we get the paperwork signed and we'll be set."

Sky nibbled on her inner lip, pretty sure marriage to Kane was not going to be that easy.

HOURS LATER, SKY sunk beneath the hot, fragrant bubble bath in the Jacuzzi tub just as the sun started to set.

"Sky Wilder." She tried out the name. It still didn't seem real. The whole afternoon seemed tinged with unreality. But in twenty minutes, she and Kane had been married, and the judge had signed off on a name change for Montana Kate Wilder, and she was now Sky Wilder. Kane and his attorney and financial planner had done all the paperwork for passports, birth certificate for Montana, college fund, life insurance beneficiary, insurance and his will.

Her head had spun. His life seemed so complicated.

As each form was signed, Kane had grown more and more relaxed.

She'd wondered aloud if there shouldn't be a prenup. His attorney had hesitated and opened her mouth to speak, but Kane had said firmly said "no." Even statistical divorce rates wouldn't mess with Kane Wilder. Then when they'd been filling out the name change forms for Montana he'd asked her about her middle name.

"Why Kate? Is that a family name?" he'd asked, puzzled.

Sky had laughed a little—the tension rolling off her finally. "Really?" she'd demanded. "You and your big brain should be able to figure that one out."

He continued to wait for an answer, as did the three other people in the room. Montana knew. She'd jumped up and down in excitement.

"K for Kane," Sky clarified, "and ate for eight seconds that you ride."

And then she'd seen Kane turn away and wipe something

from his eye.

The rest of the day had flown by. She and Colt had made good progress packing up her apartment and her studio. Colt was going to build wooden crates to transport her sculptures to Jonas's gallery. She'd met his other brother Laird and his fiancée Tucker who'd been so beautiful and vibrant and funny that both she and Montana had felt dazzled. They'd helped her pack up her small bunkhouse before dropping her off at the hotel. Kane had texted her several times during the day and called twice to tell her he was delayed.

She didn't mind so much. It was just awkward. She'd changed out of the dress again at the courthouse, and Kane had dropped them off at her house. His brothers had been there along with Tucker, but he hadn't mentioned their marriage so neither had she, which meant what, exactly? More secrets? More hiding away only legal this time?

Sky nearly hummed in pleasure as she stretched full out in the bath. She heard a faint pop, but was too tired to deal with any more surprises. She didn't even have the energy to turn on the jets for a quick massage.

"Champagne?" A crystal flute appeared in front of her.

Sky didn't drink a lot because of her mother, but it was her wedding night, although since she hadn't seen Kane all day, she wasn't sure what the night would hold.

"As long as you promise that if I ever drink more than one glass…no make that two glasses of wine, cut me off. My mom drinks. A lot." She'd meant to make a joke of it, but it wasn't funny. And she got scared sometimes. She had a little girl to take care of. What if she lost control? People said it was a disease. She could catch it.

Kane was silent. She'd shocked him. Smashed another crack in her perfect family picture. Infidelity. Addiction. Dead perfect son. Unresolved grief and anger. The nuclear American family.

"I will always take care of you, Sky."

She still didn't open her eyes. She wasn't quite ready to face him or the rest of her life. So she didn't know that Kane was naked, until he climbed in the tub with her.

"Cheers." He clinked classes with her.

Sky's eyes flew open.

"Strawberry?" Kane held out a strawberry, dipped in chocolate and lightly dusted with crystalized sugar.

"I know you tried to make this day special," Sky said carefully although the day had seemed bizarre mostly because he hadn't been there except for the actual vows part, and that had been so…so…impersonal with the judge jumping up from his desk where he'd been eating a spinach and strawberry salad to marry them. "And the dress was lovely and Montana was thrilled, but…" She didn't want to sound ungrateful, but she also hadn't wanted to rush into marriage like she had some aggrieved relative wielding a shotgun.

"Seriously, Sky. I couldn't wait six months to marry you or whatever amount of time you think we should wait to make it legal. I had to act now so that you and Montana are safe. Being my wife instantly gives you rights—money, life and health insurance, ability to act on my behalf if I can't. You'll also have an easier time negotiating anything with the AEBR over your art, access, being with me backstage—more respect from the sponsors. I won't tolerate you being tossed out a side door with Montana because some zealous security guard took my instructions too literally."

"What instructions?" she asked curiously because all the rest of it was too overwhelming. She didn't want to think about Kane being injured. He was so vibrant and alive. And the amount of money he wielded freaked her out as well. There were so many changes ahead, and Kane didn't seem to want to give her any time to process any of it.

"If I get injured, you can make decisions for me and be with me in the hospital, make decisions over my care," he said, ignoring her question. "If I get killed, you have access to my life insurance within two days."

"Stop." Sky pressed her hand over her mouth. Her stomach was churning. "Just shut up right now, Kane. I mean it. It's bad luck to talk like that."

"Baby." He leaned forward and pulled her up on his lap so she could wrap her legs around his waist. She meant to hold herself back, but the heat in his eyes, the intensity in his deep voice, low and warm, melted her resistance.

"I don't want to scare you, but I'm in a dangerous profession. High injury rate, and you know from what happened to your brother that mistakes or bad luck can be fatal.

Already this season, a few riders are out. I doubt my favorite rider Rory Douglas—we all called him Gramps, such a mentor to me, to all of us—will make it to the end of the tour. He's really struggling with injuries new and old. He's only thirty-eight, a young man, but this profession is hell on the body."

Sky could barely breathe. Kane had a beautiful body. He was so vital. The thought of him damaged, hurting, unable to ride or even enjoy reasonably good healthy cut deep.

"Have you thought about what you'll do when it's over?" she whispered.

He nodded decisively, and it was so Kane, that her heart lurched. Of course he had a plan. "But I'm rethinking some things, and a lot depends on you."

Sky liked the sound of that.

"But I can't rely on hope to keep me healthy and you and Montana taken care of. I need to be prepared. You need to know what to do in case I can't."

"Kane, please…" She touched his cheek. "We're naked in a bath with champagne that we didn't get a chance to have this afternoon. Can't this wait?"

"You need to know. Colt and Luke are co-executors of my will. Obviously I rewrote it so you get everything instead of my mom and Luke. I know Colt makes you a little nervous, but he's so solid, and he has no loyalty to my mom. She keeps trying to reach him, but so far he doesn't want to play happy family. I was shocked as hell he showed up to drive me home. He'll make sure you don't have to deal with..."

Sky leaned up and kissed him, halting his flow of words. "Please. I don't want to think about it right now."

"I know." His fingers trailed under her jaw and he tilted her face up so he could kiss the tears that spilled down her cheeks. He chased a few with his tongue. "That's why I did the thinking, but as for the rest—where we live, how we manage the time and distance—that's for both of us to decide. I just needed to make it legal and to provide for you and Montana."

"We're married," she said. "Like a business deal. Because it was practical."

His gray eyes searched hers. Regret lingered, but determination shone through. "We'll make it work. We had to make it right, Sky."

She rolled her eyes at the R word.

"But, Sky, baby, you took all my options by not telling me you were pregnant. You took away our choices together. Newton's Law."

He held out the strawberry again, and this time she took a bite of the huge berry swirled with dark and white chocolate. Flavor burst in her mouth. Delicious. And there was a gorgeous liquor in the berry. She was for the first time in her life heading toward tipsy and she so didn't care. She held out the strawberry for him to share, careful to keep the liquor from spilling out. His mouth brushed her fingers as he finished all but the stem. He chewed and swallowed while holding her eyes.

"Which one?" she whispered. She'd always found his quirky math and science references endearing. Her husband was a hot bull rider and a nerd.

"The third one."

"And which one is that?" She was pulling his chain, but Kane was way too earnest to ever get that, and Sky found she got a little of her equilibrium back.

"For every action in nature there is an equal and opposite reaction."

He leaned forward and tried to kiss her.

She didn't feel quite ready for that, and he could tell.

"What's wrong? Are you mad that I was gone most of the day?"

"No," she sighed. "I know you have many demands on your time."

"You and Montana are my first priority," he said quickly.

And he probably believed that. But… "I just don't feel married," she finally said, not wanting to hurt him, but also wanting to strive for honesty and openness between them.

"It will take time."

She pressed her lips together and looked down at her bare finger.

"Is it a secret?" she finally asked.

"No, of course not."

"But you didn't tell your family."

"No."

She waited. And waited. So much for honesty and openness.

"So it is a secret."

"I want to get married for real," he said. "In a church or on the property my brothers have. We're trying to get together enough land so that we can each work it how we want—bull breeding, horse breeding and training—hell, Laird even wants to grow hops and brew beer and distill organic whiskey or something like that, but I want to marry in front of my family so that they can be your family and Montana's family."

Tears filled her eyes.

"So I didn't want to tell them until I proposed, but I didn't want to wait to legally marry you."

Sky looked at him. Sincerity shone through.

"We really got it backward," she said softly, leaning in toward him so that her mouth was so closer to his, and her fingers held on to his shoulders. "Baby, marriage, proposal, family wedding."

She stared down at his chest, the honed muscles, the half-moon scar on his left side that was new and wasn't, she hoped, part of a bull hoof.

"My head is still spinning," she told him.

"Mine too."

"Really?" Kane had seemed in total control since he'd entered the gallery except for his aberrant stalking off into the desert.

"I just now feel I can breathe again," he said. "When I saw you at the gallery my brain just..." He made an exploding sound and flexed his fingers like a starburst. "Gone. I was gone. I kissed you again because I couldn't really help myself. It was like four years hadn't happened, and then I turned around, saw our little girl, I just...I just..."

For the first time he broke eye contact. "My world just collapsed. I..." he spread out his fingers again "...I was not functioning. All I had was instinct. And this anger. I'd always sworn I wouldn't be that man who walked away from a kid, and suddenly there I was. A stranger. A man you couldn't trust. A man who didn't know his kid."

"Kane, we've gone over this, and I'm so, so sorry," Sky breathed. "But it's my first wedding night."

"Your only wedding night," he growled and pulled her more firmly onto his lap.

She lifted herself up and teased his erection by rubbing up and down it. Shock waves danced along her clit and through her bloodstream.

"You said I'd have two wedding nights. The legal one and the family one, and I intend to take full advantage."

"You can have a hundred wedding nights as long as they are all with me."

And then he kissed her. And she kissed him back, losing herself to his heat.

"I missed kissing you," Sky said when she could finally

talk again. The water rippled around them, and Kane's erection was like a flaming sword between them, one that she intended to sheath in herself for hours tonight. "You always make me feel like I can fly. I want to fly with you."

"Let's get out of here. I have to have you and we'll make the floor too wet," he whispered harshly in her ear, already standing and lifting her with him.

"I know it's very cavewoman of me, but I absolutely love how strong you are."

Kane barely bothered with a towel. He carried her to the bed, even managing to grab his glass of champagne. Sky managed to snag the bowl of strawberries as they left the bath. Kane laid her carefully down on the silky sheets, which she could feel grow damp behind her back.

"Don't worry, baby, all your heat's going to dry everything off." He spread her out, and then sat back on his heels to look at her.

"Trying to decide where to start."

Sky dipped her finger in the champagne and then traced her lips.

"Here?" she whispered. She did it again, only this time she dripped the champagne on her nipples. "Maybe here?" she asked. Then she dipped again and spread her legs. "Or here?"

Kane's eyes glittered. "All of it. I want it all."

Sky picked up the glass and deliberately spilled some down her body. "It's yours. Everything is yours." She reached for a strawberry from the bowl and tucked it slightly in her slick, heated entrance.

"Jesus, Sky," Kane breathed. "You kill me—you really do."

"I hope not. I want you to feel, very, very alive when I make you cum." She lay flat on the bed, only elevating her head with her elbows behind her.

"I hope you are very, very hungry, Kane."

SKY SHOULD BE sleepy. She'd been so keyed up for the hospital's art auction and dinner last week that she hadn't been able to sleep and since Kane had come striding back into her life, sleep had been even more scarce, and yet tonight they'd made love three times almost without a break. They'd been so hungry for each other, as if they'd been starved and were now gorging. Kane had been so tender and then assertive, almost rough, and she'd loved every minute of it.

Now she lay tucked into his body, his arms wrapped tightly around her. One hand was splayed against her stomach, and one finger traced her small scar over and over so she knew he wasn't asleep.

"I want to have a baby with you," Kane said into the dark of the room. "I want to feel it grow and kick. I want to run out to the store at midnight and get you crazy foods if you have a craving."

She laughed even though she knew she shouldn't encourage him.

"Kane, you are crazy," she said. "We just got back together two days ago, and now you have us married and are talking about another baby."

"I know what I want and I move fast."

"More like you strike," she said, and she should be way more disturbed than she was by this conversation. "Cobras are slower. And I didn't crave weird food. I hardly had an appetite, and had to force myself to eat. Brown rice noodles in vegetable broth was the only thing that stayed down until the third trimester."

He rolled so that they were facing. His hands were gentle on her face.

"I want to cut the cord."

"And bury the placenta facing north."

He started. "Did you do that?"

She laughed. "No. I barely acknowledged I was having a baby so I was no earth mom. I nursed because it was free and easy."

"I want to taste your milk."

"I love your kinky ideas," Sky said. "But can we learn to manage our first child together before we embark on another?"

"So you'd consider another baby?" Kane asked, triumph in his voice.

Somehow Sky felt conned. She wanted to make a joke about diapers, but then she thought that wouldn't be kind. For all she knew Kane was jonesing to change a diaper or hopefully a hundred. She leaned forward and kissed him, putting a promise into her kiss.

"Kane, I love you. I do. I never stopped loving you, but we don't even know where we are going to live or what our life will look like in another month or two. You're packing all of our things except for what fits in a couple of suitcases, off to Montana. I don't know where we'll live in Montana. I don't know where we'll live if we go on the road with you. I don't know how I'll do my art. Colt said he could convert one of the barns to a studio for me, but..." She trailed off. "All of that is logistics. I'm still figuring out how we are as a family."

"You love me?" he whispered. "Even after all I put you through?"

Her whole practical speech and that was what he got out of it? Her unconscious revelation that had come out as a declaration, but it was true. Loving Kane was what she'd always done best. Even when he hadn't loved her. And he still didn't love her. It hurt. Her heart felt like someone had stomped on it, but she had to get up and keep going. Open and honest. She'd survived without love before, her whole life, and she knew Kane cared for her. He did.

"Always," she said simply. "Forever."

Chapter Fourteen

THREE DAYS LATER, Sky was sitting in the makeshift AEBR managerial office in the Phoenix arena on a Skype call with the headquarters, pinching herself. Rather than being upset with her sculpture *The Ride*, corporate wanted to commission something similar only much larger for the corporate offices. No tattoo. Shirt and vest. Sky had nearly laughed, but now it was all she could do to not jump out of her seat.

She promised to get back to them with some preliminary design sketches soon. She also had an all-access badge to photograph a variety of riders as well as backstage scenes. She couldn't publish anything without AEBR permission, and they had the right of…blah…blah…blah. They'd send her a contract. Sky would have Kane's attorney look at it, but she had a commission. And a purpose. She wasn't just Kane's wife masquerading as his hanger-on baby mama, girlfriend.

She ended the call and spun around in the chair.

"Yes." She jumped up and fist pumped the air, but before she could get too fired up, her phone rang. She crossed her fingers hoping it was Kane and that he was done with the autograph signing at a massive western wear and sporting goods store chain so that and she could tell him her great news.

"Hey! Are you done? Guess what?"

"Sky."

Oops, Jonas.

"How are you? So good to hear from you, Jonas." She infused her voice with more warmth. "You must be so busy with the auction Saturday night."

"Tell me you are going to attend. I have a ticket for you."

"Ahhh." Sky paused at the door of the office, intending to leave so that she could head back to the hotel. She had planned to attend before Kane had burst back into her life with the subtlety of a bucking bull.

"The answer I'm looking for, Sky, is yes. Bring your cowboy if you must, but he can buy his own ticket."

"Kane's riding Saturday night."

But only if he makes it to the finals.

It was disloyal to even think like that, and if he didn't make the finals it was because his ass or some other part of him kissed the dirt, and the thought of that really made her ill, although she had seen him tossed off more than she cared to remember. But he always thought he could make it to the bell. Definitely a life lesson there.

"Riding what?"

"A bull."

"You're serious."

"Very. That sculpture really was of him Jonas. He really does that." Ugh she was practically gushing. "I took a bunch of pictures of him and of other riders the summer I..." she didn't want to say followed him "...did my research."

"You did a hell of a lot more than research," Jonas said drily, and Sky could practically hear him rolling his eyes. "Bring him after. The live auction won't even start until nine or so. Maybe he can get there early and do a little publicity to gin up the bidding."

"I'll talk to him."

"What, he has you on a leash? You can't go to promote your own art without him?"

"Jonas," Sky said, pressing her lips together tightly because she should be able to promote her art, but this thing with Kane was so new she could hardly not watch him ride in his hometown. "I'm watching him ride on Saturday night. I promised, and it's his hometown. I said I'd talk to him about the auction to see if we can make it, and I will. No promises."

Long, tense silence. "You still delivering the sculpture series to the gallery tomorrow?"

"Yes," she said. "Of course."

"Good. I have a collector in town. He's very interested and very loaded."

Sky squeezed the phone, nearly hanging up in the process. "That's good news, Jonas," she said aiming for caution but her voice squeaked a little.

"See you tomorrow, and I want to hear a yes about Saturday." He disconnected before Sky could mutter what had become the theme of her life—does anyone ever ask?

KANE HEADED TO the dressing room area where he'd stashed his equipment bag and usual changes of clothes. He'd hated leaving Sky and Montana alone most of the day. The day had seemed flat and dull without them. Hopefully tonight, Sky would agree to attend the sponsor event at Cactus Whiskey Distillery, one of the larger sponsors for the Phoenix AEBR show.

Part of him didn't want her to come because he knew a lot of the bull riders would be there and some would hit on her reflexively just to fuck with him. And a lot of the sponsors and the employees wouldn't hesitate to hit on her either. She'd been so shy when they'd first hooked up four years ago that he had kept her apart from most of his world to protect her, but also, he grimaced wryly, he'd discovered he was a possessive and jealous jerk, and he'd wanted to squash that part of his personality. Hard to be jealous when you kept your girl to yourself. But now she was his wife. And he trusted her.

No more keeping his personal life totally separate. He was all in with Sky and he wanted her to be all in with him and his world. And that meant more public events. Together. He had a plan for tonight that she might not love, but it would solve one looming problem that she would hate a lot more.

"Gage." Kane stopped in surprise. Gage was in the dressing room, straddling a bench and checking his bull rope for any fraying parts, trimming it, and he had some rosin ready. Usually riders worked their ropes Friday and Saturday late afternoon to settle themselves into their routine. Get their head in the game.

Gage bent over his rope, his expression shuttered, obviously deep in thought, and those thoughts were clearly not good. Kane had been there himself more often than not.

"You tight?" he shocked himself by asking.

He wasn't the last bull rider on the tour who would open up or inspire a confidence, but he definitely wasn't in the top ten. Or twenty. Gage noticed.

He straightened and looked up, his features smoothed—polite but distant.

"Kane." He went back to his rope, pocketknife steady as he cut off the stray frayed threads. "Heard you got some changes in your life."

"That's a fucking understatement." Kane laughed, nearly jumping out of his skin to hear it. What the hell? He was happy. Happy. Downright giddy like his first season on the tour when he was learning so much—how to ride, how to focus, how to manage his higher center of gravity and keep his body on the right plane, how to read the bulls and counter each move, how to be tough, pace himself and to take care of himself. Before all the marketing and money bullshit that tried to interfere with the raw exhilaration of the rides.

Weird.

Obviously because Gage stared at him, his hands still on his rope.

"Changes are good, right?" Gage asked cautiously as if he were worried that by asking a follow-up question he would be breaking some kind of personal bull rider code.

"Yeah," Kane said, feeling like something that had been locked up tight inside him cut loose a little, making it easier to breathe. He never shared his shit with anyone on the tour. He'd been closest to Gramps—Rory Douglas—but Rory seemed to be getting injured more, emotionally pulling away. Kane liked other riders, respected even more, but he'd been so used to keeping his distance in an effort to keep his focus, he'd forgotten the concept of camaraderie, like he'd had when he'd first joined the tour before he'd rocketed up the ranks and the sponsors and money had come pouring in and the target on his back got bigger than a billboard.

"I got a daughter."

"I heard." Gage went back to his rope.

Kane pulled on his work gloves and pulled his pocketknife out of its holder hooked to his belt.

"Must have been a shock," Gage said neutrally.

"Hell yeah, but a good one. I'm going to ask Sky to marry me."

"That's good." Again it sounded like a question.

Kane felt defensive. "She wasn't a hookup," he said. "We've known each other for years. I was friends with her brother in high school." Kane stopped splicing off the frayed ends of his rope because he'd likely cut himself or his rope if he didn't. Now it sounded like he'd taken advantage of Sky—probably because he had. Too late now. Focus on the future. Gage didn't seem to have the same trouble concentrating. He took off one glove and ran his palm up and down his rope testing the remaining stickiness.

"But you didn't know about the baby?"

For Gage, who usually kept as much to himself as Kane did, this was one of the longest conversations they'd had and the hint of astonishment in his voice kept Kane talking.

"No. Having more than a little trouble getting over that, but…" he flipped out his knife again and returned to the inspection of his rope "…I will. Have to."

Gage nodded, thoughtfully. "Not much choice," he finally said. "A man has to live up to his responsibilities."

"Damn straight."

Which he would have done the second she'd told him she was pregnant. Anguish shot through him, but he pushed it down.

Don't go there.

"Actually…" Kane surprised himself; he was getting

downright chatty. "I wanted to ask her to marry me years ago. She traveled on tour with me for a summer. Best time in my life."

"Why didn't you?"

"I thought she was too young. Nineteen. In college. Wanted to go for her MFA so I thought I should keep it casual. See her on a few breaks, summers. Wait. Not suck her into this life until I was getting ready to finish with the tour."

Gage looked shocked at that that admission. TMI no doubt, but he smoothed his features out immediately. Went back to stoic cowboy. Kane knew he should shut up, but he was all in now. Had more shit on his mind that he couldn't really talk to anyone about. He knew Gage had some pressing parental issues of his own as well as a family tragedy. They sure had that in common. Between his and Sky's family they had a fucking soap opera playing twenty-four-seven.

"You're not thinking of walking away at the end of this year are you?" Gage asked still staring.

"Nope."

"Casey is. Cody is," Gage said as if testing the words and the concept of leaving. Rumor had it that Gage was here to prove something. Possibly he wasn't coming back after the finals either. If he made it that far, which it looked like he would since he was hot on Kane's ass this season. Twice he'd even bumped ahead. Kane hoped he would—make the finals and stay on tour.

Kane would be facing his exit possibly sooner than he was ready, but he had a strategy. Always. No matter how long he rode and his luck held out and his body held up. He knew how much money he needed and what he'd do with the money when he was finished. Only now, those goals were under review. Had to be.

"You know how you have this dream and you keep the dream tucked up tight inside you, and you only take it out and look at it when you're alone?"

Gage didn't look up at him, but his hands, busy with his rope, stilled and the rope fell on the bench. Gage's hands hung there, empty. He stared at the rope, but nodded.

"Well I had this dream, this promise I made to my mother. A vow, really. Sacred. Like a blood oath—she's my blood, my mother. I owe her. She went through hell for me, and I wanted to do something to bring her peace. I was sixteen. Ten years ago."

Gage was looking at him now. His face spasmed a little as if Kane were hitting too close to home.

"I've been keeping that in my sights since I got on the AEBR. The goal. Always that—win, get the sponsors, do what they want, do what the AEBR wants, carry their water, because I got this goal, this dream I have to achieve. No room for failure."

Gage's eyes stayed steady on his. He swallowed almost convulsively. Yeah Gage kept his shit locked up tight, but he had it. They all had it, and it was probably time Kane started acting a bit more like a mentor, instead of a selfish bastard. Bastard. He tasted the word. It was literal for him. But not for his daughter. He'd made sure of that Monday. His first opportunity and he'd seized that fucker and wrung its neck.

He could die tomorrow or Saturday or even tonight driving to the event. No one knew when the reaper came to call, but bull riders were in more peril than any other athlete, period. But Montana would know that she'd mattered to him. That he'd wanted to be her daddy. That he'd loved her mom enough to make a commitment to her. And he was damn straight going to keep it until the day he died.

"But now I got my own family, and my mom's dream..." Kane shrugged, not quite able to articulate what had been eating at him since he first wrapped his head around the fact that he had a child, that he was going to make Sky his wife. "I don't know if that dream, that vow's feasible anymore—all that energy and that time required and nothing left over for me to give to my wife and daughter."

"Dreams can change," Gage said, but his voice was heavy, his eyes dark and far away.

"Not easy," Kane said ruefully after a long beat of silence where they were both probably thinking, somewhat grimly, about their futures, "to give up a dream, even if it's not mine."

His mom would be... He couldn't begin to imagine how angry his mom would be, how dramatic, accusing. He'd never let her down. Ever. Everything she'd wanted, he'd done—except this. But now he had a wife, a child. He wanted more children, and they had to come first.

"Not easy," he repeated more to himself, "but bull riders don't live easy."

"Amen to that," Gage said. "Afuckingmen."

SATURDAY NIGHT. PACKED stadium. The crowd was freakin' ready to rumble. Kane felt the energy hum through the floor, hit the soles of his boots and shoot through his body, a life current like he was his own personal lightsaber. The anticipation pulsed through the arena. The restless roar was electric. The smell of bulls. Dirt. Sulfur from the accelerant that would be lit to make the lines, all of them leading through the bull riders to the AEBR logo in the middle of the arena.

It was cheesy, but Kane still loved this part. The drama, the tension, the anticipation. The fucking fire. He stood on a line of fire most Friday and Saturday nights. And he was supposed to look like a badass while he did. They all got to pose like none of them had completely left all remnants of childhood behind, yet they were still Men with a capital M. They were goddamn bull riders, the baddest of the bad of cowboys. Kane was one lucky bastard. He was also jacked up. Tonight was his.

Yeah, Sky would probably prefer private, but fuck that.

She deserved romance and grand gestures. She was his wife. He was going to propose so that everyone knew he meant it. No more hiding her away. No more pretending. He belonged to her and she belonged to him, and he'd had a ring designed that had cost more than his first truck. He wanted it seen across a room. Hell yeah, she was his. He'd been raking in stupid amounts of money over the past five years, and he'd invested most of it, saving, planning. Felt good to cut a little loose and do something because he wanted to and it felt good and she was his girl.

He lined up in the chute. Fuck there was tension here. The good kind. Riders were focused on their rides, their bulls. Their plan to keep their ass glued to the bull. The small talk and jokes had been shut down like a faucet thirty minutes ago. No drip, drip. Kane usually didn't talk two to three hours before his ride, but obviously that didn't fly with a three-year-old and he so didn't care.

He felt it. He was going to stick it tonight and he was going to win. Tonight would be fucking fantastic. The happiest night of his life. He could feel it in his bones.

Lights went out. The roar of the crowd was deafening and lit up Kane's blood. It would suck when he had to say good-bye to this. He loved challenges. He loved to grit it out and win.

But he'd find new challenges. No doubt. Just like when he stood on top of the chute looking down at the bull. Definitely no room for doubt there either.

The cowboys filed out to their places on the line. Names announced, tip the hat, cowboy pose and then the fire. It was a primal spectacle that he had yet to tire of. They were modern-day gladiators and the heartland arenas were all fucking coliseums. He felt the energy burn through him, and he wanted to scream from his soul and toss his hat in the air. It felt goddamn awe-inspiring to be alive.

SKY WAS ON her feet with the crowd. Montana was in her arms yelling 'Daddy' when Kane's name was announced. Tucker and Laird were beside her cheering Kane on. She wasn't sure where Colt was. Kane briefly appeared on top of the chute fence looking down.

He was riding a Triple T bull—Dunkirk. It was the bull's first season in the AEBR, but he was already making a name for himself. No bull rider had yet to stick him. That made Sky nervous but probably thrilled Kane.

Sky had been amazed by the heart and the resourcefulness of her new family and how they had so eagerly welcomed her and Montana into their lives.

Hallelujah.

Sky looked around the arena. Kane must be bursting. His family in the audience. His hometown. His family's bulls from their growing stock-contracting program. Couldn't live shinier than that.

"Please be all right, please be all right," Sky now whispered, the memory of him in the dirt last Saturday still fresh in her mind.

"He's going to kill it," Tucker screamed. "Go, Dunkirk!"

"You are not cheering the bull," Sky whispered.

"Usually," Tucker said, tossing her long red ponytail.

"Always," Laird chimed in.

"Well this time I'm cheering the bull and the rider, but my twin and I do like our one hundred percent bulls and we need our AEBR stock to keep scoring high. Our stock company is new to this level. Go, Dunkirk!" she shouted again.

Trying hard not to gnaw on her nails, Sky saw Kane drop down but then he jumped up again. The chute crew seemed to be focused on something.

"Oh God. Oh God." Sky wanted to hide her head.

"Stay up," Tucker hissed. "You're a cowboy's cowgirl and you have to be tougher than anyone else."

Kane adjusted his helmet. His hold-hand glove. Handed his rope to his brother, Luke, who'd flown out yesterday. Luke and two men were talking, readjusting the bull. Kane popped down fast.

"I don't think I can watch," she whispered. She also didn't think she could turn away.

"You need to watch," Tucker said. "This is televised. Kane's on top again—going into the final in first place in his hometown. Look adoring and smile. Nice dress."

She did look good. She'd picked out the strapless red dress that was fitted lace on the bodice, but flowing, asymmetrical diaphanous tulle on the bottom. In keeping with the bull rider theme, she'd bought red cowgirl boots with silver details. She'd seen them in one of the boutiques attached to the hotel and though the price was astronomical, she'd charged them to the room. Kane kept reiterating that what was his was hers so she thought she'd give that concept a test run tonight. Kane hadn't complained. His eyes had glowed with approval and then he'd pulled her in for a kiss.

"I want you to model the boots for me later tonight—just the boots," he'd growled in her ear.

To keep the theme western, she wore a tight, cropped denim jacket with embroidered red roses and rhinestone details. She'd left her hair down so that it fell in waves.

For a moment she just soaked in the excitement of the arena. The novelty of her new life. Married. The concept no longer sounded or felt so foreign although Kane hadn't told his family, nor had she and Kane exchanged rings. She knew she shouldn't care, and it wasn't like she was jonesing for a diamond, but it was hard to take words like committed and forever seriously without a symbol. Maybe she'd make him a ring for the ceremony with his family.

She saw Kane give the nod and then the gate flew open and the tan bull launched out practically horizontal. It rolled left, spun right and then proceeded to lurch forward, kick its back legs high, coming down hard on the front legs, and then the bull turned a tight circle and balanced on hind legs before kicking off and lifting its hindquarters startlingly high. The turns were wicked sharp and fast and Kane seemed to extend out from the bull, his posture erect, his core aligned with his pelvis so he never got shifted off his plane of balance. His left hand stayed high, never once flopping toward the bull or his body.

Sky felt dizzy just watching, and how the heck could eight seconds last like ten minutes?

"Show-off," Tucker yelled. "He spurred Dunkirk twice. Rock star."

The bell and the light went, but Kane stayed on.

"Get off." Sky felt her throat close off in panic.

And then Kane hurtled off the bull, barely brushed the ground before he was off and vaulting the fence. He waved to the crowd, tossed his helmet to Luke, and took out his mouth guard.

Instead of Kane's song, there was no music. Jessie was cued up to do the bro-victory stuck the ride dance, but he'd taken off his microphone. As the bull trotted friskily into the chute, Kane jogged over to Jessie. The score flashed. Ninety-two. Kane didn't even look at it, but several AEBR officials started filing into the arena with the buckle and the check and the speeches.

"I know I usually do a little dance right about now." Kane spoke into the microphone, his deep voice warm and amused. "It's my thing, and Jessie is a great dancer and all but, I gotta confess, I found me a new dance partner."

The women in the audience went crazy. The AEBR staff smiled, a little uncertainly. The PR staff, especially, looked stiff.

"Shit," Tucker breathed. "He's going to do it now."

That didn't sound good. "Do what?"

"Sky." Kane looked up at her and crooked his finger.

Her blood washed to her toes. No way. He wouldn't do this. He wouldn't do this publicly, would he—well he would, but not to her, right? And without Alicia's approval?

"Breathe and get out there." Tucker gave her a push toward the arena fence like she was supposed to vault down there like a real cowgirl.

The cowboy on the horse rode over and before Sky could really process that Kane was going to do something very, very public, the cowboy held out his hand. Laird lifted her over the fence and even if she'd had the inclination to run, and she did, oh she definitely did, she knew she could never leave Kane hanging. She was over the fence and on the ground.

The crowd was cheering and then a Black Keys song came over the loudspeakers. Kane stood center of the arena smiling at her. She covered her mouth with her hand. This wasn't happening—but it was. A laugh broke out as the first chorus sang out about love keeping you waiting. She used to jam out to the *Lonely Boy* song while cleaning the trailer or sketching while she waited for Kane to return.

He did a little dance spin and held out his hand. Before

she could panic, Sky took a step toward him, then another then she did a 'slide, roll, down,' move that got the crowd warmed up.

"So we gonna dance or have a dance-off?" Kane asked. The crowd laughed.

"Dance," she said softly. "You're crazy."

"I think you told me that more than once before and I'm view it as a good thing."

Gosh, he was so good at this, and when he took her in his arms and did a fast-paced Texas two-step that had them whirling around, Sky let him have his fun and take over. She'd missed this. It had been a long time. Too long. And it felt so good to move with him, and watch him in his element that she almost forgot thousands of other people were watching them.

After sixteen counts, Kane twirled her and then lifted her with one arm so she slid across his back and came to a stop in front of him again. She smiled, still a bit bemused. Kane was lucky they were in public because Kane in chaps was a delectable sight, and she vividly remembered how she used to ask him to put them on when they were alone, just so she could watch him walk, and then she'd take them off him painfully slow until he was cursing with lust and impatience.

Kane dropped to one knee.

The arena was eerily silent considering so many people had been screaming and cheering a minute earlier. A lot of the bull riders were filing out in the chute staring at them.

The film crew was getting obnoxiously close.

"Sky Gordon, I wanted to ask you this question four years ago, but my timing left a lot to be desired," he smiled ruefully. "Sometimes I can be a bit slow."

A ripple of laughter worked its way around the crowd.

"Sky, would you please make me happy forever by marrying me?" He pulled a ring out from deep in his jeans.

This was happening. Really happening. She was on TV in front of thousands of people getting proposed to by her still-secret husband. Please let this be a commercial break. Sky couldn't even breathe so she stupidly bobbed her head.

"This is the part where you're supposed to say yes." His eyes warmed.

It was silly to feel so undone. They were already married. But the ring was so beautiful and Kane was making a public declaration and all her words seemed to tangle in her throat.

She stuck out her hand. He slid the ring onto her finger, but all she could do was stare at him. He was so beautiful.

"Still hoping for a yes."

"I love you," she mouthed.

Something flashed deep in his eyes, and pink stained his high cheekbones—a pale, pale pink under his golden skin.

"Is that a yes?"

She bit her lip and focused only on his face because if she thought about what they were doing right now, she'd probably hyperventilate. "Yes," she managed to squeeze out through her throat closed tight by emotion. The crowd erupted and Kane stood and pulled her close. She held on like she'd never let him go.

"I already got my prize," he whispered in her ear. "Getting the buckle and the money and congratulations seems like overkill."

Chapter Fifteen

LESS THAN AN hour later, Sky slipped out of the Uber with a shaky thank you after paying and tipping using the app on her phone. She stomped down the tears that threatened. She was not being childish or petty, but she had to let Kane know that she was not going to just go along with everything the way he wanted, especially when it came to her career.

The ring felt weird on her hand. Heavy. But so beautiful. The square-cut diamond caught the light and glimmered. Hope for the future, she thought, although she didn't feel exactly buoyant with optimism at the moment.

She'd wanted Kane to come to the end of the auction with her. She wanted to thank Jonas for his support and for inclusion of her western collection in his gallery. She wanted to introduce him to Dr. Sheridan, who had been the one who had first noticed her work and invited her to donate to the auction. He had been so interested in *The Ride*, and she thought he'd be surprised and happy to meet the actual inspiration for the original sculpture. And she was hoping to meet the "off the hook rich" potential client Jonas had enthused over.

And now she was here to do all those things but alone.

Kane had been suspicious and more than a little reluctant to attend the auction. Thinking he was just tired from the ride and all the adrenaline, she patiently waited while Kane speed-showered and signed some autographs, posed for pictures.

"I really want to go, Kane," she'd said near his ear when he was ready to leave. "I know, Sky, but we just got engaged. Tucker and Laird are going to keep Montana tonight. I thought we could spend the time more..."

"The engagement was for show," she'd said.

"It meant something to me," he'd said after a long pause.

She'd sighed. The night had gone from scintillating with promise to feeling thick and dark and tangled. "You've done your work. What about mine?" she'd asked quietly.

He'd slipped his arm around her and began to walk. "Is that why you dressed up tonight—the auction?"

"Is that why you proposed tonight—the auction?" she'd countered, feeling a cold dread slither inside her and dig its sharp fingers into her heart.

"No, I proposed because I wanted to do it properly, and publicly. You said I'd kept you hidden away, and I wanted to show you that wouldn't be the case anymore."

Sky had stood ballet straight and dug for courage. She had to go into this marriage and be the strong and respected woman she wanted to be, and she couldn't do that without veering away at the first hurdle. She wanted a partnership. She'd chosen her words carefully. "Kane, it's important for me to be there."

"I understand the importance of your work, Sky. And I admire it, and I want to support your career. I will support it, but the auction, the invite, the donation—there's more at work there than you think."

"What's that supposed to mean?" He'd suggested that once before, and now Sky truly felt insulted.

"It's not as black and white as you think. There are undercurrents at work."

"Because my work doesn't belong with the work of the other artists?"

"I didn't mean it like that. Don't put words in my mouth I'd never say."

"Kane, congrats." The owner of Cactus Whiskey Distillery she'd met last night hurried over, slapping Kane on the back. "Great win tonight. Exciting to watch. Know I'll see you in the finals in Fort Worth."

"I aim to be there," Kane said politely, his marketing smile in place. His voice even changed, the cadence slightly more country, easygoing.

"You don't mind if I steal him for a few minutes, little lady?" The man turned to her, but he already had his hand ready to steer Kane toward a knot of men much further back down the hall. "After all you're going to be spending a lot of time with him in the future."

Kane's eyes shot to hers, gauging her mood. Sky smiled politely, showing the even, white teeth her parents had paid a lot of money for. She too had a social smile.

"Go right ahead," she said sweet as could be.

"Sky," Kane had said. "You can wait in the VIP tent or with…" His words were lost because she'd turned around and started walking away. Wait and VIP tent had not been in her future.

So now, Sky walked into the hotel and took the escalator up to the ballroom. She was a featured artist. She belonged here, and she wouldn't let Kane's suspicions or her father's voice from the past squash her back down.

She texted Jonas and felt relieved that he met her at the entrance.

"Perfect timing," he said. "*The Ride* is up for bid, and there are a lot of paddles being raised.

"Maybe we should stay out here until it's over," Sky suggested. "I can't watch."

"Better get used to it, Sky. I think you are going to have a lot of patrons vying for your art in the future."

"Thank you, Jonas. You believed in me so early."

"No-brainer." He snagged two glasses of champagne and handed one to her. "Dr. Sheridan may have brought you to my attention, but I needed no persuasion. To an artistic partnership."

Sky clinked his glass, and gulped a little.

"Where's your cowboy?"

"Doing cowboy things."

Jonas laughed. "I hope that doesn't mean he intends to steal another piece of art."

"No, that would be bandits. Cowboys are the good guys."

"I'm not really in agreement there, but Dr. Sheridan did show me your cowboy's winning ride tonight on his phone, which scared the crap out of me, and I was blocks away, and even though I still think he's an arrogant pain in the ass, he's your problem so let's forget about him and mingle."

Kane was not an easy man to forget, and Sky didn't even try. She hated being here without Kane, but she'd felt like she'd had no choice. She'd needed to make a stand. Hopefully he wouldn't carry her off again. Hopefully he'd realize how important meeting potential clients was to her.

"I know Dr. Sheridan wanted to meet you. He'd hoped the cowboy would also come."

"Jonas, the cowboy has a name. It's Kane, and we got engaged tonight."

Jonas looked at her ring and then her, his face concerned. "Congratulations," he paused, clearly thinking something through. "Why didn't he come with you tonight then?"

She kept her smile in place. "Like I said, busy with cowboy things."

"Are you okay?"

"Never better," Sky lied. "Let's mingle."

KANE DIDN'T EVEN bother putting his game face on. He'd texted Colt fifteen minutes ago, and yes, Sky was at the auction, and yes, she was with Jonas, and yes, Colt agreed to stay put to keep an eye on her, but no, he had not managed to secure the winning bid for *The Ride*.

"Why not?" Kane demanded the minute he entered the ballroom and spotted Colt looking like security against the wall. "I told you to bid whatever it takes."

"I don't think you meant that much dough."

"I don't care how much it went for. I wanted it," he said knowing he sounded like a sulky teen. He felt like shit. Sky had ditched him at the first opportunity without explanation, and he needed to ice himself. That had been a mother of a ride.

"I wanted you to bid on the sculpture until it was mine."

He saw his biological father, lording it over the room, his eyes, so cold like a shark's watching, waiting. Manipulative bastard. Colt had better not have backed down to him.

"Some things you just can't control," Colt said philosophically. "Like Sky."

"That's for damned sure."

"Laird said you proposed and she said yes and now…?" Colt didn't make eye contact, which was probably good, because Kane felt primed for a fight. Not that he would fight, but he really, really wanted to. "Even I don't fuck up that fast," Colt said.

"I didn't want to come tonight," Kane admitted. He hated saying anything because more explanation would be warranted. He couldn't get the hell out of Phoenix fast enough. Tonight would be good. Now would be better.

"Why?"

"Million reasons."

"Tell me one."

"What did it go for?" Kane asked.

"Two hundred K."

"No fucking way."

"Way."

"Who bought it?"

"Some guy."

"That narrows it down a lot."

"He had long black hair."

Sky was now enthusiastically talking to his biological father, who was smiling. Probably right before he ate her. Kane was about to charge in, but Colt caught him by the shoulder. His very fucking sore shoulder that needed ice. And a lot of tape. And then he needed to stretch for about an hour or three.

"Let her stay," Colt said.

"WTF!" Kane said. "She doesn't know who that man really is."

"Probably because you didn't tell her."

That was true. Kane swore.

"I don't know who he is," Colt said, and Kane flinched guiltily. "Besides, you know when you pose with all those women, and the pictures go round and round on the internet, and you say you're working, not fucking?"

"Yeah."

"Sky's working. Back the fuck off. I'll get her home."

Everything about that idea felt wrong except it was right. He kept pushing. Needing to get her back, needing the emotional intimacy that she'd given him so easily before. Needing to be an instant family with her and Montana. He needed so much. Everything from her. And what was he giving back?

Two other couples joined Jonas, Sky and his biological father. Then Dr. Sheridan's wife and three daughters rounded out the group. Kane felt sick to his bones. Glad he hadn't eaten yet. He'd been starved and had wanted to take Sky for a romantic dinner but he wouldn't be able to get anything past the knot in his gut his bio dad and daughters always created. It took all of his control to not go over there and do something stupid.

It burned him to see them so friendly to his wife. Sky laughed at something his bio dad said, smiled at what were technically his half sisters. She looked beautiful and confident and he didn't have the right to ruin it for her.

She looked up and met his gaze. Then she smiled. Kane felt gutted. He didn't deserve her. He never had.

"I'll take you up on that offer," he snapped at his brother. "Make sure she gets home. I owe you big." He spun on his heel and walked back out of the room as if he hadn't a care in the world, but then he mocked himself. He'd always been about image.

BACK AT THE hotel room, Kane set the timer on his watch once again and climbed back into the ice bath. Ice had a way of clearing out the junk in his head as well as alleviating the pain in his body and reducing his inflammation. He'd fucked up with Sky. Again. How could a man who was celebrated at being smooth with women act like such an idiot?

He heard the key in the lock. Closed his eyes. Waited. Nothing. What was she doing? He stayed in the bath five minutes and then deciding he'd prefer to let Sky swing at him sooner rather than later, he got out of the bath, toweled off and put on a pair of boxers.

He wasn't sure what to expect. Sky in a pair of hip-hugging worn sweats and braless in a razorback tank packing up a suitcase was not it.

He strode to the door and stood in front of it, arms crossed.

"What were you doing in the dark?" she asked looking past him to the dark bedroom and darker still bathroom.

She was leaving him. Really leaving him. He repeated the

words internally, tasted them, tried to make them real.

"I know I fucked up," he admitted.

"No, Kane, you weren't open." She folded the last of Montana's tiny clothes into the suitcase after pulling out one flowery pair of leggings and a plain pink T-shirt and cute little panties that said Monday on them. His heart lurched.

"You told me you wanted us to be open with each other. I told you everything. My every fear. My childhood story. The fact that I never met my biological father. The fact that your biological father tried get a meeting with you through me."

"Christ, not him again. He ruins everything."

"No, you ruin it," Sky informed him stalking to a closet to pull out the larger suitcase he'd bought her. First she put her dresses, including her wedding dress and the dress she'd worn tonight, in the garment bag.

"Why didn't you tell me Dr. Sheridan was your father?" Sky demanded.

"I hate him."

"That's not productive," she said. "And that's not really what I asked. Why didn't you tell me that the man who was in charge of the fundraising campaign for the new hospital wing, the man who approached me about my art, was your father?"

"He was trying to manipulate you," Kane said.

Sky stood up and came over to him.

"I'm not stupid. And I'm definitely not taking any of

your broody man crap. The only way we are going to work is if you open yourself up to me. You demand everything from me—every thought and fear and hurt—and then you just stand there pretending that you're perfect. Well, I'm not a teenager with a crush anymore. I'm not a nineteen-year-old desperately in love with a man who never once told me he loved me, but showed me in a millions ways even if I was too inexperienced and insecure to understand it then. I am a woman, and I love you. I love you when you ride a bull that sets the arena on fire. I love you when you fall. I love you when your geeky nerd boy emerges, and I love you when you fuck up like tonight. You don't have to be perfect so get on board with that and stick the ride that's going to be our life."

She walked back to packing calmly as if she hadn't just cracked his heart and his head wide open.

"If you love me, why are you packing?" he asked quietly, more afraid of her answer than of any other moment in his life.

"Because you said you wanted to get an early start to Clovis tomorrow. You bought us so many clothes it's going to take me some time to…."

The rest of the words were muffled as he picked her up and held her hard against his bare chest.

"I'm sorry, I'm so sorry," he whispered, pressing his lips against her silky hair. "You are the only woman I've ever loved and I keep screwing up over and over again. It's like I'm trapped in a time loop. Are you crying?"

Sky looked up. Her eyes were shiny.

"And there's my geek, my sweet and my screw-up all lumped together." She pressed a kiss to his chest. "Seriously, Kane, you're not really screwing up, you're just human. You're not perfect, and I don't want you to be."

"Clearly that's not going to be a problem."

Sky opened another drawer where there was some lacy lingerie Kane had bought her.

"I don't think you need to pack up everything tonight," he said softly, his hand covering hers.

"Nice try, cowboy. Tell me about Doctor Sheridan."

"I hate that he used you," he said bitterly. "He ruins everything."

Sky, her hands full of lacey panties faced him. "Seriously? He brought my work to the attention of an established art gallery owner with connections all over the world. I don't care why Dr. Sheridan chose my work, just that he did."

"You're not pissed that he used you?"

"I just had some Brazilian cowboy tycoon—and I didn't even know those existed—bid two hundred thousand dollars on my first sculpture. Jonas has six more of my sculptures in his gallery, and already sold two and is negotiating over a third so pretty sure I'm okay with his meddling."

"You're so practical," Kane breathed.

"Clearly you're not at the moment so give," she tossed her panties in her suitcase. "Tell me about him. Share. Heal."

"My mom worked at a barista stand at the hospital one summer because they had a child care facility that was available for all employees so she could put Luke there, and she could work, and study for her general ed classes when it wasn't busy. She liked the job because it was clean and safe and friendly and she said the doctors tipped good. Not all they did good obviously."

"Kane," she whispered her voice broken, and he hated himself just that much more. "Why didn't you tell me about him? You saw the flyer."

He laughed but it wasn't funny. "That flyer gave me my life back so I really ought to be on my knees in gratitude to him even though he's still a manipulative jerk."

"Maybe he's finally ready to make amends," she said softly. "People change. He's older now. Maybe he really wants to be part of your life. He seemed so pleasant. He took me aside and asked about you. How you were. What your plans were for the future."

"Probably so he could hijack them and claim them for himself. He pulled that stunt when I earned a scholarship to Pinnacle Peak Day High School. Same thing when I was offered a scholarship to an Ivy. He said he'd made some calls. He hadn't done dick. I looked into what the new wing of the Austen Sheridan clinic is focusing on and guess what it is? It's too easy."

"Sports medicine."

"Ding. Ding. Ding. You are correct. Robotic surgeries,

physical therapies, rehab from surgery and injuries, physical training, nutrition all geared toward athletes from teens up. Gee, I wonder what he wants with me? Free advertising."

"Kane, I'm sorry." She took his hand and pressed it to her cheek. "I was hoping he was trying to make a bridge."

"If he did, I'd burn it down. So many of my childhood memories involved my mom making me write letters and send pictures to him that he'd return then through his attorney unopened. She'd also make me dress up to try to ambush him somewhere. It was humiliating, but my mom was relentless. She got obsessed. Finally, she got some help through legal aid, and that's what later spurred her to become an attorney, but even with that good, it was still a nightmare."

Sky wrapped her arms around him and held him close. He shivered.

"Ice baths. I'd forgotten about those."

"Alive and well, but hey, the night wasn't an epic fail. I proposed to the girl of my dreams and she said yes."

"That sounds promising," Sky said, looking up at him and fingering his hair.

"And the girl of my dreams happens to be my wife, and I'm crazy head over ass in love with her."

"She's pretty intense about you too."

"And the girl of my dreams gave me a beautiful and brilliant daughter."

"Speaking of that," Sky walked to the nightstand, opened

up the drawer and took out the box of condoms. "Oops," she tossed the box in the trash can. "I'm all in with this marriage Kane Wilder, family barn wedding, three or four kids, whatever you want."

"Really?" He breathed feeling like his heart was on fire. "You're sure. I don't want to push you."

Sky laughed. "Pushing's what you do best, but don't worry, I'm learning to push back."

"You are, and I gotta say, it makes me hot as hell."

"Don't we have a proposal and a win and a big sale to celebrate tonight in our hometown?"

"That's a lot of celebrating," Kane said. "I remember something earlier about boots."

"Not sure I remember that," Sky said. "But you could tell me you loved me again."

"I loved you four years ago, Sky. I didn't know what to do with that. I was just blindsided by how fast you fit into my life and how much I wanted you there. I wanted you to stay on the tour with me, but it's a hard life and a boring one, and you were destined for so much more."

"I would have stayed," she said. "But now I am glad that I have my degree, and I have the beginnings of a career."

"Pretty sure a six-figure sale is more than a beginning."

"That was for charity, but Jonas does have another buyer interested and who wants to view my sculptures, and with the AEBR commission, I will be busy. Looks like I might need that studio in Montana after all."

"So Montana?"

"If you're there, I'm there."

"I'm thinking two more years tops on the tour, what do you think?"

"What happened to retiring at thirty?"

"You. Montana will be entering kindergarten in two years. We might be expecting another baby or two by then. It would be nice to have a home base. My mom's wanted me to try to restore the Wilder family ranch: Wild Winds. It's been eating away at her, the thought of it being sold out of the family, but I think it's better if we all start fresh. There's land that borders the small former cattle ranch that Colt inherited coming up for sale. My mom will be pissed but I can talk to my brothers. We can build up a ranch with land north of town, away from the Wilder land and the McTavish land. Clean start if you want."

"I want."

"So we'll travel together until the tour ends this year as long as it works for you and Montana and then after the finals we'll re-evaluate over the break and spend time with family."

"That sounds perfect, Kane. You've given me a family—your brothers. Their wives."

"Hardest thing I've ever done in my life was walk away from you that day four years ago," Kane said. "I was afraid that if I didn't walk away fast and never look back I wouldn't be able to let you go."

"And now I'm here to stay."

He pulled her in tight and held her.

"I love you, Sky Wilder. Crazy deep, but I'd love you in those boots just a teensy bit more."

AEBR Finals Fort Worth October 2017

"DADDY, I HOPE you win," Montana said as he swept her up in his arms before he headed down to the chutes.

He smiled at his little girl, but then he looked at his wife. Thought of how she'd woken him up before dawn—saying that she'd had a really vivid dream with lots of sound and color and that she'd been having those for the past week or so, and just as he'd woken up enough to process that she was telling him that for a reason and that he should pay attention, she'd pulled out a box—a pregnancy test.

He jacked up in bed and she'd laughed at his shock and eagerness.

"You said you wanted to be in on every part," Sky had teased. "Does that mean you want to watch me pee on the stick too?"

"Hell yeah." He'd reached for her, feeling excited, scared and a little sick with nerves, but she'd rolled away from him shaking her head.

"You can watch after. You're pervy enough, and I don't want you getting any more ideas."

"I'm always full of ideas," he'd objected following her to the large master bathroom.

Because of all the events surrounding the finals, they'd been in Fort Worth for the entire week staying in a very upscale hotel. Kane's family had joined him, even his mother who was still upset that he was giving up on the dream of restoring the Wilder family ranch as it was rumored her father teetered on the edge of bankruptcy.

Kane had managed to purchase three of the five parcels of ranch land he'd been interested in to add to the existing one that Colt had reluctantly inherited from his stepfather. And on the most southern part of the property closest to town where there was a barn that was still in excellent condition—that Kane had suggested Sky use as her studio—they'd been married by local pastor Sam Zabrinsky, who had married Kane and Colt last Christmas and who would marry Laird and Tucker this Christmas. It had been sweet, simple, and very personal as they had written their own vows.

And after the finals they'd live at the ranch during the off-season, make improvements to the property to accommodate all four Wilder brothers, their families and their dreams. They also planned to start the remodel on the existing ranch house that had good bones and vintage charm but needed serious updating.

Mid-January would see him, Sky and Montana back out on the road as the 2018 tour started in a new trailer he was having customized.

Kane had waited at the closed bathroom door, his heart pounding until Sky had opened it, and they had stared at the stick together. Hours later he still felt giddy that the word pregnant had appeared on the white stick so quickly.

"Do you hope you win too, Daddy?" Montana asked, the question launching him back to the present.

"I already did, baby girl. Win or lose this ride, I've already won."

And he had, he thought, as he made his way down to the chutes, lots of people lined up, wishing him luck, high-fiving him, touching his shoulder, wishing him the best. He felt the familiar calm settle over him, like he was in a bubble. He checked his helmet and tucked it under his arm as he made his way to the chute. Ran his gloved hand lightly down his bull rope that he'd re-resined earlier in the day, a ritual that always had centered him, only this time, he'd done it while Sky had sat beside him, taking pictures, leaning against him and talking softly, trying to trick him into telling her about the long overdue honeymoon he had planned.

Gage waited by the chute. They were two-tenths of a point apart going into the final round, but really, almost anyone in the final round could seize victory. Kane had gone into the finals and won it twice already, once from behind and once far, far in the lead. He'd drawn a rank Harper Bull so that should be fun. A Wilder Bull in the final would be better, but he'd get his shot at that dream someday, he predicted. Luke and Tanner and Tucker were determined and working hard despite last year's setback.

"I know your brother Luke's up there for you today, but

I wanted to say good fortune. I almost want you to win as much as I want to, seeing as we are both burying some ghosts."

Kane found himself laughing. "If it's not me, then I hope it's you." He shoulder-bumped Gage, whom he'd become closer to since May. "But as for ghosts, I slayed those bastard spirits. Feel like a better man."

Gage's face, so often set in fiercely determined lines, relaxed. A small smile touched his lips.

"Think you can beat me?"

"Hell yeah. If not this year, then next."

"Cocky asshole."

Kane agreed.

"But best attitude to think you can win." Gage nodded his approval.

"I not only think I can win, I know I already have," Kane said thinking about Sky, his little girl and the other baby just entering their lives.

He paused at the bottom of the chute, popped in his mouth guard, fitted on his helmet and snapped it into place. Sky was hoping for a boy this time for him, but Kane was good with another girl. He smiled remembering how Cody had laughed at the news Kane had surprisingly shared with him earlier in the day. Cody hadn't missed a beat and told him. "No way you'll throw a boy. You think too goddamn much and are a moody, angsty fuck."

Then he'd body-slammed Kane and squeezed his shoulder—man code for congrats. "So don't fuck it up out there and stay out of the well."

High praise and maybe the beginnings of a friendship from Cody, and Kane realized that he was enjoying himself. It wasn't just about the technicalities of the ride and the score and gaming the sponsors anymore. It was the challenge and the people and the pageantry as well that drew him.

"You going to ride or just think about it?" Luke peered down at him from the top of the chute, snagging the bull rope from Kane.

Kane vaulted up, heard the announcer with his yearly stats—awesome—and his two previous world championships. The crowd noise was so deafening he couldn't hear the rest. Somewhere out there in the family section Sky sat with his mother, brothers and their wives and Parker and Montana.

He kept his head down, breathing deep and watching the bull—judging the edgy restless movements of the beautiful beast—definitely pissed and ready to rock and roll. Good, well so was he. The power of the animal was palpable. When everything was set, he let his boot touch the back of the bull to warn it he was coming aboard. The reaction was a strong shift to the side. The flex of muscle was truly awesome.

He thought he should take a photo up here next time for Sky. She could capture that flex of muscle—make it look alive. Maybe somehow capture the coiled tension of the bull rider and the bull right before they melded into one.

For eight seconds.

A murmur went through the men at the top. Approval and caution.

Kane dropped down and immediately set his feet angled back so they couldn't catch on the bars and wrapped his rope. He pulled and wrapped and pulled tighter again and again. He tested the grip. The smell of bull, dust, popcorn and resin filled his nose and the feel of the bull's energy translated to his body.

One more adjustment of the grip and he rocked up higher on the bull. Set his thighs, his ass, flexed to give himself space to move with the bull. His left hand was already up. He shifted his pelvis forward, tested the distribution of his weight. Felt good. He felt set as if a pole went through the top of his head, his body and pelvis welding him in place. He shifted up, back, side to side and felt the quiver of the muscles beneath him. He ran through the visuals of the bull's last five rides, pictured himself on top, thighs tight, ass floating slightly above to better counter shift.

Yeah.

Kane nodded.

Slide of metal. Powerful enough thrust to launch the bad boy rank bull clear of the gate to start the clock.

The End

The American Extreme Bull Riders Tour

If you enjoyed *Kane*, you'll love the rest of the American Extreme Bull Riders Tour!

Book 1: *Tanner* by Sarah Mayberry

Book 2: *Chase* by Barbara Dunlop

Book 3: *Casey* by Kelly Hunter

Book 4: *Cody* by Megan Crane

Book 5: *Troy* by Amy Andrews

Book 6: *Kane* by Sinclair Jayne

Book 7: *Austin* by Jeannie Watt

Book 8: *Gage* by Katherine Garbera

Available now at your favorite online retailer!

About the Author

Sinclair Jayne has loved reading romance novels since she discovered Barbara Cartland historical romances when she was in sixth grade. By seventh grade, she was haunting the library shelves looking to fall in love over and over again with the heroes born from the imaginations of her favorite authors. After teaching writing classes and workshops to adults and teens for many years in Seattle and Portland, she returned to her first love of reading romances and became an editor for Tule Publishing last year.

Sinclair lives in Oregon's wine country where she and her family own a small vineyard of Pinot Noir and where she dreams of being able to write at a desk like Jane Austen instead of in parking lots waiting for her kids to finish one of their 12,000 extracurricular activities. …

Thank you for reading

Kane

If you enjoyed this book, you can find more from all our great authors at TulePublishing.com, or from your favorite online retailer.

Made in the USA
San Bernardino, CA
04 December 2017